D1608253

A PLAIN
MALICE

An Appleseed Creek Mystery

Amanda Flower

DEDICATION

For Nicole Resciniti
no one fought harder for Chloe and Timothy's
Happily Ever After

ACKNOWLEDGEMENTS

This novel exists because of you, the readers, who asked for it. Thank you for your love of Appleseed Creek and continued support of my writing. I couldn't do this without you.

Special thanks to my agent and friend Nicole Resciniti, who fought long and hard for this story and went to extraordinary lengths to make sure it ended up in print.

Thanks to my editors Julie Gwinn and Marisa Cleveland. I'm so happy that you both were part of this book.

Hugs to my dear friend Mariellyn Grace. Your edits and voice of reason have saved me more times than I can count and go way beyond my writing.

Thank you to the Burns and Queen families, especially Mike, Cathy, and Meredith, who answered my endless questions about dairy farming. Any mistakes in the manuscript are my own.

Love my mother, Rev. Pamela Flower, who edited this novel before she went home to be with the Lord. I'll keep writing because you asked me to. And love to my family, especially Andy, Nicole, Isabella, and Andrew. You put up with a lot so I can live my dream. Thank you.

Finally, I thank God in Heaven for allowing me the opportunity to finish this series. It ended in an unexpected way, but it is a happily ever after.

CHAPTER ONE

A luxury cobalt blue passenger bus sat in the middle of the Troyers' yard. Toddler-sized white lettering announced, "Blue Suede Tours" across all four sides of the vehicle. A balding bus driver stood a few feet away wearing an equally blue polo shirt and drinking a Diet Coke. With a foul expression, he watched his southern passengers wander the grounds. The tourists milled around the Amish dairy farm, pointing at the black and white Holstein cows, plain dresses on the line, and push lawnmower leaning against the tool shed. *English* people wandering the Troyer farm were not common place, but then again, I hadn't visited the farm all that much since Becky's argument with her parents about cutting her hair over Christmas.

Five shiny black buggies sat on the opposite side of the driveway from the blue bus. I parked my Beetle in between two of the buggies, but before I got out, I gave myself a mental pep talk. *I could do this.* When I'd visited the Troyers before Becky cut her hair I'd had a sense of peace on the Amish farm because I felt like I finally found a place to belong. That all changed when the Troyers saw Becky's shoulder-length blonde locks. Her short English hairstyle was her statement that she not only left the Amish way of life but would never return.

When Becky left her Amish home I gave her a place to stay, and after some time, her family came to accept me as her friend. Maybe because they thought I gave her a safe place to live until she was ready to return to Amish life. I gave her a comfortable English home. Perhaps, I made it too easy for her to make the opposite decision. I suspected that was how her parents felt.

I grimaced. Timothy, their oldest son and my boyfriend, was also a complication. He left the Amish years before I met him, but I knew the Troyers wanted him to return to their way of life as much as they wanted Becky to return. I, who would never be Amish, stood in the way of their hopes for their two eldest children.

As I unbuckled my seatbelt, I spotted Timothy talking with a stout English man a few yards away. The medium-height thin man wearing the same blue polo shirt as the bus driver gripped a neon yellow umbrella in his hand like a riot club. Overhead, the periwinkle sky was clear and cloud free. It was a perfect spring day. The umbrella wasn't needed as raingear. Perhaps, crowd control?

Sunlight reflected off Timothy's white-blond hair giving him a halo effect. The sleeves of his long sleeve T-shirt were pushed up, revealing his muscular forearms, permanently tanned from hours of laboring in the sun.

Bang! Something hit the door on my side of the car. I jumped in my seat and smacked my wrist on the bottom of the steering wheel.

Grandfather Zook's concerned face peered at me through the open window. His long white beard spilled over the windowsill. "Chloe, are you all right? I'm sorry to scare you so. One of my braces got away from me and walloped the Cockroach." He glanced at the side of the car. "No harm done. What were you doing still in your car? There's work to be done."

Heat rushed to my face. Did Timothy's grandfather catch me staring at his grandson? I willed myself to stop blushing, but it was no use as any true redhead knew. Grandfather Zook backed away from my VW Bug's door on the metal braces he used to help him walk. I stepped out of the car, and as I shut the door, I slipped my car keys and cell phone into my jacket pockets.

Across the yard, the man with the umbrella stalked away from Timothy, muttering under his breath. He was too far away for me to make out the words but clearly whatever Timothy said had not been welcome news.

Timothy spotted me standing with his grandfather, and his face lit up. I felt a smile curve my own mouth. He started our way, but a cluster of elderly tourists stopped him with a flurry of questions. He gave me a half smile and then chatted with the visitors.

Grandfather Zook cleared his throat. "I used to look at my sweet wife that way." He winked at me. "I'm happy my grandson has found someone to love as dearly."

His comment only made me blush more. My fair complexion would be my undoing. That much was certain.

"Chloe!" a high pitched voice cried.

Seven-year-old Thomas Troyer and four-year-old Naomi raced to my side. The wisps of Naomi's blonde hair escaped her braid and flew behind her like silken thread. Thomas's Amish bowl-shaped hair bounced in tandem with his energetic steps. He reached me first and threw his arms around my waist. "Where have you been? We haven't seen you in weeks and weeks. And when we do, you never stay."

My heart constricted as Naomi wrapped her arms around me on my other side. "We missed you, Chloe. Don't you like us?"

Naomi's question was harder to digest than her brother's. When I had moved to Appleseed Creek eight months ago, she was only three and couldn't speak a word of English since she wasn't in school yet. She'd learned English because the Troyers spoke it when I visited since I didn't understand Pennsylvania Dutch. Now, she spoke it almost as well as Thomas, who I suspected came out of the womb bilingual with something to say.

"I've missed you too. I'm sorry I haven't visited lately." I swallowed a lump in my throat. "I've been so busy this school year."

Grandfather Zook frowned at me over the children's heads. Yes, I was busy as the Director of Computer Services at Harshberger College, but we both knew that wasn't the reason I'd avoided the Troyer farm. I stayed away because Mr. Troyer, and even to some extent Mrs. Troyer, didn't want me there. When Timothy told me his father asked for me to help with the bus tour today, I had been hopeful things would go back to normal, but since Becky had not been invited that told me the dispute between parents and child was long from over. Some in the Troyer's district, most notably the deacon, expected the family to shun Becky for her haircut. Even though no one said aloud that was happening to Becky, her absence spoke volumes. I understood Becky's hurt. Estrangement with a parent was something with which I was all too familiar.

"Did you see the bus people?" Thomas asked.

I patted his head. His hair felt like silk. I didn't tell him that because a rough-and-tumble boy like Thomas would find the comparison insulting. "I did."

Naomi tugged on my arm. She had her favorite faceless doll tucked into her left elbow. The doll wore the purple dress I had given Naomi for Christmas. "They talk different."

I smiled. "That's because they're from another part of the country and have a different accent than we do. We probably sound strange to them too."

Thomas frowned. "They can be hard to understand."

"I'm sure they think the same of us."

Grandfather stamped his right brace into the ground, but his eyes belied his good humor. "Enough yapping. Let's head to the barn. Simon's giving an old fashioned milking lesson."

"Am I late?" I asked. "Timothy told me to be here at ten." I slipped my cell phone from my pocket. The readout said I was ten minutes early.

He started across the bright green spring grass to the barn. "*Nee,* you're right on time. It's the bus of Mississippi *Englischers* who are early. They were supposed to go to the Zug sheep farm first, but one of Zug's sheep broke out of their pasture and made a run for it. He's got to go find it."

I fell into step beside him. Thomas and Naomi still clung to my sides. "How long have the tourists been here?"

Grandfather Zook frowned. "Maybe a half hour, not too long."

Why didn't Timothy call me to ask me to come sooner?

Carefully, I stepped out of Thomas's and Naomi's arms. "Do you have any idea what Mr. Troyer wants me to do?"

Naomi grabbed hold of my hand, and I squeezed it.

Grandfather Zook gripped his braces and was careful not to put them down on any dips or ruts in the yard. "*Nee,* but I'm sure there is plenty for you to do. My daughter,

Ruth, and Ruth's friend Anna Lambright have been in the kitchen most of the morning." He lowered his voice. "You'd think the tour director didn't feed them by the way they ate my daughter's cooking. She had to send Anna home for more eggs and flour, so that Martha could bake more muffins." Grandfather Zook edged around an indentation in the lawn. "I had hoped Becky would come with you."

Naomi gripped my hand more tightly at the mention of her oldest sister's name. As young as she was she still felt tension between Becky and her parents even if she didn't know the cause.

"She's working at the restaurant today," I said, hoping Grandfather Zook would leave it at that.

"Strange that Ellie wouldn't give her the morning off. She knew this tour was coming through." Ellie Young was the proprietress of Young's Family Kitchen and Flea Market, the largest Amish business in Knox County, and a close family friend to Grandfather Zook and the Troyers.

"I don't think that was the issue." I let my statement hang in the air.

Thankfully, Grandfather Zook dropped the topic at least for the time being.

Ten yards from the barn, I saw Bishop Hooley standing with Deacon Sutter. The two men studied the tourists milling around the Troyer farm. Bishop Hooley smiled and stroked his brown grizzled beard as he watched the travelers. In contrast, black-bearded Deacon Sutter looked like he was ready to excommunicate everyone within a twenty foot radius, including the non-Amish. I nodded in their direction. "What are they doing here? Isn't this the last thing they would want to see in the district?"

Grandfather Zook dug the end of his brace into bright green grass. "The tour was Bishop Hooley's idea."

I pulled up short. "It was?"

The older man nodded. "*Ya.* Bus tours like this have been traveling through Holmes County for decades. The bishop contacted some travel agencies and found one to come to Knox County instead of Holmes. If it goes well, this could go on all spring and summer."

"Deacon Sutter was okay with that?" I stole a glance at the deacon. He glared in return.

Grandfather Zook shrugged. "He might not agree with the bishop, but he won't cross him. What the bishop says goes."

I wasn't so sure about that. "Why did the bishop do this?"

"He saw this tour as a way to attract tourists to our district. Many times they pass Knox County on their way to Holmes." He snorted. "Holmes County doesn't have anything we don't have."

I smiled. "Just a few thousand more Amish and five times the businesses."

Thomas and Naomi ran ahead. Again wisps of hair flew behind the small girl.

Grandfather Zook tugged at his beard. "There is that. It is *gut* for the district. Bishop Hooley is turning into a fine bishop." He grinned. "All the families taking part will get a portion of the money the district earns from the tours. I think that's why my son-in-law agreed to participate. We could always use the money."

We'd almost reached the large white dairy barn. The familiar scent of dry milk, manure, and hay washed over me, and the sound of the cows mooing mixed with the German-sounding Pennsylvania Dutch and Southern drawled English voices. Thomas and Naomi dashed into the barn. I touched Grandfather Zook's arm. "Is the farm in financial trouble?"

"*Nee.* It's not in any more trouble than usual, but it is hard to compete with those big corporate farms buying up land. They're so large they can undersell us until we go under. They can take a loss on the sale of milk, we can't. After all the small farms go out of business, they can hike their prices."

I stared at Grandfather Zook, surprised by his bleak comment. He was more cheerful after the attack that sheared off his beloved beard.

He must have noticed my expression. "*Es dutt mir leed.* I'm sorry. We're here to promote the farm. Instead I am scaring you."

"I'm not scared."

He laughed. "You're face tells me something different."

Thomas and Naomi stood just inside the barn door as if too shy to enter. This was nothing new for Naomi, but Thomas was typically more fearless.

"Aren't they sweet? Don't you love the little girl's dress and the little boy's suspenders?" an African American woman with close cropped gray hair asked. "My, I wish I could take a picture of them. The photo would look so nice in my country style kitchen. I know right where I'd hang it too. Between the buffet and my plate collection."

"Now, LeeAnne, you know the Amish don't like their photographs taken," her companion, a white woman with a half dozen rings on her fingers and beads around her neck, said.

LeeAnne lifted her tiny digital camera. "One little picture won't hurt."

Grandfather Zook cleared his throat behind them.

The two women turned around and a blush flew up both of their cheeks.

"Those are my grandchildren you are talking about," he said.

The lady's hands with the rings fluttered into her face. "I'm so sorry. We were only saying how much we would like a photo of them. We would *never* take one. We would *never* disrespect your culture like that. Isn't that right, LeeAnne?"

LeeAnne hastily tucked her small camera into her tapestry purse, which was large enough to conceal a bowling ball or two. "Raellen is right. We would never do that."

Grandfather Zook folded his arms, trying to look gruff but failing horribly at it. "*Gut.* Because I would hate to have Chloe escort you off the farm. She's in charge of security today."

The two women looked my petite frame up and down.

"She's a lot tougher than she looks," Grandfather Zook said in a conspiratorial whisper. "She's taken down murderers."

Technically, that was true, but it was attributed to good timing and wits, not brute force.

The women whispered to each other as I followed Grandfather Zook into the barn.

Because of their herd of dairy cattle, the Troyers had one of the largest barns in the district. Despite its size, which could hold up to forty head of cattle, the building felt claustrophobic with the dozen or so tourists roaming the interior. Most were in a half circle around Mr. Troyer and one of his cows. Like his children, Mr. Troyer was blond, but his hair had darkened with age, and gray streaks ran throughout his beard and the hair visible under his black felt hat.

Timothy's father squatted on a three-legged milking stool in the middle of the room demonstrating how to milk by hand. Typically, Mr. Troyer milked six cows at a time with the milking machine in the milking parlor, an adjoining building at the rear of the main barn. A propane generator powered the milking machine and refrigerated the seven hundred gallon milk tank next to the milking parlor. I guessed Mr. Troyer thought it would be more "Amish" to show the Mississippians the by hand method. A calico barn cat watched a few feet away from Mr. Troyer's stool. He clicked his tongue at the cat. The feline opened her mouth, and Mr. Troyer squirted milk into it. The crowd cheered at him.

"Isn't that the sweetest thang?" a woman murmured.

Several tourists held small plastic cups of milk in one hand and one of Mrs. Troyer's muffins in the other. Half-empty trays of blueberry and cranberry muffins sat on a cafeteria-length table to the right of the barn's main door. Grandfather Zook was right. The Mississippians hit the muffins hard. Not that I could blame them. Mrs. Troyer was a world class baker. "Mr. Troyer is giving free samples of the milk too?" I whispered to Grandfather Zook.

He nodded. "That was Timothy's idea. He said the tourists would like to taste the real thing. Not that watered down stuff they buy at the grocery store."

I frowned as I watched a man take a big swig of milk. It left a white mark on his *Just for Men* black mustache. "It's not pasteurized?"

Grandfather Zook chuckled. "You are still a city girl. The milk is fine to drink. You've had it straight from the cow many times when you've visited and didn't even know it. It won't hurt these Dixie folks."

I cocked an eyebrow. "Dixie?"

"I know the song." He hummed the tune. "I wish I was in the land of cotton."

Naomi pulled on my arm. "Isn't it funny when *Daed* feeds the kitty like that?"

I gave her a squeeze. "It's very funny."

Thomas stood beside the muffin table stuffing muffins into his pants pockets as if he were a squirrel hoarding nuts for the winter.

A woman in an ankle-length denim dress stood a few feet from Thomas and gripped the edge of the table. I took a step in that direction. Was she fainting? Her Ronald McDonald red-headed friend held a paper plate. "Ruby, are you all right?"

Beads of sweat gathered on Ruby's upper lip. "Dizzy," she slurred.

Her friend set her plate on the table. "It must be the close air in here. Let's go outside, so you can catch your breath."

Ruby nodded as if she were underwater. She stumbled toward the open barn door and swayed. Her sway turned into a fall as she collapsed to the barn's dirt floor, hitting her head on the side corner of the table as she went down. Muffins and little cups of milk went flying in all directions. Her friend screamed.

Across the barn, the mustached man with the neon umbrella fell. He gripped his chest. The plastic cup of milk he held in his hand crashed to the floor, spilling milk onto his blue polo shirt. Ruby started to writhe on the dirt ground. Naomi gripped my leg so tightly that she cut off circulation.

"Chloe, get the children out of here!" Mr. Troyer bellowed.

I scooped up Naomi and grabbed Thomas by the hand. I took them from the barn. Thomas dragged his feet and the muffins he gathered fell from his pockets onto the grass. I looked back hoping that Grandfather Zook would follow, but I didn't see him.

CHAPTER TWO

Naomi buried her face in my neck. Her hot tears trickled down the front of my cotton jacket. "Shh. Shh." I tried to sooth her.

Thomas tugged on my sleeve. "What's wrong with those people? Are they sick?"

Sick was an understatement. "I don't know, Thomas."

He inched back toward the barn.

I grabbed him by the back of his suspenders. "No, Thomas, stay here with me."

For once the seven-year-old did as he was told. I reached into my pocket for my cell phone and dialed 911. "We need an ambulance." I told the dispatcher the address. "Two people have fallen seriously ill."

"What are their symptoms?" the sheriff's department dispatcher asked.

"Heart attack, maybe? The man clutched at his chest. The woman looked like she was having a seizure."

"Did anyone try to assist them? Turn the woman on her side, so she doesn't swallow her tongue," she asked in a calm voice.

I felt sick. "I don't know. They are inside the Troyers' barn. I'm standing in the yard with the children. I don't know what happened after I left the barn."

"Do you know their medical history, Miss?"

Naomi's small frame quivered against my body. "No, I've never seen them before. They're tourists."

"Stay where you are. An ambulance is on the way."

"Thank you," I paused. "Can you call Chief Rose too? I think she would like to be here for this."

"Do you suspect foul play?" Her voice was sharp.

"It's possible," was all I managed to say. I had no proof, only suspicion.

Mrs. Troyer burst out of her house and called to her children in their language. Naomi wriggled out of my arms. Both she and Thomas ran for their mother. As grown up as Thomas claimed to be, he still needed his mother's comfort when he was afraid. I would love to have my own mother to comfort me at a time like this, but that wasn't possible.

Their thirteen-year-old sister Ruth stood in the kitchen doorway with her arms crossed. Anna, Ruth's closest friend, peeked over Ruth shoulder. Her face paled. After her sister's sudden death in December, this couldn't be bringing back good memories for her.

Tourists poured out of the barn. The women cried, and men murmured to each other in a low timber.

Two Amish men and a lanky Amish teenager with sandy-colored hair joined the bishop and the deacon. The men spoke to the elders in their language, but the teen stood a few feet away. His eyes trained on the Troyer's back door where the girls stood.

Sirens blared as two ambulances turned in the Troyers' long driveway. The EMTs whooshed by us as they raced into the barn.

A few minutes later, Timothy stumbled through the open barn door. His neck bent down.

I jogged over to him. "What happened? How could they both fall at the same time?"

"Chloe—"

"Are they okay?"

He grabbed me by the upper arm. "Chloe, they are dead."

"Dead?" I stepped back from him but didn't go too far as he still had a hold of my arm. "Both of them?"

He nodded. "We tried CPR on both but couldn't get any response. Maybe the EMTs can revive them."

"But how is that possible for them both to fall like that? Had they been sick? Did someone say anything about that?"

"I don't know." He released me. "They both fell ill just after drinking a cup of *Daed's* milk." He let his last statement sink in.

"You don't—it couldn't be the milk that did this."

His expression was pinched. "That's exactly what everyone will think. It's what they already think." Timothy wrapped his arms around me, I suspected more to comfort himself than to comfort me. "It's what Greta will think. I can promise you that," he said as Chief Greta Rose's police cruiser rolled onto the property.

The petite, curly haired police chief jumped out of her car. Officers Nottingham and Riley climbed out of a second patrol car but stayed a few feet behind the chief. They knew this was her show. Officer Nottingham was a young guy close to my own age of twenty-four. He had perpetually wind-blown hair that looked like he'd just surfed in on some wave even though the closest beaches were hours and states away. In contrast, Officer Riley was just what you would expect to find in a small town Midwestern cop. He was middle-aged and grumpy with a slight paunch hanging over his duty belt.

Despite her small frame, the police chief walked with the swagger and confidence of a gun slinging cowboy. She shook her head as she approached. "Humphrey? Why am I not surprised?"

I grimaced and noted she wore teal eyeliner. Her love of brightly-colored eyeliner was legendary in the county.

She nodded at Timothy. "Troyer." She hooked a thumb at the tour bus. "What's with the Smurfmobile?"

Timothy stared at her as if she spoke Farsi. Smurfs were not part of his childhood.

"It's the bus the tourists arrived in," I said.

"Interesting color choice," the cop in teal eyeliner said. "Tell me what is going on here."

Timothy told the chief about the bus tour and had just gotten to the part where the two people fell when an EMT poked his head out of the barn door and whistled. Chief Rose's head snapped in that direction. The EMT frowned and shook his head. The chief sighed. "It appears the victim is dead."

"Victims," Timothy corrected. "Two people from the tour bus died. The tour director, Dudley Petersen, and a woman. I don't know the woman's name."

An EMT jogged back to the ambulance and pulled a medical kit from the open bay.

"I heard someone call her Ruby," I said.

The chief sighed again. "You two stay here. I will want to talk to you—"

Mr. Troyer rushed out of the barn and threw milk from a galvanized bucket onto the trampled grass.

Chief Rose broke into a run. "What are you doing?"

Timothy and I raced after her.

Mr. Troyer froze, and droplets of milk fell from the bucket's rim.

Chief Rose placed her hands onto her hips. "What are you doing?" Her steely voice would have brought a drug dealer to tears. It only confused Timothy's father.

Mr. Troyer removed a handkerchief from his back trouser pocket. "I'm dumping the milk. It's bad. I don't want anyone else to drink it and become ill."

Chief Rose glowered at him. "You're destroying evidence."

Mr. Troyer pulled his neck back. "*Nee.*"

"Greta." Timothy's voice held a warning.

She pointed a finger at Timothy. "Don't get involved, Troyer."

Officer Nottingham stood a few feet away with his SLR camera.

"Nottingham, take the bucket from him," the chief ordered.

Nottingham hung the strap of his camera over his shoulder and carefully removed the bucket from Mr. Troyer's hands.

"Is there any milk left?" the chief asked.

Mr. Troyer stood ramrod straight. "Not that I gave the guests. That was all of it. I threw it all out. It was the right thing to do."

The chief's eyes narrowed into teal painted slits. "No, Simon Troyer, it was not the *right* thing to do. You've made my life a lot harder."

Nottingham peered into the pail. "There's some liquid sticking to the sides of the bucket, Chief. There may be enough to test."

"Good." She turned. "Riley, run back to the squad car and grab the evidence kit. I want to see if we can salvage any of this milk before it's all washed away."

The older officer held onto his duty belt. "It's going to be contaminated, Chief."

"I know that, but I want backup to test if what's in the pail isn't enough." she snapped. "Hurry up. The ground is soaking up the evidence."

Officer Riley jogged back to the squad car.

"Nottingham, start collecting the names and personal information from everyone here. No one leaves until we question them. I'm going inside to take a look at the scene."

The improbable redhead who was with Ruby when she fell stood a few feet away. A cluster of women, including LeeAnne and Raellen, who wanted to take photographs of the Troyer children, surrounded her, so that I could only see the side of her bright red head. The women murmured platitudes to her. Whatever they said didn't appear to be working as the woman's sob escaped the semicircle.

Timothy followed the chief to the barn but waited outside when she shot him a dirty look. Officer Nottingham carried the milk pail to his squad car. After it was stored away, he cupped his hands around his mouth. "Your attention please. We know that you are all eager to leave, but we need to speak with each one of you first. Please be patient."

His announcement caused a flurry of conversation to run through the group.

Officer Riley returned with the evidence kit, but even I could see most of the milk had absorbed into the ground. He removed a small spade from the kit and collected a dirt sample where Mr. Troyer had dumped the milk.

I inched away toward the women clustered around the redhead.

"I want to go home," Ruby's friend wailed. "Today. I want to go home today."

"Pearl, you need to calm yourself." LeeAnne fished through her enormous purse and handed Pearl a tissue.

Pearl clutched the tissue but did not dab at the mascara running down her cheeks. "My cousin is dead. I knew this trip was a mistake. I kept telling her it was a mistake."

Raellen twisted one of the strands of beads around her index finger, so tightly I was afraid her finger might turn blue. "Is there anyone we can call for you? Ruby's husband? Any children?"

"Ruby and I are both widows." Her eyes cast down to the grass. "Neither of us has any children."

While Nottingham moved among the tourists, gathering their names and numbers and asking them what they knew about the two dead Mississippians, four EMTs checked the temperatures and blood pressures of the other bus passengers. Timothy carried wooden folding chairs from one of the sheds and began setting them up on the grass. The Troyers only used the chairs on the Sundays when district church services were in the Troyer home. Timothy helped an elderly woman into one of the chairs. Reluctantly, I left my eavesdropping post and went to help him.

Before I reached the shed, Chief Rose stuck her head out of the barn. "Nottingham, get in here and take photos of the scene. Riley, take up where Nottingham left off in the questioning. Make sure you look at their cameras and phones. Tourists take pictures. Maybe someone captured something on film."

"They weren't supposed to be taking photos while on the farm," I said.

She eyed me. "That doesn't mean they didn't."

A red-faced, heavy-set man stomped toward the police chief. "Is it the milk? Did that Amish man poison us?"

A collective gasp swept through the tourists. The EMTs ignored the outburst and focused on the task at hand, and Timothy continued to bring out chairs with a clenched jaw.

Chief Rose stepped all the way out of the barn. "Right now, everyone on this property is a suspect. Understood? We will make sure you all get the best medical attention, so that no one else falls ill."

"I feel a little woozy," an African-American woman wearing red plastic-framed glasses murmured in one of the chairs.

A man—I assumed her husband—placed a hand on her shoulder. "My wife is diabetic."

An EMT stopped taking the blood pressure of another man and knelt in front of the woman.

"See," the red-faced man said. "Another person is about to keel over. Who will be next? Me?"

"Mr.—" the chief began.

"French. My name is Jimbo French, and I'm here with my wife Bobbi Jo." He pointed at an equally heavy woman wearing a shearling jacket and sitting in a chair next to the diabetic woman.

The chief held onto the barn's doorframe. "Mr. French, as soon as we record your statement and the EMTs say you are ready to transport, you will be heading to the community hospital."

"Community hospital?" he blustered. "I don't like the sound of that. I want to go to a real hospital, not some back water clinic."

The chief jabbed a fist into her hip. "It is a *real* hospital. The closest *city* hospital is over an hour away. Do you want to wait that long to be checked out? Because if you do, we're going to need to you to sign a waiver that says you refused our advice in case you die. We can't have your family suing us."

Jimbo placed his hands on his ample stomach. "Is this how you northerners treat visitors? It's shameful." He pointed a meaty finger at Mr. Troyer. "I hope you Amish are prepared for a lawsuit because that's what you have coming to you."

Behind Jimbo, the Knox County coroner's SUV turned onto the Troyer land.

The invisible rod that held up Mr. Troyer's back and his pride gave way. His shoulders slumped forward and my heart broke for him. Simon Troyer was a beaten man.

CHAPTER THREE

C hief Rose scowled as she watched the Mississippians line up to climb back onto the blue bus. "Well, Humphrey, this is one for my memoir. I have a bus full of Mississippians who want their stomachs pumped after drinking Simon Troyer's milk. The hospital staff is going to love me for sending them their way." She folded her arms. "And I thought this was going to be a quiet spring."

The Knox County coroner, whom the chief simply called "Doc," and his team examined the bodies inside the Troyer barn. Chief Rose had told them to wait to bring the body bags out until after the tourists were off the property.

Ten yards from the barn, the EMTs packed their equipment. Timothy and his father were inside the Troyer home along with the bishop and deacon. The other Amish men left shortly after Officer Nottingham questioned them, but the unknown Amish teenager slunk around the periphery of the farm. I needed to ask Timothy who he was.

"Do you think more of them will get sick?" I asked the chief.

She slipped her aviator sunglasses, which were a tad too large for her small face, over her eyes. "Hard to say, but the EMTs believe whatever caused the two peoples' deaths would have reacted in others by now. With that said, we're not taking any chances. Two dead southerners in my town are more than enough, thank you." She folded her arms. "There was some remnant of milk in the bucket and in the cups. I hope there's enough for the techs at the sheriff's crime lab to test. It doesn't look good for your boyfriend's father."

I unclenched my hands. "If it was the milk that made them sick..."

"Point taken."

I shaded my eyes from the sun. "Mr. Troyer wouldn't hurt anyone. You can't believe he would do something like this on purpose."

Chief Rose looked me straight in the eye. We were the same height, five-four, and my pale, lightly freckled face and worried hazel eyes reflected back to me in the lenses of her sunglasses. "I would think by now, Humphrey, you should know anyone is capable of murder. You have certainly seen your share."

I had seen more than my share.

The line shuffling onto the bus moved slowly. Impatience masked many of the faces as if they were in a hurry to leave. I didn't fault them. Not many people were comfortable around death.

At the back of the line, a woman wearing a pink floral blouse touched a hand to her chest. "My pacemaker skipped a beat."

The man in a blue Polyester jacket and an impressive set of jowls cupped her elbow with his hand. "Are you feeling poorly, Bitty?" He waved to Chief Rose. "My wife's ill."

"What's wrong, ma'am?" Chief Rose asked. "Do you need assistance? We can have the EMT check you out here again before transporting you to the hospital. Did you drink any of the milk?"

"Oh no, I'm lactose intolerant. I can't touch the stuff," Bitty said, sounding perfectly fine and basking in the attention.

In front of her, Jimbo helped Bobbi Jo onto the bus.

Her husband adjusted his large camera bag on his shoulder. "Bitty, let's climb onto the bus. We will be at the hospital in no time, and the doctors can check out your pacemaker."

Bitty gave him a wobbly smile. "All right, Charles." She let her husband help her to the bus.

A tiny elderly woman, who was no more than five feet tall and somewhere between eighty and eighty-five years old, tugged on the chief's sleeve. Chief Rose peered down at the older woman. "Don't you worry about Bitty." She gripped her three-prong cane but stood so straight I wondered if it might be a prop. "She's been complaining about her ticker since she boarded the bus in Tupelo. If you ask me, it's all an act. It makes her husband set aside that annoying camera for three seconds to focus on her."

"Gertie," the tall thin woman behind her said. She was considerably younger than most of the group members. I placed her at mid to late fifties, maybe just shy of sixty. Her hair was styled in a messy pixie cut that went well with her tiny features. She wore designer jeans and a cashmere sweater. Most of the bus passengers were more of the wrinkle-free poly-blend set. "Maybe Bitty really isn't feeling well."

Gertie snorted. "Melinda, you always see the best in everyone." She released the chief's sleeve. "When you are as old I am you can tell when someone's pulling your leg."

"And how old is that?" Chief Rose asked.

I scowled at the chief. She should know it was impolite to ask a woman—any woman—her age.

Gertie stomped her cane into the grass. "I'm one hundred years old."

I gaped. "You are?"

"Surprised, ain't you?" She grinned, showing off square teeth which were far too perfect to be real.

"You look good for one hundred," the chief said.

"I should." Gertie pointed a bony finger at the Appleseed Creek chief of police. "It's all about clean living, exercise, and the grace of God."

The driver stood in the bus's open door. His bald head shone in the sunlight, and his polo shirt had "Blue Suede Tours" embroidered on the left breast pocket in white. All of the passengers except for Gertie and Melinda were on board. "This bus is leaving. If you want a lift to the hospital, you had better get on now."

Melinda touched Gertie's arm. "Come on, Gertie." She smiled at the chief and me. "Thank you for your help. I know this must be so difficult for all involved."

Gertie made her way up the bus's steps with Melinda's hands out ready catch her. Gertie didn't need the extra help; she moved with the ease of a fit fifty year old.

As the bus pulled away, Chief Rose said, "If I'm that spry at forty, I'll be pleased."

"Me too."

Chief Rose cracked her knuckles. "This could be the case that breaks me."

"Why's that?" I asked.

"Because, Humphrey, most of our suspects are on the bus, a bus bound to leave Ohio someday soon. Unless, I can find evidence to hold them here or figure out another way to keep them here…" she trailed off, looking through me.

My stomach clenched. I didn't like it how she called the southern travelers *"our* suspects." I didn't want anything to do with this.

Officer Riley carried a basket of Mrs. Troyer's leftover muffins to Chief Rose's car.

Happy for the distraction, I asked, "You guys taking those back to the station for a snack?"

Chief Rose rolled her teal-lined eyes. "They are evidence too. I suspect whatever made those two people so deathly ill was in the milk, but we have to test the muffins too to rule them out."

I swallowed. So much for a distraction.

The chief whistled at Officer Riley. He lumbered toward us. When he was within earshot, she said, "Go meet up with the bus at the hospital. I want every last one of those tourists accounted for. We need to keep an eye on them."

Officer Riley saluted and turned back to his car.

"You think it could be someone on the bus," I said.

"Humphrey, right now it could be anyone." With that, she headed back to the barn.

Across the property, Mr. Troyer sat at a picnic table answering Officer Nottingham's questions. He must have emerged from the house while Chief Rose and I were talking to Gertie and Melinda.

There was no sign of Mrs. Troyer and the children. Grandfather Zook was MIA too. I knew the elderly Amish man must be up to something because he typically liked to be in the thick of things.

My smartphone felt heavy in my jacket pocket. Should I call Becky at Young's and tell her what had happened? Surely, Ellie would allow her to leave the restaurant under the circumstances. Would Mr. Troyer want her here?

Would her presence make things worse? *I'll call her after the police leave.*

Bishop Hooley and Deacon Sutter came out of the back door of the farmhouse. The bishop's face was drawn while the deacon wore a hint of a smile, an expression I immediately distrusted. A knot tightened in my stomach. If there was anyone in the world who would want to hurt the Troyers, it was the deacon. The Amish were God-fearing people, but they had disputes within their communities just like the English do. Decades of animosity boiled between the deacon and the Troyer family, and it only grew worse when I arrived in town. The deacon had no use for the English and would love nothing better than for me to leave the county. Thankfully, Bishop Hooley, who held the real power in the district, didn't feel the same way.

Chief Rose emerged from the barn and joined Officer Nottingham and Mr. Troyer at the picnic table. I ambled in that direction, hoping that I would be overlooked. No such luck. Chief Rose frowned at me as I inched closer, but to my relief, she didn't order me to leave.

All of Officer Nottingham's concentration fixed on Mr. Troyer. "Where did the milk come from?"

The Amish man sat perfectly straight on the backless seat and met the officer's gaze. An intense scrutiny like that would cause me to flinch, but Officer Nottingham showed no emotion. Despite his young age, he was a seasoned cop who had seen too many things to be intimidated by an Amish man's glower.

"It's my milk," Mr. Troyer said. "It is from my cows." His voice was flat and without feeling, and his face was expressionless. Shock. He had to be in shock.

Officer Nottingham wrote something in a tiny notebook. "How old was the milk?"

Mr. Troyer folded his hands on the rough tabletop. "It was fresh. From that morning's milking. I set it aside special for the *Englischers*, who were coming."

More notes went into the notebook. "What do you mean you set it aside special?"

"Normally, it would have gone into the milk tank with the rest of the milk, but I didn't add it to the tank."

"Why did you do that?"

Mr. Troyer's knuckles turned white. "My son, Timothy, said that it would be good to give the *Englischers* a taste of farm fresh milk. I wanted them to have the freshest we had."

Officer Nottingham's head snapped up. "After you collected this special milk, what did you do to it?"

"Nothing more than set it inside the refrigerator we keep in the milking parlor..."

"What time did you do the milking this morning?"

Timothy's father crossed his right thumb over his left. "Same time that I always do. Five."

"And how were the cows this morning?" The young officer scribbled in his notebook. "Were they acting normal? Anything strange or off catch your notice?"

Mr. Troyer glanced up and made eye contact with me. His face was blank, and my heart sank. For a moment it was like looking into my own father's blank stare. No love, no approval, no emotion. I mentally kicked myself. Things with my father were better. I visited him and his family in Southern California in January. Over the trip, I had an opportunity to talk to him as I'd never done before. I even surprised myself when I told him about Timothy and his family.

"*Nee.*" Mr. Troyer dropped his eyes to his hands. "I mean, no, no there was nothing odd. The cows were fine and acted normal."

"Was the milk unattended at any time throughout the morning?"

Mr. Troyer glared at him. "No."

I inwardly groaned. Wrong answer, Mr. Troyer. The Amish man wasn't doing himself any favors. Not that I wanted him to lie, but he didn't have to make it so easy for Chief Rose and her officers to suspect him.

"That can't be true," I jumped in. "The milk parlor is on the other side of the barn. If the family was in the house, someone could have tampered with the milk, and no one would have known. Unless the milk was taken into the house, it wasn't attended the whole time."

Mr. Troyer's jaw twitched. Maybe I should have kept my mouth shut.

"Is this true, Mr. Troyer?" The chief asked.

"*Ya*, I mean, yes," he said.

Officer Nottingham played with the cap of his pen. "What's your relationship with the deceased?"

Mr. Troyer wrinkled his brow. "I don't know them. I met them this morning. I spoke to the man briefly when he arrived because he was in charge. I never spoke a word to the woman." Mr. Troyer stood. "I need to return to work. The cows are agitated."

Chief Rose held up a hand like a traffic cop. "You can't go back into the barn just yet, Mr. Troyer. The coroner is not finished working in there, and before you go back inside, an inspector from the state department of health, who is on his way here, has to give his okay."

"Health inspector?" I asked. "What's this about?"

Chief Rose frowned at me. "The inspector has to test the cows and the milk in the main milk tank to make sure it's not contaminated."

Mr. Troyer pressed the knuckles of his right hand into the tabletop. "There is nothing wrong with the milk in the tank."

"Are you sure about that? Whatever made Dudley Petersen and Ruby Masters ill could be in that milk as well."

"I told you I kept the milk the *Englischers* drank separate from the rest. It was in the parlor's refrigerator. It was never added to the tank. There's nothing wrong with the milk in the tank." He repeated and closed his eyes as if to regain his composure. "I don't want you testing my milk."

"Two people are *dead,* Mr. Troyer." Chief Rose slapped her hand on the tabletop. "You have no choice. It will be tested. Do not touch it. Do not throw it out. Do not add any milk to it. Don't go back into the barn until the health inspector gives his blessing."

"Where should I put my milk from my cows? They must be milked twice a day no matter what the inspector says."

The chief straightened. "The cows will need to be tested too."

Mr. Troyer's face was beet red. "There's nothing wrong with my cows. We give them *gut* care."

"Sir," Chief Rose's voice was steely. "We have to test them to prove that. No one is going to buy your milk if there is the least bit chance of contamination. We are doing this to help you."

Mr. Troyer stared at her for a long minute. "*Ya*, I am sorry. Two people have died. Do as you must." He walked away.

Officer Nottingham jumped out of his seat. "I wasn't done with the interview."

Chief Rose waved him back into his seat. "Let him go for now. We know where to find him."

A coroner's assistant rolled a stretcher with a body bag out of the barn. I cringed but was relieved that Chief Rose had the foresight to ask them to wait until the bus left the farm. As painful as it was for me to see this, I couldn't imagine how the tourists may have felt. This was someone they knew. Two EMTs, who hadn't left the grounds yet, helped the assistant load the first body into the back of his black SUV. The assistant went back into the barn. The elderly coroner brought the second body bag out.

Chief Rose jogged over to him. "What do you think, Doc?" the police chief asked.

He removed latex gloves and tucked them into a black fanny pack strapped to his waist. "My cursory glance is cardiac arrest. I won't know what caused it though until we have test results back."

She folded her arms. "When will that be?"

He adjusted his glasses. "I'm not even back at the lab yet, Chief, and I have several other cases ahead of yours."

"Doc, my case has to have priority. If I don't close up this case in the next few days, I never will. The bus is only in Knox County for a few days unless you can find something to keep them here."

"I'll see what I can do, but the other cases belong to the sheriff. You might want to give him a call and sweet talk him into letting me put yours first."

Chief Rose grunted, and Doc toddled away.

"Chief Rose, you can't believe Mr. Troyer had anything to do with this." I stepped in her path. "He doesn't even know any of these people."

The sun disappeared behind a cloud, and she pushed her sunglasses to the top her head. They nestled in her short poodle curls. "Wishful thinking does not become you, Humphrey."

"It's more likely the killer is one of the other passengers on the bus."

"Thanks for stating the obvious, but the first rule of being a cop is you have to have an open mind. If the milk in the tank tests clean and there is nothing wrong with the cows, that's good news for the Troyers. I'm doing these tests to help him, not to hurt him."

I gave a sigh of relief. "So you're not convinced Mr. Troyer did it?"

She shook her head. "Then again, I'm not convinced he didn't do it either."

Perhaps the sigh was premature.

CHAPTER FOUR

Finally, the crime scene began to clear out. Chief Rose's officers drove away in their squad car behind the ambulances, black SUV, and Doc's pickup truck. Chief Rose was the only public servant left on the property.

Bishop Hooley spun his black felt hat in his hand in front the police chief. "Ch-Chief Rose," the bishop said with his characteristic stutter. "When will the travelers be able to continue with their Amish Country tour?"

She cocked an eyebrow at him. "You think they will want to continue the tour after what happened here today?"

He replaced his hat on his head. "B-but it is all planned. We have m-many places in the community to show them."

Deacon Sutter, standing next to the bishop, smoothed his dark beard. "I told you, Bishop, this tour idea would lead to trouble. All *Englischers* bring to our community is sin and corruption." He gave me a pointed look.

At least I didn't have to wonder where I stood with the deacon. His feelings were clear and consistent.

The chief slipped her aviator sunglasses over her eyes again. "I don't know if the tour will go on. I will have a hard enough time keeping them in the county." A small smile played on the corner of her lips. "However, I will do my best to convince them to stay on schedule. It will help your community, Bishop, but more importantly it will also help my investigation. I need them here."

Why did I have a bad feeling about the chief's smile?

A white-paneled van with the Ohio State Department of Health seal on the side of it pulled into the Troyers' driveway as Chief Rose was leaving in her squad car. The two vehicles stopped, and Chief Rose spoke with the driver for a moment before waving good-bye to him and turning onto the county road.

Three inspectors piled out of the van in hazmat suits and face masks. The tallest walked over to me. "Is this your farm, Miss?"

I swallowed. "No. I'm a family friend."

"Where's the owner?"

I glanced back at the house and saw Mr. Troyer's face in the window. "He's inside the farmhouse."

The inspector turned toward the house. "He's welcome to observe our tests if he would like, but he doesn't have to."

"I don't think he wants to," I said.

The inspector nodded. "This shouldn't take too long." He waved to the two other men in white suits.

Inside the barn, the cows mooed. I imagined needles being stuck in their hides. Would the health inspectors test all forty-some cows?

Unable to listen to the cows, I went in search of Timothy and Grandfather Zook. I found it odd they weren't there to see Chief Rose off or meet the state inspectors.

I walked around the outside of the main barn and peeked in the buggy and horse barn. Grandfather Zook's horse Sparky ate from the trough in his stall and Mr. Troyer's two buggy horses and his work team kicked up dirt. They could hear the commotion in the dairy barn. Timothy and his grandfather weren't there.

I left the buggy barn and headed to the milking parlor. As many times as I had been to the Troyer farm I had never set foot in the parlor. Going there felt like an invasion of Mr. Troyer's private domain.

An open air breezeway covered the twelve feet between the main barn, where the cows lived, and the milking parlor. The breezeway didn't have any walls, but the roof offered the cows some shelter and protection from the worst of the rain and snow during the colder months.

The barn's large back door was closed, but the door to the milking parlor was cracked open. I peeked inside and found Timothy and his grandfather inspecting the floor. Mabel's plume of a tail thumped the ground when she saw me.

"What are you two up to?" I asked.

Grandfather Zook jumped and one of his braces fell from his arm.

I bent to pick it up. "I didn't mean to scare you."

He slipped the brace back on his arm. "I thought you were the lady copper."

"Chief Rose left, as did the coroner and Deacon Sutter and the bishop. The health inspectors are the only ones left. They said their tests won't take long."

Timothy pursed his lip. "I hope that's true."

Timothy's half collie, half German shepherd, half who knew what, shaggy black and brown dog got up from a horse blanket by the door and sniffed my hand.

"Hello, Mabel, what are you doing in here?"

"*Daed* told me to close her up in here while the tourists were on the grounds. He thought some of them might be afraid of dogs."

I laughed. "Afraid of Mabel?"

I scanned the room as Mabel licked my hand. The floor was cement and there were two raised cement platforms on either side the main floor. There were three narrow metal pens on either platform. Each pen had a clean milking machine, hanging from a metal hook and waiting for the next use. A bottle of weak iodine solution sat on a shelf by the parlor door. The iodine was used to sanitize the cow's udders before milking. It looked like any modern milking parlor, but the milking machines and the stainless steel refrigerator against the back wall were powered by propane not the power grid.

"Those lab coats stalking about give me the willies." Grandfather Zook shivered. "Reminds me of when I had polio."

"What do you mean?" I asked.

"When there was an outbreak of polio in my Amish community in Pennsylvania, the state sent a dozen of those lab rats to the community to test us. It was terrifying. Remember, when I was a child we had a lot less contact with the outside world. They said it was because of our 'inbreeding' that we got sick. Many of my friends and siblings were sent to *Englischer* schools to make them more *Englisch*. They didn't send me because I already had the disease. I suppose in their minds I wasn't worth making *Englisch*."

Timothy stared at his grandfather. "I never knew that. You never told me that before."

I shivered. "That's terrible. How old were you?"

"Nine." He chuckled. "It was a long time ago. *Gott* has given me many blessings since, but I hope you don't mind if I give those lab rats a wide berth." He adjusted his hold on his braces.

I peeked out the door and saw one of the health inspectors searching the ground around the barn. *What was he looking for?* "I won't let them come near you," I said.

Grandfather Zook grinned. "You *are gut* to me, Chloe. My grandson is a lucky man."

Timothy's face spilt into a smile, and I blushed. The fact that Timothy wasn't the least bit embarrassed by his grandfather's statement made my heart jump.

I cleared my throat. "So what are you two doing in here?"

Grandfather Zook bent his head in a conspiratorial way. "We are looking for evidence. My eyes aren't as good as they used to be, so I asked for Timothy's help."

"Evidence?" I scanned the dusty cement floor and didn't see anything amiss. The back door of the milking parlor stood open. Through the door, I saw the back pasture. Beyond the pasture there were the woods that separated the Troyer farm from the Lambright farm, where Anna lived. "Why's that?"

He fluffed his snow white beard with the back of his hand. "Early this morning, I heard a noise behind the barn. It may have come from the milking parlor. At the time, I thought it was a deer or a barn cat, but now, I wonder. We're looking for tracks. The cop lady always looks for tracks."

I examined the ground. There were blurry tracks on the floor, but it was impossible to tell if they were there from the morning or from our shoes. "What time did you hear the noise?"

"Just about six o'clock. I was in the main barn feeding the barn cats—Simon says they can fend for themselves, and that's true, but it doesn't hurt to do them a kindness.

Naomi was with me and she heard the noise too." He patted the barn's white-washed siding. "I was right on the other side of this wall." He hobbled over to the open door that led to the breezeway and pointed. "My workshop is right about there. He pointed at the south corner of the barn. The cats eat in my workshop, so that's where we were standing when we heard the noise."

Grandfather Zook made wood handicrafts which sold to the Amish gift shops in town to earn a little extra money for the family.

I peered through the door. "That's a ways away, Grandfather Zook. It's hard for me to believe whatever you heard came from the milking parlor. It would have to be awfully loud. What did it sound like?"

Grandfather Zook cocked his head. "It was a bang, like a rake handle hitting the milking parlor wall."

A sound like that would get my attention too. "You didn't go look?" I asked.

He shook his head. "Naomi was scared and wanted to go back inside the house. When I told her to run inside without me, she started to cry. I agreed to go with her because I thought it was an animal knocking something over. The old farm makes a lot of noises, and there's no telling what critters are on the land at any given time." He frowned. "I wish I had gone to see what it was. I would have stopped whoever did this."

Naomi may have saved her grandfather from confronting a killer.

"With all the spring rain," Timothy said, "had someone or something been back here I would have thought there would be a track between the barn and milking parlor."

"Did you see any tracks in the mud?" I asked.

Timothy shook his head.

I stepped away from the open parlor door. "Did you tell Chief Rose about the noise?"

Grandfather Zook turned from the door to face me. "*Nee.* I wanted to see if I could find some type of proof first. I know the lady cop likes her evidence."

This was true. I wasn't sure if I should be horrified or amused that Grandfather Zook, an elderly Old Order Amish man, knew that. It was certainly a sign that the Troyer family had too much interaction with the Appleseed Creek police.

Timothy ran his hand through his white-blond hair. "We've been searching for twenty minutes and haven't found anything outside or inside the parlor. I'm beginning to wonder—"

Grandfather Zook shook his finger at his grandson. "Don't you start thinking your *grossdaddi* was hearing things. I know what I know. I only wish I had had the good sense to investigate when I first heard the noise. Then, this all could have been avoided."

Timothy blew out a breath. "You said yourself it could have been another barn cat or a deer."

Grandfather Zook snorted. "I'm going to keep looking."

"Timothy's father did say he stored the milk for the tourists in the refrigerator here around five in the morning. If someone was here at six, they could have tampered with it and left before the bus arrived," I said.

"That's not the only time," Timothy said. "It was so chaotic when the southerners first arrived. Since they were an hour early, we weren't ready for them. Someone could have slipped in here unnoticed and put something in the milk."

"But wouldn't that person have to have known your father set the milk aside for the tourists?" I asked. "Did either of you know?"

They both shook their heads.

I fondled Mabel's ears. "Did you hear anything, girl? Did anyone come inside here while you snoozed?"

Grandfather Zook leaned heavily on his braces and chuckled. "If someone did she would have licked him to death."

Mabel gave me her best doggie grin. Lassie she was not.

My cell phone rang. As I retrieved it from my jacket pocket, I saw Chief Rose's name on the readout. Why was I not surprised?

Timothy examined my face. "Who is it? Your dad?"

I sighed. "No. It's Chief Rose."

"I thought she just left," Timothy said.

"She did." I put the phone to my ear and stepped out the back door of the milking parlor. "Hello?"

"Humphrey, get your behind down to the hospital now," the police chief ordered.

"What? Why? What's wrong?"

"These tourists are what's wrong. They need a new tour guide." She sucked in air. "You."

"Me?" I squeaked.

Timothy touched my shoulder, and I turned to face him. His brow was knit together in worry. "What is it?" he mouthed.

I shook my head.

"Yes, you," Chief Rose snapped. "I need a new guide or these people are going to bolt."

I gripped the phone to my ear. "They still want to go on the tour?"

"Let's just say I talked them into it." She sounded a little too pleased with herself in my opinion.

I knew that smirk on the chief's face would lead to trouble. "I wouldn't know what to do."

"Humphrey, it's not rocket science. You stand on the bus and tell them about our quaint little town and introduce them to the Amish farmers and convince them to buy buggy-shaped paperweights they don't need. How hard can that be?"

There has to be a way out of this. "I'm not a tour guide. I'm a computer geek."

"You're not a detective either, but you like to pretend you are," she said.

I grimaced and knew the chief referred to the few times I'd meddled in her investigations, sometimes with her blessing, sometimes without it. Her voice turned sharp.

"You know more about the Amish living in this county than English folks who have lived here for generations. I need you." She paused. "Do it for the Troyers. If the bus people stick around, I will have more suspects."

"Isn't there someone else you can ask? There has to be a real travel agent in Knox County. Isn't there an AAA office in Mount Vernon? Maybe you should call them."

"Don't you want to help your boyfriend's family? I'm surprised, Humphrey. This is your chance to be trapped on a bus with all those lovely suspects, perhaps even clear the good name of Troyer's father."

Or be trapped on a bus with a murderer.

"You want me to do that?" I asked. "You want me to investigate while I'm on the bus?"

"You might as well make use of your time. I certainly can't do it. They aren't going to say anything incriminating in front of me or one of my officers. Remember everything they say and report back to me. This should be one of your easier assignments."

A light wind whipped across the pasture. The grass bent low in submission to it. I shivered. "What if they suspect I'm reporting back to you?"

"Humphrey, you look like a human replica of Raggedy Ann. No one would suspect you of anything more devious than forgetting to say 'thank you' after someone passes you the salt."

I chewed on the Raggedy Ann comment and reflexively touched my hair to reassure myself it wasn't yarn-like.

"How many passengers are there?" I squeaked. "I didn't count when they were here on the farm."

"Fourteen. The bus seats thirty-five. See, I'm not even sticking you with a full bus."

"Thanks." I pulled my car keys out of my jacket pocket and balanced them in my hand.

Timothy arched his brows in question.

"Fifteen if you count the driver," the chief said.

Which I do. I thought of the irritable-looking man in the blue polo shirt.

"Where are they staying?" My tone was resigned.

"The Dutch Inn right here in Appleseed Creek."

That made sense since it was the largest inn in town. Hotel options were few in Knox County. There were a couple chain hotels in Mount Vernon or bed and breakfasts dotting the small towns, but none of the B&Bs were large enough to hold fourteen people plus a bus driver.

"Listen to me." The chief's patience ran thin. "If you don't do this, these people will leave and the only suspect left is Simon Troyer." The threat hung in the air. Chief Rose had me, and we both knew it. "If you care about the Troyers as much as you claim to, you don't have a choice."

I locked eyes with Timothy. His brow drooped in concern, and even though he was only twenty-seven, I saw the beginning of light wrinkles feathering out from the corners of his eyes caused by sun and worry. Like she said, I really didn't have a choice. "I'll be there in twenty minutes."

CHAPTER FIVE

L eaving Grandfather Zook and Mabel at the Troyer
farm to continue to search the grounds for evidence,
Timothy drove me to the hospital.

I straightened my seatbelt's shoulder strap while
Timothy turned onto State Route Thirteen, heading into
Mount Vernon. "When I first arrived at the farm this morn-
ing, you and Dudley were talking. He didn't look happy."

"He wasn't," Timothy said.

"What were you talking about?"

"Dudley wanted the tourists to have an opportunity
to walk through the house. I told him that wasn't part
of our portion of the tour. There may be other Amish

families that invite them in, but *Daed* would never be comfortable with that many strangers in the house at one time."

"That seems reasonable. Why was he so upset about it?"

"I guess the district he used to take tours to in Holmes County always included a home tour. He said if the district didn't provide one, he wouldn't have his tours stop in our district again. I told him that was something he would have to take up with the bishop." Just inside of Mount Vernon, Timothy stopped his truck at a red light. "He didn't seem to want to talk to the bishop."

"That's odd. The tour was the bishop's idea."

The light changed to green. "I thought so too."

Another questions struck me. "Who was the Amish teenaged boy on the farm?"

Timothy turned his head toward me for a half second. "Amish teenaged boy? Who are you talking about?"

"I don't know. That's why I'm asking you. He looked about sixteen and sort of gangly."

"I didn't see anyone like that there."

"You didn't?" I asked. "I saw him a couple of times with Amish men and then later by himself."

"Maybe he was a son of one of the men."

I wrinkled my forehead, not sure why I was so concerned with the boy. Then, I remembered how he'd watched Ruth and Anna so intently as they'd stood in the kitchen doorway. "Maybe Ruth knows who he is?"

"Maybe," Timothy said seemingly unconcerned about this little mystery. He drove up the small hill to the community hospital. Most of the Mississippi folks waited on their tour bus and scowled out of the windows at anyone who happened to walk by.

I placed my hand on the door handle. "You don't have to come with me."

He shifted in his seat to face me. "One of these tourists may have killed two people. Do you think I would let you ride in a bus alone with them?"

"I'll be fine. Chief Rose wouldn't ask me to do this if it put me in any kind of danger."

Timothy barked a laugh.

I tightened my grip on the door handle. "You need to go back to the farm and help your family."

"There's nothing that I can do there. *Daed* refuses to talk me about it. *Grossdaddi* is wandering around the farm hunting for the source of the mysterious sound."

"I know but..." I trailed off.

He shifted away from me. "You don't want me to come with you?"

I squeezed his arm. "No! No, it's not that."

"Then what?"

"They know you are Simon Troyer's son."

"So." He shut off the ignition and slipped the pickup's key into his hip pocket.

How do I say this nicely? "They think your father killed their friends. They might not welcome you onto the bus."

Timothy's face fell as if he realized I was right. "I can't let you go alone. I don't want anything to happen to you."

I couldn't help but smile at his concern. It felt strange to have someone worrying about me. "I'll be fine. And remember Chief Rose—"

Timothy snorted. "Wouldn't put you on the bus if she thought you were in danger. I know."

I opened the door and paused before hopping out of the truck. "Whoever did this isn't going to do anything in a bus full of tourists. There would be too many witnesses."

He leaned across the bench seat and brushed his lips across mine. "Just remember I said this was a bad idea."

I patted his cheek. "I'll remember."

Timothy and I climbed out of the pickup and joined Chief Rose and the bus driver waiting outside of the bus. The police chief with arms folded and her aviator glasses hiding her eyes said, "Took you long enough, Humphrey. I want—"

"His father murdered my cousin!" Pearl cried from the open bus window.

The police chief muttered something under her breath I didn't catch, and Timothy took a huge step back from the bus.

"Humphrey, I don't remember asking you to bring Troyer. Are you two attached at the hip?" She made a show of examining our legs.

Timothy closed his eyes for the briefest of moments as if to stop himself from saying something he would regret. "I'm not staying. I'm just dropping Chloe off."

The chief nodded. "Good. I need to keep these folks as calm as possible. The more riled up they are, the more likely they'll leave. I won't be able to convince a Knox County judge to write an order to keep them here unless I have hard evidence. I need more time to get that."

"Can we get going already?" the bus driver asked.

Chief Rose pointed a thumb at the bright blue bus. "Go fire up the Smurfmobile."

The bus driver gritted his teeth and stomped to his bus.

"What is this Smurfmobile stuff?" Timothy asked.

"There's not time to explain pop culture to you, Troyer. Humphrey will give you a lesson later." She pointed a finger at me. "We need to have a powwow before you saddle up."

I followed her a few steps away. Timothy was close on my heels. Chief Rose frowned at Timothy but didn't tell him to leave. "Officer Riley thoroughly questioned every passenger before letting them back on the bus, and so far, I have nothing to hold them. That's why you're here. You're going to have the perfect opportunity on the bus to gather information about these people. See what you can find out. Did anyone have any hard feelings for either victim? Did anyone see anything peculiar or was anyone behaving oddly at any point during the trip?"

"You're asking Chloe to investigate," Timothy said.

The chief gave Timothy a look. "She's going to anyway. I might as well benefit from it."

"She's right," I said.

"See." She smiled triumphantly at Timothy. "Report everything you learn to me. If you think something is particularly important, don't wait. Call me immediately."

Timothy flexed his hands. "I don't like this."

"Don't worry, Timothy," I said. "It's just one day."

The chief shook her head. "Wrong. This trip goes on for four days."

My mouth fell open. "What?"

"Yep, I signed you up for the entire trip through Knox County and portions of Holmes County too. The tour company was pleased, especially when I told them you'd work for free. I said it was the least we could do to help them deal with the tragedy. When the bus moves on to Indiana, you are off the hook. We have to solve this case before that happens, if we ever hope to solve it at all."

"I don't know anything of the Amish in Holmes County," I argued.

"The culture is basically the same." She shrugged. "Buggies, cheese, quilts, and pies. No big deal."

"I can't just blow off work to lead this bus tour."

She gave the tiniest of smiles. "I know your semester ended last week. What do you have to do?"

"Dean Klink isn't going to go for it." Even as I said this, I knew it was only wishful thinking.

She smiled. "You leave the dean up to me."

A piercing whistle came from the direction of the bus. "Let's go. We're burning daylight," the driver bellowed.

"Be charming. You'll have a great time," the chief said.

I straightened my shoulders.

We were a few steps from the bus when, Timothy squeezed my elbow. "Are you sure you want to do this?"

"I have to. It's for your family." I bit my lip. "Maybe if I help your father, he will accept me again."

"Chloe, he does accept you."

"I have to do this for Becky too. Maybe—"

"Today!" the driver bellowed.

"It's going to be a long trip." I pecked Timothy on the cheek and dashed for the bus before he talked me out of it.

I stumbled onto the bus as I saw the interior. Nothing could have prepared me for it. I'd thought the outside was blue, but the inside was *blue.* It looked like blueberry girl from *Charlie and the Chocolate Factory* blew up in there. Every inch of it was the same cobalt blue color from the floor to the seats, to the ceiling. On the back walk there was a German shepherd-sized white outline of a man's dance shoe with Blue Suede Tours written in white beneath the shoe, apparently the company logo. The front row was empty. It felt like suede. It had to be imitation leather because it covered every seat. At least, I hoped that it was. The tour company officially took the theme one step too far.

I held my hand out to the driver. "I'm Chloe."

"You're late." He pulled the lever to shut the bus doors and revved the engine. Chief Rose was right. He was a charmer.

I gripped the railing. "I'm so sorry about your loss."

He blinked at me. "My loss? I didn't lose anything."

"Oh, I meant the guide, Dudley. He was your coworker."

"He might have been that, but it doesn't mean he meant anything to me. Dudley Petersen was a thorn in my side. As far as he was concerned, I couldn't do anything right. 'Hudson, you're driving too fast. Hudson, you're driving too slow.' Dudley was like having a gnat in my ear twelve hours a day for three years. Truthfully, I would have preferred the bug."

"Oh." I clung to the closest handrail. "What about his family?"

"What about it? I don't know anything about the guy. He never mentioned a family, but we were not exactly chums, you know what I mean?"

"What about the woman who died?"

He narrowed his eyes. "Are you going to lead this tour or keep running your mouth?"

I stepped back.

"Time is money, and I don't have very much of either." He ripped a piece of paper from his breast pocket and handed it to me. "This here is the itinerary Old Dudley made."

I unfolded the paper. It said the Mississippi gang would be in Central Ohio for four days just as the chief said. I swallowed. That meant we had to find who framed Mr. Troyer in four days. After leaving Ohio, they were headed to their next destination in Shipshewana, Indiana. It appeared they were doing a thorough tour of Amish Country, which began in Lancaster County, Pennsylvania. It was a long trip. The group had already been together for five days. Two weeks on a bus through Amish Country with these people didn't sound like that great of a time to me.

After the Troyers' dairy farm, the next item on the itinerary was a stop at Deacon Sutter's place. "Care if I make some adjustments to this?"

"As long as we start moving and I get paid, I don't care what you do."

"Then, I have the perfect place." I told him the address, hoping Ellie wouldn't mind.

CHAPTER SIX

As Hudson turned the bus out of the hospital's parking lot onto Coshocton Ave, the main shopping district in Mount Vernon, I turned and waved to the passengers. "Hi, everyone. I'm Chloe."

"We can't hear you!" someone called from the back.

"I'm Chloe," I shouted.

"We still can't hear you. Are you mumbling on purpose?" the same man with sparse gray hair and a pronounced nose asked.

Hudson shoved a thin microphone at me with his right hand. "The mic, the mic. Use the mic. Half of the bus uses hearing aids, and the other half needs to."

"Let's try this again," I said into the mic. "Hello, everyone. I'm Chloe Humphrey, and I will be leading the remainder of your tour through Ohio's Amish Country."

"What about the tour after Ohio?" a man with a bulbous nose shouted from the back of the bus. "Who's going to lead the tour when we get to Indiana? We paid good money to see this tour from beginning to end. I'm not going back to Mississippi until I see all of it or get all of my money back."

Other disgruntled voices in the group agreed.

"Tell 'em we're working on it," Hudson said out of the side of his mouth.

I covered the microphone. "Are we working on it?"

"Just tell them. You don't want this group to get restless. Trust me. They'll eat you alive. They have dentures. It won't be pretty."

I made a face. "That's yet to be decided," I said into the mic. "But rest assured we are working on it."

Nose didn't appear satisfied with that answer. I suspected he planned to ask every day until we could give him the new guide's name and social security number. There was some rumbling from the back, but no more shouts. That was progress.

"Because of," I paused, "the sensitive circumstances, there has been a small adjustment to today's schedule. We will skip the Sutter farm and go straight to our lunchtime destination, Young's Family Kitchen. There's an enormous

Amish flea market on the property, and you will have plenty of time to eat, shop, and mingle with the Amish."

"Shop?" my heckler in the back called. "That's the last thing my wife needs to do. She's already spent my life savings on this trip. Do you know that she bought an entire dining room set, table, chairs, and buffet in Lancaster? They are being shipped to my home as we speak."

A silver-haired lady in the seat next to him punched him in the arm. "Fred, stop your complaining. Just think of how nice it will be when the kids come home for the holidays."

"It won't be paid off until I'm long dead. I bought that life insurance for my burial, Nadine, not for a new dining room set."

She smiled and shook her head. I had a feeling Nadine had done that many times over the last sixty years.

Fred gave her a withering look. "That's fine, just have me cremated and stick me in a shoebox. That's all I ever meant to you anyway. Better to save money that would have been used for a proper burial for a new sofa."

Nadine laughed. "Oh, Fred, you're too much." She smiled at me. "Don't mind him, Sweetie. He's just a jokester."

From the scowl on Fred's face I wasn't so sure about that. "Oh look," I cried with relief. "There's Young's now." The large parking lot was full with buggies and automobiles. Locals and visitors packed the flea market and restaurant on a gorgeous spring Saturday like today. The enormous Amish restaurant that boasted a twenty foot long buffet, a bakery, pie shop, and gift shop loomed over the parking lot.

Behind the restaurant was the Youngs' prize business, the flea market. Most of the vendors in the market were Amish, but the Young family opened their doors to English sellers as well. In the flea market, a shopper could buy everything from Amish kettle corn to mint condition Beanie Babies to a new tractor. Over the winter, Timothy enclosed the flea market's three pavilions to make them all weather safe, so the Young family could rent the space to vendors year round. Only open a month, the enclosed pavilions already earned the Youngs a twofold increase in profits. This was great news for Timothy too. He was a carpenter by trade and Young's Flea Market was the first project he'd taken on as a general contractor. Because of Young's, he received countless calls for contracting jobs within Knox and neighboring counties.

If the demands of his business continued to grow, Timothy would have to find a new workshop space. Right now, he worked on site or out of the garage of the old purple Victorian house he rented with another former Amish guy, Danny. Purple was not Danny's or Timothy's color choice.

"Not soon enough," Hudson said under his breath. "If Fred keeps this up, I might lose him somewhere. He can hitchhike back to Mississippi."

"I heard that," Fred bellowed.

"Course you did," Hudson muttered.

"Heard that too."

Chief Rose had scoffed about this easy assignment. Obviously, she had not seen Hudson and Fred in action before she put me on the bus. Then again, maybe she had. To my relief, Hudson pulled up in front the restaurant's door. The passengers gathered their jackets and handbags before they disembarked.

Hudson snapped his fingers to get my attention.

It was my turn to scowl. Snapping fingers didn't work for me.

"Before I open the door," he said. "You'd better tell them when to return to the bus. As soon as they hit the pavement, they'll scatter. They may look like a slow bunch, but they can move quickly when a meal's involved."

I covered the mic. "When should I tell them to come back to the bus?"

"Hey, open the door. We're not getting any younger," Fred crowed.

"Yeah, open the door," Jimbo chimed in.

Hudson's jaw twitched. "I don't care. Pick a number before one of the old biddies smacks me in the head with her pocketbook."

I turned back to the anxious crowd. Many stood in the aisle waiting to exit. Hudson was right, they wanted out. "Be back on the bus at three o'clock, then we'll head back to the inn."

The driver opened the door, and they charged. I hopped off of the bus to avoid being trampled. Fred was the first off. No surprise there. "Hurry up, Nadine," he said to his wife as she gingerly navigated the bus steps. "We need to get in line for lunch, or we will be here all night."

I gave Nadine my hand to help her down the last step. "Thank you, dear," she said. *How did a sweet lady like Nadine end up with such a grump like Fred? Another case of opposites attract?*

I greeted each guest as he or she disembarked. Gertie took my hand. "Thank you, Chloe. By the way, I forgot to tell you my real secret for living over a century."

Behind her Melinda sighed.

"What's that?"

"I've eaten two pieces of fish jerky every morning for the last seventy years. It's an old family recipe, and I cure and dry it myself. It keeps me young and fit."

"I've never heard fitness attributed to jerky before," I said.

"That's because you're not eating the right kind. I eat one hundred percent Mississippi fish jerky. It makes all the difference." She shot her thumb toward the bus. "I never leave home without it. I got a stash back on the bus. I'll give you a taste later. It will change your life."

My stomach turned at the thought. "That's a very kind offer."

"Gertie, you're holding up the other passengers," Melinda said.

Gertie pursed her lips. "I'm over a hundred years old, so that makes me the closest to death. They can wait."

"I hope you and your daughter have a lovely lunch. I recommend the fried chicken," I said. "It may not compete with your jerky, but it's very good."

Gertie wagged her finger at me. "Melinda isn't my daughter."

I blushed. "I'm so sorry, I shouldn't have assumed."

Gertie was unconcerned. "She's my companion. I pay her to travel with me."

Melinda's face turned bright red.

I smiled at Melinda. "That sounds like a fun job. I'm not well-traveled. I've been to California and a few other states. I hope to visit Italy this summer. My best friend Tanisha lives there."

Gertie beamed. "Melinda and I went there three years ago for my ninety-seventh birthday. Oh, the Italian men, were they ever taken with me! I can tell you stories that will make your toes curl. We had pip of a time, didn't we, Melinda?"

"A pip," Melinda deadpanned.

Melinda gave an all-suffering sigh and followed Gertie up the short walk into Young's.

Ruby's cousin, Pearl, was the last person to exit the bus. Although Gertie was one hundred, Pearl seemed to be twice Gertie's age and did not have the centurion's energy. She hunched forward as she navigated the bus steps. I offered her my hand to help her down the steps. She thanked me quietly as tears gathered in her light brown eyes.

"I'm so sorry about your loss." I didn't know what else to say.

She took a shuddered breath. "I don't know what I'll do without her. She was all the family I had. Should I go home? How will I get there?"

"If you need to make arrangements to return home, I'm sure the travel company can help you. There's an airport just an hour away."

Her eyes were bloodshot. "What about Ruby? I can't leave her here alone. Who would take care of her arrangements?"

She had a point, and Chief Rose wouldn't be happy with me if I encouraged a prime suspect to skip town.

Tears gathered in Pearl's eyes. "I don't think I can face the rest of the tour."

"I can take you to the inn if you would like some time to rest."

A tear slid down her heavily powdered cheek. "I would appreciate that. It would be nice to lie down and make some phone calls. There's so much to do. I need to call the funeral home, the church, and..." She trailed off as the enormity of her task settled on her shoulders.

Hudson placed his hand on the door closer. "How are you going to get her there? You're not taking her in my bus."

I glared at Hudson. "I have no intention of driving your bus."

"Good." He moved to shut the bus's folding doors.

I grabbed the door. "Wait! Pearl, is there anything on the bus that you will need before we go?"

An SUV behind the tour bus honked and the driver shared a rude gesture.

Pearl flushed. "I do have a small carry-on under my seat."

"I'll get it for you." I jumped onto the bottom step. "It will take me two seconds to grab her bag."

"Fine," Hudson grudgingly agreed.

As I climbed onto the empty bus and realized this might be the only time I'd be on it without passengers. I should look for clues. Trouble was I had no idea what to search for. I wished Chief Rose had given me more direction on this investigation.

Umbrellas and folded jackets lay on the empty seats. Small roll bags with the Blue Suede Tours logo of a blue shoe were embroidered on the front of it were tucked up the seats. The Mississippi tour group was a neat bunch. There were no confession notes or smoking guns left behind.

Hudson watched me in the rearview mirror. "What's taking so long? I've got to eat too, you know."

I shuffled to the back of the bus and retrieved Pearl's bag; it looked like all others, but had Pearl's name and address on the luggage tag. Under the seat next to hers was another bag. I flipped over the luggage tag. It was Ruby's. Before I could change my mind, I took that one too.

CHAPTER SEVEN

I climbed out of the bus with two roll bags, not one. Tanisha would be proud. She taught me the key to pulling anything off—good or bad—was confidence.

Hudson shut and locked the bus door behind me and revved the engine. I stepped clear of the bus just before he peeled away from the curb.

"You have two bags there," Pearl said.

I adjusted my grip on the roll bags. "I grabbed Ruby's too."

Tears appeared in her eyes again. "That was so thoughtful of you to do that for me."

I hadn't grabbed the bag for her but didn't argue.

A man cleared his throat as he brushed passed us to enter the restaurant and muttered about people always "standing in the way." Inside the restaurant, there was a line to be seated—Jimbo wasn't going to be happy about that— but many of those waiting sat in white rockers on the restaurant's wide front porch.

Without my Beetle, we needed transportation. Maybe I should have lined that up before I offered to take Pearl to the inn. I led Pearl to the side of the porch, so we didn't block the door and removed my cell from my pocket. Pearl stood in a daze as I texted Timothy. "Where are you?"

A text came back. "At Young's."

"I'm here too. Can I borrow your truck?"

"Meet you out back."

I smiled at Pearl, whose head appeared even more Crayola crayon red in the sunlight. "We've got a ride to the inn."

"That's nice," she murmured and reached for her roll bag.

I studied her face as I handed it to her. *Was she going into shock?*

I led Pearl into the restaurant. The place was packed. Ellie, the owner, and her son Uriah must be pleased. I wove through the people waiting to be seated. As we reached the host stand, a burly man stepped in front of me. "Hey, no cutting! Get back in line."

I frowned. "I'm not staying, I'm just passing through."

Aaron Sutter, who was both Timothy's best friend and Deacon Sutter's son, watched the exchange from his wheelchair beside the host's podium. His bowl haircut was longer than the last time I had seen him, and his bangs hid his eyes.

The man folded his arms. "We've been waiting here for over twenty minutes for a table. If you think you can waltz in and take our place, you have another thing coming."

Aaron straightened a stack of menus in his lap. "She's not here to eat. She's a friend of the owner."

The man grunted and stepped out of my way.

"Thanks, Aaron." I gave him a small smile.

He simply nodded and handed the stack of menus to an Amish teenager who seated guests.

Sadness washed over me as I led Pearl through the dining room. Even though Aaron was Timothy's best friend, I had seen little of him since Becky told him she was never returning to the Amish community. I kept an eye out for Becky. She was supposed to be working, but the place was so crowded I couldn't pick her out from the other servers running in and out of the kitchen in matching Amish dresses.

In the stainless steel professional kitchen, none of the Amish cooks questioned me as I led Pearl through their domain. They diced vegetables for the salad bar, stirred huge vats of beef stew, and dropped chicken legs into the fryer. All the while, chatting with each other in Pennsylvania Dutch as if they were in their home kitchens. Pearl and I went out the back door, and the heavy door banged shut behind us as we stepped into the small private parking area behind the restaurant.

Timothy's blue pickup waited right outside the kitchen door. He leaned against the hood of the truck and looked like a Stetson advertisement in scuffed boots. All he needed was a cowboy hat. The thought of Timothy in a cowboy hat made my heart race. Mabel sat at his side, completing the look.

"If I had known you were coming to Young's I would have followed you here instead of going back to the farm to get Mabel," Timothy said. He nodded to Pearl but didn't say anything to her. An unspoken question lingered in his eyes.

I scratched Mabel between the ears. Her eyes closed in doggy bliss. If only it were so easy to please my Siamese cat, Gigabyte. Only Becky knew the way to his feline heart, through his stomach. "The next stop on the itinerary was Deacon Sutter's farm. I made an adjustment."

"Ahh." He nodded. "Young's is a good choice. There's plenty to do here to keep the tourists busy well into the afternoon."

Pearl didn't look up from her hands which clutched her roll bag. I held Ruby's bag, and I itched to see what was inside of it. "Can I borrow the pickup to take Pearl to the Dutch Inn? It's been a terrible day for her, and she needs to rest."

He fished his keys out of the hips pocket of his jeans. "I can take you there."

My eye flitted in Pearl's direction. "I think it's better if I take her on my own."

Timothy dropped the keys into my palm. "Okay." Timothy circled to the back of the pickup with Mabel on his heels. He reached into the truck bed and pulled out his red toolbox. "I have a few small jobs to do for Ellie, so it's no problem if you're gone for a little while. I should be done when you get back." Timothy cleared his throat and nodded to Pearl. "It was nice to see you again."

She refused to look at him and only clung to the handle of her bag more tightly.

Timothy raised his eyebrows at me, and I shook my head. With his index finger, he touched the luggage tag of the roll bag I held, and his eyebrows shot up even higher in question.

"I shouldn't be gone too long," I said. "Hudson, the bus driver, knows I'm taking Pearl to the inn. You can tell any of the passengers that's where I am if they ask."

He nodded. "Will do."

I opened the passenger side door, shoved Ruby's roll bag into the tiny backseat, and helped Pearl into the truck. Timothy squeezed my fingers as I climbed into driver's side.

I turned out of Young's parking lot and onto the county road in silence. The Dutch Inn was only fifteen minutes from the flea market by car. If I wanted to ask Pearl about her cousin, I had better do it quick.

Pearl beat me to it. "I hate to travel. This trip was Ruby's idea. She tried to talk me into a vacation like this for over thirty years. I finally say 'yes,' and she's dead because of it."

"Pearl, this isn't your fault," I said. *At least I hope, it's not.* I paused at a four-way stop. "Does Ruby go on trips like this often?"

She stared out the windshield at the farmland whizzing by. "Yes, she's been on dozens all over the country and Europe. She is—was—so adventurous. I always wished I could be more like her."

I wrung my hands back and forth on the steering wheel. "How do you know the other people on the bus?"

"I don't know them. Ruby and I met them the day we left Tupelo."

I passed a wagon buggy on the road. "How did you join the tour then?"

"Ruby saw an ad in the local paper and signed us up through the travel agency. I was so angry at her, but finally, I relented. I could never be angry at Ruby for long." She turned her head away to face out her window. "She has done too much for me."

"Blue Suede Tours is an interesting name for a travel agency," I said. "And they *really* like the color blue."

Pearl chuckled softly at my comment. "It got its name from Tupelo."

I gave her a blank stare as I paused at another stop sign.

"The birthplace of Elvis Presley. He had a song. *Blue Suede Shoes.* That's where the name comes from. There are many Tupelo businesses that are named after one of Elvis's songs."

"Did Ruby use Blue Suede Tours before?"

She folded and unfolded her hands on her lap. "I don't think so. Like I said, she found the trip in the local newspaper."

"Was she sick? Did she have any health problems?"

"She had a heart murmur, but she'd had it for decades. It was well controlled by medication. It's hard for me to believe that's what caused her collapse. And if that was the cause, why did Dudley keel over at the same time?"

An excellent question.

The stone face of the Dutch Inn came into view. It was small by Holmes County standards. Several of the large Amish Inns there boosted over one hundred rooms, indoor swimming pools, and health spas. The Dutch Inn was a simple country inn with modest but clean accommodations. It sat two miles as the crow flew from the center of Appleseed Creek and resided on several acres of fallow farmland. The back balconies held a vista of the unplanted fields and banks of the winding Kokosing River.

What the Dutch Inn lacked in amenities, it made up for in gardens. The grassy center of the circular driveway boasted a sea of daffodils, ranging from light lemon yellow to deep goldenrod. I smiled. Yellow was my favorite color and daffodils were my favorite flowers. I always wished they lasted a bit longer than a few short weeks of spring. Beyond the daffodil garden, there were flowerbeds of spring bulbs: tulips, hyacinths, and flowers I didn't know by name on either side of the inn. "What a pretty spot," I said.

Pearl said nothing. I parked the car in the small lot to the left of the building. A patrol car was the only other vehicle in the parking lot. I should have known Chief Rose or one of her officers would check out the inn. Ruby's roll bag, sitting in the backseat of Timothy's truck, should go to Chief Rose. I hoped Pearl had forgotten I'd taken it from the bus. Outside of the pickup, she gripped the handles of her roll bag as if her life depended on it.

Pearl and I entered the lobby that was also decked out in spring flowers. By the door, a bouquet of pink hyacinths sat in a bowl-shaped vase. A massive river stone fireplace was the focal piece and dominated one wall. The walls were butter yellow and the carpet was cream and charcoal. The carpet repeated the silhouette of an Amish buggy within a two by two diamond. I was afraid that if I stared at it for too long the buggies on the carpet would begin to spin and cause motion sickness.

A plump Amish woman with strawberry blonde hair peeking out from under her bonnet and reading glasses hanging from her neck smiled at us from behind the curved wooden registration desk. Beside her was an Amish girl close to Ruth's age. The girl held an enormous orange Persian cat in her arms. Chief Rose was on the other side of the counter and jabbed a fist into her left hip. "Are you a mind reader, Humphrey?"

"No," I replied.

"I was just about to call you and ask you to bring Mrs. Kennerwell to the inn."

Pearl tightened her grip on her roll bag. "Do you need me for something, Officer?"

The chief's face softened when she looked at Pearl. "I do. Officer Riley is upstairs searching Dudley's room. We would like to go into your room and search Ruby's things with your permission."

Tears gathered in Pearl's eyes. "Yes, I suppose that will be all right." She swallowed. "I am in number eight just down the hall."

"Can we go there now?" the chief asked.

Pearl looked to me.

"Do you want me to come with you?"

She nodded.

I followed Chief Rose and Pearl down a short hall to the left of the lobby. The elevator binged and opened as we passed it. I blinked as the teenaged Amish boy, whom I saw at the Troyer farm that morning, stepped out of the elevator carrying a basket of folded towels. I stopped, and the boy looked at me quizzically.

Chief Rose and Pearl were halfway down the hall.

"Didn't I see you at the Troyer farm this morning?" I asked the boy.

He stared at me but said nothing.

"Humphrey, are you coming?" the chief asked.

I turned to look at the chief. By the time I looked back at the teen, he and his basket were gone. I hurried to catch up with Pearl and the chief.

Officer Riley stood outside of Pearl's door.

"Pearl," the chief said. "Can you unlock the door for us?"

Pearl's hands shook as she put the old fashioned key into the lock. The end of the key slipped off the metal.

I took the key from her hand and unlocked the door. The door swung in. The room was a simple and clean space with white cotton curtains, two twin beds, and a small attached bathroom. The highlight of the room was the tiny patio off the back that led to the garden. The patio faced west, so Pearl could watch the sunset over the Kokosing.

Chief Rose and Officer Riley entered the room first.

"Which bed and suitcase belonged to Ruby?" Chief Rose asked.

Pearl pointed to the far bed, closest to the French doors.

Officer Riley pulled latex gloves out of his back pocket and set Ruby's suitcase on the bed. He unzipped the back and began to methodically rifle through the contents.

Pearl wrung her hands. "I'll wait in the lobby. This is more difficult for me than I thought it would be."

"No problem," the chief said and looked at me.

I curved an arm around Pearl's shoulders and led her from the room.

Pearl sniffled. "Thank you, Chloe. You are very kind."

When we reentered the lobby, the Amish woman, girl, and cat were still behind the registration desk. The teen-aged boy was nowhere to be seen.

I parked Pearl on the sofa in front of the fireplace and approached the desk. "Would it be possible to get Pearl a cup of tea?"

The woman with the strawberry blonde hair nodded. "Ivy," she said to the girl, who I assumed was her daughter because she had the same color hair, "Go make Mrs. Kennerwell a cup of tea."

"*Ya, Mamm*," the girl murmured and turned to go taking the cat with her.

"Leave Cheetos here. She won't want any cat hair in her tea, and he's shedding his winter coat right now."

Ivy frowned but then set the cat on the counter. The cat spread out on the smooth surface like a wooly blanket.

I let the feline sniff my hand. "Cheetos?" I asked.

The woman laughed. "He belonged to our *Englisch* neighbor who moved to England and couldn't take her cat with her. We got the name as well as the spoiled cat. Ivy adores him."

"I have a Siamese at home."

She smiled. "You should tell Ivy that. She loves all cats. If she had her way the inn would be overrun with them."

She glanced at the large cat, who leisurely washed his face with his right paw. "Cheetos is more than enough I think." She reached across the counter to shake my hand. "I'm Jane Shetler."

"Chloe Humphrey."

She slipped her glasses onto her eyes. "You're that *Englischer* girl who solved Katie Lambright's murder."

Heat rushed to my face. "I—umm…"

Jane reached across the counter and grabbed both of my hands. "*Danki.* Thank you for what you did. It made our community a little bit safer."

I blinked. This was not the reaction I was used to when an Amish person learned I meddled in their district's business. "You're welcome. Katie's sister is Ruth Troyer's closest friend. I am friends with the Troyer family."

Jane nodded. "Yes, I know this. Ivy is a classmate of Ruth and Anna. Ruth's older brother Timothy is courting you."

I blushed but wasn't surprised she knew. "Yes."

"Are you working for this tour group now?"

"Well, I—I'm subbing until they can find a replacement tour guide." I swallowed.

"*Ya,* the police chief told me what happened. It's terrible." Jane removed her glasses, and they hung from their chain again. "Sounds like being a tour guide to this group may be a dangerous job."

I hadn't thought about it that way. I hoped Jane was wrong.

CHAPTER EIGHT

I petted Cheetos' back, and the cat purred. "When we were walking back to Pearl's room, we passed a teen-aged boy in the hallway."

Jane nodded. "That must have been my son Ephraim. Both he and Ivy work here at the inn."

"I saw him at the Troyer's farm this morning."

She played with the simple chain holding her glasses. "I don't see how you could have. Ephraim has been working at the inn all day."

"That's odd. The boy I saw looked just like him. He wouldn't happen to have a brother, would he?"

Jane brow creased. "*Nee,* he does not."

Ivy returned Pearl's tea.

"I'll take it to her," I said.

Ivy nodded and picked up Cheetos again. The large cat purred.

I carried the tea to Pearl. "Here's some tea."

She clutched her roll bag in her lap. "Thank you. Can you set it on the table there?"

I placed the teacup and saucer on a woven coaster. "Is there anything else I can do?"

She shook her head.

"Mrs. Kennerwell?" Chief Rose entered the lobby.

"We've finished our search. You're welcome to go back to your room." The chief removed a paper list. "We confiscated Ruby's medications. This is a list of them here. The coroner needs to know what was in her system and what health problems she may have had."

Pearl accepted the piece of paper without looking at it. "I understand. I think I would like to go lie down now."

"Of course," the police chief said.

I walked Pearl back to her room, holding her cup of tea and was relieved to see Officer Riley gone. Chief Rose and her officer had been neat. There was no indication they had searched the small room.

Pearl perched on the edge of one of the beds. "Thank you so much for your help. I could use the rest and the time to make some phone calls. If I feel up to it, I will come out for dinner. When is that?"

I set the teacup on the nightstand between the two beds and slipped the tour itinerary out my back pocket. "It's right here at the inn at six o'clock."

She nodded. "I will see how I feel."

I hesitated. "Do you want me to get you anything else?"

She shook her head. "No, I'm fine."

I opened my mouth to say something else but changed my mind. It was too difficult for me to pry into this woman's life so soon after the loss of her cousin.

I set her key on the dresser. "I will see you later then."

Chief Rose waited for me in the lobby.

"I have another of Ruby's bags in Timothy's truck," I said.

"You never disappoint," she said. "Show me."

As Chief Rose and I stepped out the front door of the inn, I felt three sets of eyes on my back, including Cheetos.

In the small parking lot, Officer Riley placed the medicine he had taken from Ruby's luggage in the trunk of the patrol car. I unlocked Timothy's pickup and retrieved the bag from the backseat. The chief placed it on top of the hood of the patrol car. "How did you get this?"

"I went into the bus to retrieve Pearl's bag when she said she wanted to come back to the inn. I spotted Ruby's too, so I grabbed it."

"You stole it."

I blushed. "No. Pearl knows I have it."

She arched an eyebrow. "Let's take a look." She removed a pair of latex gloves from her shirt pocket.

Officer Riley ambled over to us.

"Do you think there's something in there that will tell us what happened to Ruby and maybe even Dudley?" I asked.

"Patience, Humphrey, I won't know until I've opened it."

Right. Chief Rose was one of the least patient women I knew.

She unzipped the bag and removed a beige cardigan, a water bottle, a pair of thin slippers, two paperback novels, a toiletry case, and a leather-bound notebook. Chief Rose flipped through the notebook. I held my tongue even though there were a thousand questions sitting on its time. She peered at me. "It's a diary."

"Really?" I leaned forward.

"Don't get too excited. It's more of a log than insights into her deepest thoughts." She cleared her throat and began to read. "Today, we left the inn at Birds-in-a-Hand. Before we left we had breakfast in the breakfast room. It was a buffet. I had coffee, scrambled eggs, sausage, rye toast, and butter. Pearl ate pancakes and bacon." She closed the leather volume. "The whole thing is like that. It's a running menu through Amish Country. I wonder if they had flakey biscuits in Intercourse. I can hardly wait to find out."

"There must be more to it than that."

"Doesn't look like it, but I will give it a closer read-through to make sure. I can't wait to read what they had to eat at McDonalds in Pittsburgh." She unzipped the toiletry case. One by one, she set the items on the table. Nail clippers, a compact, Aspirin, hand cream, and prescription pill bottle. She held up the prescription pill bottle. "Heart medicine. We found another bottle of this in the room. We'll take this to Doc. If she had a weak heart, that could explain why she reacted so quickly to whatever killed her."

"Pearl mentioned Ruby had a heart murmur," I said.

The chief sighed. "Why didn't she tell us that at the scene?"

I shrugged. "Shock? Do you know what caused them to collapse?"

She shook her head. "We won't know anything for sure until the autopsy on both of them and any tests Doc has to run on their stomach contents and samples from Troyers' farm."

I grimaced at the mention of stomach contents. "Doc has to know something..."

She frowned. "This doesn't go any further, but Doc thinks some type of chemical reaction was involved. The question remains if that chemical reaction was caused by bad milk or some type of poison. And before you ask, Doc was unwilling to speculate if a poison was used or what that poison might be."

I thought of Pearl. "Pearl is concerned about the arrangements. She is a long way from home."

Sympathy crossed the chief's face. "I can understand that. We can't release the body until the investigation is complete, but she can start contacting a funeral home. The home will be able to make arrangements to transport the body. It might help Pearl feel better to do something."

Another thought struck me. "What about Dudley? Who is going to care for his arrangements?"

"We don't know that yet. We're trying to find a next of kin. I called Blue Suede Tours." She rolled her eyes when she said that name. "To find out who that might be. There was no family listed in his personnel file. The owner of Blue Suede said he was going to see what more he can find, and he said he would handle the arrangements if necessary."

"That's awfully nice of him."

"I think the gesture is more out of self-preservation than good nature. He must be sweating bullets over the idea of a lawsuit. One of the reasons he's letting the tour go on is he wants me to find the killer. If I do, someone other than him will be held responsible, or at least it will give him a strong case if Blue Suede Tours is sued."

Where I thought the owner did actions out of the kindness of his heart, Chief Rose suspected an ulterior motive. Sadly, her suspicions were likely closer to the truth.

"Did you learn anything from Pearl while the two of you were alone?" the chief asked.

"From what Pearl says, she and Ruby didn't know anyone else on the trip. Who would do this to an elderly lady like Ruby? It doesn't make sense."

Chief Rose tapped her fingernail on the metal table-top. "Maybe the killer didn't."

"What do you mean?"

"Maybe Dudley was the target," the chief mused. "Ruby was an unfortunate accident. This makes it even more important that we talk to someone who knew Dudley well, so we can piece together his story. Ruby's story is pretty much in place. She was a seventy-some year-old woman, widowed ten years ago, and had no children. She came on this bus tour with her first cousin Pearl, also a childless widow. Both women live in Tupelo, Mississippi."

I placed a hand on the hood of the patrol car. "That's her whole life summed up? How sad."

The chief frowned. "It's what we know so far."

"I asked Hudson a little bit about Dudley, but he either doesn't know much or doesn't care. He made it clear he and Dudley were not close."

The chief repacked the roll bag and handed it to Officer Riley. He carried it to the police cruiser's trunk without a word.

"I guess this means you plan to keep the roll bag too," I said as Officer Riley tucked the bag into the trunk along with Ruby's medicine.

"Yes." Concern crossed her delicate face. "Humphrey, we have to get to the bottom of this before they leave for Indiana." She pointed a finger at me. "I want you back on the bus. Find out who hated Ruby and Dudley. You're not getting off the bus until you can answer that question."

As I left the inn, I wondered if the real question I should be asking was, "Who hated Simon Troyer?"

I drove Timothy's pickup down a quiet county road, or, it would've been quiet, if a beat-up green pickup hadn't been coming from the opposite direction. Six months ago the sight of that truck would've sent me peeling toward the police station. Now I viewed it in a friendlier manner, but I didn't know if I would ever lose the first immediate stab of anxiety when I saw it.

The truck's owner, Curt Fanning, beeped his horn, and I pulled over to the side of the road.

Curt did an illegal U-turn and stopped his truck behind me. In the rearview mirror, I watched him hop out of the cabin. He wore a gray flannel shirt over jeans and a white T-shirt. As always, dog tags belonging to his father, who died in combat during the First Iraq War, hung from his thin neck. His trademark goatee was shorter than it had been the last I'd seen him. At first my enemy, Curt was now, if not a friend, a friendly acquaintance. He'd recently started visiting the same Mennonite church that Timothy, Becky, and I attended.

I rolled down the pickup window. He smoothed his goatee with his knuckles and straightened his stance. "Where you off to, Red?"

"The Dutch Inn. I have a friend staying there."

He placed a hand on the side mirror. "I see you have Bugg—Troyer's truck." A strange look crossed his face so quickly I wasn't sure I even saw it, but I did know Curt almost slipped and called Timothy "Buggy Rider," a perceived slur that he had thrown at Timothy many times before. Although I had made peace with Curt, Timothy and Curt's truce—if you could call it that—was much more fragile.

"I'd let you borrow my truck if you ever needed it," Curt said.

"That's nice of you to offer."

"I would…" He trailed off, leaving me wondering what he would do. He stepped away from the truck. "I was on my way to town to talk to the chief, but then I thought better of it when I heard about those two tourists dying at the Troyer milk farm." He examined my face. "That's why you were at the inn, isn't it? About those two dead bus people? I heard they were staying at the inn."

I frowned at his insensitive way to describe the situation. Curt may have turned over a new leaf, but he was still the same Curt. It would take some time to smooth twenty-five years of rough edges.

He pointed at me, and for a millisecond, I flashbacked to the time when we were enemies. I reminded myself Curt was different now. Forgive and forget. Forgiving was the easy part.

"What did you want to talk to Chief Rose about?" My tone was sharper than I intended it to be. I tried to soften the effect with a cheerful smile. By the tic in Curt's cheek, I knew he felt the sharpness of my words.

"To see if the chief had any work for me." Curt blushed. "Seeing how I know about all of the nefarious going-ons in this town, I thought I could be a help to her in catching some crooks."

Curt *did* know most of the troublemakers in the county. "That's good of you to offer help, Curt," I said.

He brushed the sole of his combat boot back and forth over the pavement. "I spoke with the pastor last week about…about everything I've done and told him I wanted to make up for it. He said to look for ways to offer help."

I smiled, genuinely this time. "I'm glad you're meeting with Pastor Chris. That's very brave of you to talk about your past with him."

Curt studied my face. "No one has ever called me brave before."

I swallowed and needed to change the subject quickly. "Did you talk to the pastor about Brock?"

Curt bit the inside of his cheek. "Yes, but I haven't seen Brock in weeks. He's tired of me preaching at him."

Brock was Curt's best friend and his former partner in crime when he was terrorizing the Amish and making my life as difficult as possible. Curt may have changed in recent months, but Brock had not. In fact, he had threatened me more than once since Curt gave up a life of crime. Brock believed I was the reason Curt changed, but I knew that couldn't be true. Regardless, Brock attacked me in December and was charged with assault. Since I decided not to press charges though, he was free and wandered about the county. I suppose a small part of me hoped by giving Brock yet another chance he'd turn his life around. I had been wrong.

"I'm sorry. I know he was your friend."

"He's the kind of friend that I don't need." His angular face softened. "I need more friends like you."

I shifted on the bench seat.

He leaned closer to the open window. My instinct was to back away, but I held my ground. Curt wasn't the enemy any more. "Would you like to grab a coffee with me sometime?" he asked. "There's something important that I need to tell you."

My scalp tingled. "Can't you tell me now?"

He shook his head. "I have to finish settling all the details first."

"Curt, I don't know."

"Please." He searched my face.

"Maybe Timothy and I—"

He scowled. "I want to meet with you. Don't bring Troyer. It won't take more than a half hour, I promise."

"Can I have a hint?"

He face broke into a smile. "No, but you will like it. I promise."

I bit the inside of my lip. It wouldn't kill me to have a cup of coffee with Curt, and I knew he needed support and encouragement. He didn't have much family, and his constant companion Brock had abandoned him. "Okay."

His face broke into a grin. "Great. Thank you, Red." He walked back to his green pickup, made another U-turn, and continued on his way into Appleseed Creek. He was gone so quickly. It was almost as if he thought I might change my mind.

CHAPTER NINE

B ack at Young's, I parked Timothy's pickup next to the kitchen door. The Young and Troyer families were close friends, so any time the Troyers visited the restaurant Ellie dropped everything to see them. The Troyer children believed it was because Ellie Young, the widowed matriarch of the family, had a crush on Grandfather Zook. The children loved to tease their grandfather about it.

I inhaled the scent of fresh-baked bread coming out of the kitchen window mingling with the scent of spring. A hint of rain hovered underneath the sweet smell of the blooming apple trees. I thought Ohio was always beautiful during its brief spring but there was nothing quite like spring in Ohio's farmland.

I checked my cell phone. It was one thirty. The tour group would be scattered across the property by now. I turned away from the main building in the direction of the pavilions. That's where I would most likely find Timothy. Near the entrance to the first pavilion, Hudson squared off in front of Raellen. He jabbed a finger at her, and she shook her overly ringed fist at him in return. *That can't be good.*

I wove through throngs of shoppers and jogged toward the pair.

"Listen, Lady," Hudson spat. "You aren't putting those onto my bus, and that is final."

"You're being ridiculous," Raellen argued. "The bus isn't even full."

LeeAnne watched their exchange with round eyes. A red-faced Amish teenager stood behind the pair, gripping the handles of a wagon. There were four large boxes in the wagon each the size of an old thirteen inch television. I took the wagon handles from him. "You can go," I whispered.

Relief washed over his face, and he fled.

Raellen dug her bejeweled hands into her hips. "Miss Chloe, tell this oaf of a man I can put my boxes on the bus."

Hudson's hands curved into fists. "It's not her call. She doesn't even work for the tour company."

I stepped between them before it came to blows. "Raellen, we can make arrangements to have your purchases shipped home."

She jutted out her chin. "That will cost me a fortune."

"You should have thought about that before you handed over your money, you hoarder."

Raellen and LeeAnne gasped. Raellen stuck her neck out like an angry chicken. "I am most certainly not a hoarder. My home is neat as a pin." She tugged on her friend's sleeve. "Isn't it, LeeAnne?"

LeeAnne nodded. "Yes. Raellen keeps the best house. I wished mine were half as tidy." She lowered her voice. "She even cleans the keys of her piano with Q-tips and mineral water."

Hudson closed his eyes for a moment as if he needed to gather strength. "Do you think I care how she cleans her piano? You got to find another way to cart those boxes to Mississippi, or you leave them here. I don't care. They're not going on my bus and that's final." He stomped away.

Raellen's mouth fell open. "Are you going to let him talk to me like that, Miss Chloe?"

I sighed. "Raellen, Hudson's right. I don't have a say on what can or cannot go on the bus."

Tears gathered in her eyes. "But I've already paid for these. If there was going to be restrictions on space, they should have told us before leaving Mississippi."

LeeAnne linked her arm through Raellen's. "That's right."

I pulled the wagon to the back door leading from the pavilions to Young's. "Let's see about having these shipped."

The three of us nearly collided with Ellie as she entered the restaurant through the back main door. "Chloe." Ellie placed a hand on her round middle. "I saw Timothy a little while ago and wondered where you might be. It's not often that I don't see the two of you together on a Saturday." Her eyes twinkled with humor.

Ellie was a widow in her late sixties with steel gray hair peeking out from under her prayer cap. She nodded to the two ladies behind me. "Hello. Are these friends of yours?"

I nodded. "This is Raellen and LeeAnne, they are from the tour bus."

Raellen stuck out her hand. "We were on the bus where those two people died. It was awful."

Ellie shot me a quick glance and turned back to the ladies. "I heard about that. I'm so sorry for your loss. Is there anything I can do?"

"I could use some help actually." Raellen beamed. "I've just been shopping in your lovely flea market, and the bus driver won't let me put my packages on the bus. I don't know how I'm going to get them home."

Ellie peered into the wagon. "One of the girls at the gift shop will ship them for you. I'll take you to her right now."

"She would? Bless your heart. That is so kind of you." Raellen clasped her hands.

I was surprised she didn't cut her fingers on the sharp edges of her jewels.

"It's no trouble," Ellie said.

"You go ahead, Raellen. I'll wait here." LeeAnne pointed to one of the white rockers on either side of the cold fireplace.

With Ellie pulling the wagon, she and Raellen headed in the direction of the gift shop.

LeeAnne sighed as she sat in the rocker. "It's nice to get off of my feet."

"Care if I join you?" I asked.

She smiled. "Not at all."

I settled in the rocker on the other side of the fireplace. "Are you enjoying the trip?"

"Very much." She leaned back in the rocker. "Until this morning. In fact, when we woke up this morning, Raellen and I commented on how well everything was going. I knew we should have knocked on wood. Raellen said I was superstitious to say that, but look what's happened."

"How was Dudley as a tour guide? Did you speak with him that much?"

Her black eyebrows knit together. "I won't speak ill of the dead, but Dudley wasn't the nicest man I had ever met. Then again, he was a whole lot better host than Hudson. I plan to write a letter of complaint to the tour company about Hudson."

I leaned forward. "Why? What did he do?"

She tipped her rocker toward the fireplace. "It's what he doesn't do. He's not interested in helping anyone. Many of these people need help off the bus or with carrying their luggage. Hudson won't lift a finger. He says it's not part of his job." She folded her hands in her lap. "And he's bad tempered too. It was worse when Dudley was here. Those two were like two cats trapped in a burlap bag."

"Has Hudson been in a foul mood the entire trip?"

She thought about this for a moment. "No, I wouldn't say that. In fact, our last night in Lancaster he seemed almost giddy. I had wondered if maybe he'd taken a nip."

"A nip?" I asked.

"Drank liquor," she whispered.

"Ahh." I nodded. "What did he do that made you think that?"

"He was just so cheerful I couldn't imagine what else could have made him so happy. Hudson is a grouchy soul. It's hard for me to understand those types of people. Life is too short to be in a bad mood, you know?"

"What made you think he was in a good mood?"

Her false eyelashes hit her cheekbones when she blinked. "Well, he said hello to me with a big smile and then held the elevator for me. Hudson is not the sort of man who holds the elevator for a lady." She tipped her chair forward again. "And he whistled while we were in the elevator. It was a bright cheerful tune. I was relieved when the elevator reached my floor. Hudson's cheerfulness made me uncomfortable." She shivered.

"Did you see Hudson with anyone that night?"

"No. When he wasn't on the bus, he was alone. He never joined us on any of the excursions, but I imagine he had seen them all before on other trips. I think I remember Dudley saying the Amish Country tour was one Blue Suede did three times a year."

"Did you know Ruby before coming on the trip?" I asked.

"Ruby?" She cocked her head. "I never met her before the day the bus left Mississippi. Tupelo isn't that big of a city, but it's large enough not to know everyone." She frowned. "She was a kind lady. It's a real shame what happened, but I know she had a heart condition."

It was my turn to tip my chair. "You did? How did you know that?"

"She told us. She told everyone who would listen. Ruby was a talker. You know the type. She never met an ear she didn't want to yap in."

I settled back into my chair. "When you said, she told everyone, who do you mean?"

"Everyone on the bus. When you get old sometimes all you feel you have to talk about are your ailments and your grandchildren. Ruby didn't have any grandbabies, so I guess that left her only with her ailments. You'll understand when you're older."

Something to look forward to.

"What did she say about her heart condition? Did she go into a lot of detail?"

"Oh my, yes, I can't say I remember what she said about it other than she had one." She lowered her voice. "I tuned her out after a while."

"Ellie, thank you so much for mailing those packages," Raellen said as they appeared in the hallway. "I don't know what I could have done if I had to leave that set of Depression glass here. I've been a collector for years."

"It should be waiting at your doorstep by the time you're back home." Ellie patted her arm. "I hope you all enjoy your visit in our little county."

"It's been lovely," Raellen said. "Discounting the tragedy, of course."

Ellie's eyes slid my way. "Of course." She said her goodbyes and left me with the two southern women.

LeeAnne stood. "Ready to eat, Raellen?"

"I'm starved," her friend replied.

I checked the read out on my cell phone. It was exactly two o'clock. "You two haven't eaten yet?"

"Shopping before snacks. That's our motto," Raellen said.

"That's right," LeeAnne agreed. "Would you like to join us, Miss Chloe?"

I shook my head. "I should go check on Hudson and the other guests."

LeeAnne smiled. "You're such a wonderful hostess. I wish we could have had you from the beginning."

Raellen nodded. "Dudley was the worst."

Whoever killed him must have agreed.

CHAPTER TEN

"Chloe!" Becky ran up to me just outside of the dining room. Tears were in her eyes. "Why didn't you tell me?"

I didn't have to ask her what she meant. "Becky, I—"

"I deserve to know." She stood in front of me in her Young's uniform: a plain navy blue dress and black apron with white stitching with the restaurant's name on one of the apron pockets. She looked every bit the sweet Amish girl from the neck down. Her white-blonde hair brushing her shoulders belied the decision she made to leave the Amish way. "It's my family."

"I know, I know. I'm so sorry. I wanted to call you. I thought of it, but then I got caught up with Chief Rose..." I knew it wasn't an excuse.

"So I have to hear about it while I'm waiting tables?" A tear slid down her flawless cheek. Becky was a good five inches taller than me and had the frame of a prima ballerina. She had no idea how beautiful she was. Aaron, who I spotted over her shoulder watching Becky from the host's podium, did.

"I'm sorry, Becky."

"I could have been there to help." Another tear rolled down her cheek.

I winced. Becky coming out to the farm was precisely why I didn't call her. I didn't want her father to associate her with the incident. Their relationship was already rocky enough. I knew it would heal. If I could mend my relationship with my father, then I knew there was hope for Becky and Mr. Troyer.

"Is it true? Do the police really believe my father could have killed those people?"

A couple waiting in line to be seated at the restaurant gasped and shuffled away with their two children in tow.

I wrapped my arm around her shoulders and guided her to a quiet corner of the gift shop where oak shelves held packages of dry Amish noodles and popcorn kernels.

"He would never do that," Becky insisted.

We sat on a bench beside the noodles. "Shh, shhh," I said. "The guests are watching you."

She raised her voice. "I don't care if they are."

"Becky, I don't think Chief Rose believes your dad did anything wrong. She put me on the bus with the people from the bus tour. Their guide was one of the two people who died. The other person was an elderly woman."

She wiped at her face. "So, she wants you to drive them around town in a bus?"

"I'm not driving." I dropped my voice to a whisper. "Chief Rose wants me there more to gather information."

"Oh." Her mouth formed a circle, and some of the hurt in her eyes cleared away. "What does Timothy think about that?"

I frowned. "He didn't argue against it."

"I know my brother. He's against it," she said. "How can I help? Do you think I should go to the farm?"

I didn't know, but I knew from my own experience sometimes staying away was worse because it's so much harder to reach out to someone after hours, days, or even weeks have passed. "If you want, I will go with you."

She gripped my hand. "Thank you, Chloe."

"So you really are friendly with the locals," a voice said from behind.

I turned to find Hudson glowering at us.

I gritted teeth. "Becky, this is Hudson. He's the bus driver. Hudson, this is my friend Becky."

Hudson folded his arms. "We leave in thirty minutes. The geriatrics are shuffling back to the bus. You'd better get over there to supervise."

"I'll be there as soon as I can."

He waited.

"You want me to come right now?"

"I'll meet you on the bus." He stalked away.

"You have to stay on the bus with that guy?" Becky asked.

I gave her a wry smile. "Are you envious of me of being stuck on the tour bus with him?"

She giggled.

"You said you heard about the incident while waitressing. Was the staff talking about it?"

She shook her head. "A couple from the bus was discussing it. When they spoke of the two people dying on an Amish farm, I asked where the farm was." She frowned. "I know Ellie doesn't like me to spend that much time chatting with the guests, but they enjoy it. When I asked, I never thought, I never imagined, it was my farm. I knew you were going there today for a bus tour, but I didn't put it together until they said it was a dairy farm. They said dad's milk killed those people."

I scooted away from her on the bench, so I could have a clear view of her face. "Did they say anything else?"

She thought for a moment. "They said the two women bickered a lot during the trip." She nodded. "Yes, they said that, and Pearl—I think they said the name Pearl—was probably sorry she didn't have someone to bicker with any longer."

"Did the couple say who they were?"

Becky shook her head.

"What did they look like?"

"They were a black couple."

Most of the passengers on the bus were white, but there were three African Americans, one being LeeAnne. I pulled the itinerary out of the back pocket of my jeans. On the backside of the itinerary there was a list of all the guests' names. I had met everyone on the list except Earl Kepler and Duke and Doris Kite.

I patted Becky's arm. "I'm sorry. I messed up. I should have called you right away."

She shrugged. "It's okay."

"Why don't you talk to Ellie about going home early?"

She shook her head.

"All right. Then, I will see you later. I had better go see about the bus passengers." I removed Timothy's pick-up keys from my pocket. "Timothy is around here somewhere. Can you give them to him?"

She dropped the keys in her apron pocket.

At twenty until three, Hudson had the bus at the curb in front of the restaurant. All of the passengers were already aboard.

"What took you so long?" he asked.

I guessed it was Hudson's idea of a greeting. "I told everyone to be back on the bus at three. They're early."

"This is an early to bed, early to rise crowd. Always assume that they need less time than you give them. They want to go to the inn and take off their orthopedic shoes."

"Thanks for the advice," I muttered.

Hudson smiled. "You're welcome." He handed me the mic. "Now, hit it and entertain the masses."

I took the microphone from his hand with a grunt.

At the inn, Gertie handed me her roll bag as she disembarked. "Careful with that. It has my jerky."

Melinda shook her head as she took the bag from me.

I consulted the itinerary again while they made their way to the entrance. "You will have dinner here at the inn tonight at six in the dining room."

Fred scowled. "Why doesn't this place have cable? I want to watch the game. We got in too late last night for me to complain."

I wondered if there was a specific game Fred wanted to watch or any game would do. I couldn't remember if I even saw a television in Pearl's room earlier in that day. "It's an Amish inn."

"It's ridiculous."

His wife Nadine trilled in laughter. "Oh, Fred, don't be such a grumpypuss."

To me, it looked like Fred was a professional grumpypuss.

Jane answered questions at the desk, and Ephraim stood nearby, alert and ready to help the guests with their every need. When he saw me, he slipped away again. I frowned and debated too long about going after him.

I slipped away to check on Pearl before I left. I knocked on the door. There was no answer. "Pearl? It's Chloe. I just wanted to say good-bye. I'm leaving for the day."

Still nothing. *Was she asleep?*

I hurried down the stairwell to the first floor to find Fred arguing with Jane about the lack of televisions in the inn. "Do you have cable in your part of the inn?"

Jane's friendly smile waned. "Cable?"

"Yes, for a tel-a-vision." He said the word extra slow as if he thought she didn't know what he meant.

I balled my hands into fists.

Jane's smile resurfaced, and her Pennsylvania Dutch accent became more pronounced. "What is this television you speak of? I don't know what you mean?"

Fred's mouth fell open. "What kind of backwoods place is this?"

Jane forced a smile. "You are staying at an Amish inn, and our life is plain."

He pointed a finger at her. "Who are you kidding? This place is lit up like a Christmas tree with electric lights. How Amish is that?"

"Would you like me to turn the lights off, Sir?" Jane asked.

Gertie poked her head between Fred and Nadine at the counter. "Make due, Fred. I don't have Wi-Fi."

Nadine placed a hand on her husband's arm. "Oh, Fred, she knows what a television is. She's just teasing you. Aren't you, Jane?"

Nadine and Jane shared a conspiratorial wink, and my fists unclenched at my sides. "I've seen them at Wal-Mart," Jane said.

Fred picked up his roll bag and stomped away from the desk. Nadine shouted out apologies as she hurried behind him.

I placed my hands on the counter. "Do you know where Pearl is?"

She looked confused.

"The lady who I brought here earlier today. I went upstairs to check on her and she didn't answer her door."

Jane stacked papers on the counter. "I know who you mean. You can't find her because she's checked out."

I flattened my hands on the dark wood countertop. "Checked out?"

The travelers waiting for the elevator stared at me in concern.

I lowered my voice. "How could you let her do that?"

Jane blinked at me. "What do you mean I let her? She paid for her night here even though she didn't stay. It wasn't like I could tie her down and tell her not to leave. If a guest pays, I don't ask questions."

"Where did she go? She doesn't know anyone here and could get lost!"

She slid the papers in a manila folder. "I don't know. I didn't ask."

"How did she leave here? On foot? She didn't have a car. We are still a few miles from town." Worry for Pearl's safety grew in the pit of my stomach.

"I called her a cab."

"A cab. Appleseed Creek has a cab?"

"The cab company was from Mount Vernon."

"Can I see her room?" I asked.

Jane frowned. "It's already been cleaned for the next guest."

"Humor me, Jane. This elderly woman just lost her closest relative and doesn't know a soul in Ohio. She's traveling alone and scared."

"Maybe I should have stopped her. She was determined to leave. I have to stay here while the other guests have questions. Can you check the room yourself?" She went to the back wall and selected one of the keys. She dropped it in my hand.

"Did she take her luggage with her?"

"Yes." She pointed at her feet. "She left her cousin's though. She asked me to have it loaded on the bus. It's down here."

I leaned over the counter and saw Cheetos sleeping on top of Ruby's suitcase.

I held up the key. "I'll bring this back as soon as I check the room." I spun around and dashed down the hallway.

At Pearl's room, I slid the key into the lock. The door swung open. The room was just as it appeared when Pearl and I arrived a few hours ago. Everything looked exactly the same as it had before with the exception of the absence of Pearl's and Ruby's luggage.

It should have occurred to me that this might happen. I kicked myself for leaving her on her own. *Where would the cabby take her? All the way to the Columbus airport?*

I slipped my Smartphone out of my jacket pocket, knowing what I had to do next. Chief Rose would not be pleased.

CHAPTER ELEVEN

"She left?" the police chief bellowed. "You shouldn't have left her alone!"

I stood in a small corner of the lobby and held my phone away from my ear to avoid bursting my eardrum. "You told me to return to the bus."

There was a pause. "Oh, right." She ground her teeth. "She couldn't have gone too far, and there are two taxi companies in Mount Vernon. I'll have Nottingham track her down."

"Do you think she ran out of guilt?" I hated that my voice sounded so hopeful, but someone to divert the investigation's focus from Mr. Troyer was welcome.

"Nice try. Troyer's father is still a suspect."

I sighed. It seemed the chief had me figured out. I said good-bye and slipped my phone into my pocket. Now, all I wanted to do was go home. My car was still at the Troyers' farm where I left it that morning, which seemed so long ago. I called Timothy.

There was a smile in his voice. "You need a lift?"

"Yes," I said relieved.

"All right," he said. "I'll be there in ten minutes."

I waited in the flower garden to the right of the building. The early spring flowers - tulips, small Dutch irises, and more daffodils - were in bloom. By June, the garden would be awash with colorful annuals and perennials. I touched the petal of a bright red tulip. It was hard to believe in August I would have lived in Appleseed Creek for one year. Originally I'd planned to be in and out of the rural town within that time. I took the job at Harshberger College because the position padded my résumé, which was heavy on degrees and low on work experience, and Harshberger was the only place that would hire me. Then, I met Becky and her brother Timothy, and my life changed. The thought of leaving made my heart ache.

A twig snapped to my left. I turned, grateful for the distraction from my black thoughts. A shadow moved near the corner of the inn.

Angry voices floated in my direction. "You'd better not be lying to me." A male voice said.

I edged along the side of the building with only the tiniest needle of guilt tickling the back of my mind. I eavesdropped, yes, but I did it with the Appleseed Creek police chief's blessing.

"There's nothing to worry about. What happened won't mess anything up," the same voice said.

"You'd better be right, or I'm pulling out," the second voice, which could be either male or female, rasped.

I inched around the side of the building, hoping to see who they were. At least I knew one was a man, so that narrowed down my candidates from the bus tour—if it was a passenger from the bus—considerably. There were far fewer men than women on the trip.

"And," the hissing voice said. "This had better not cost me any more money."

"It won't. What you have already paid is enough. More than enough."

I accidently kicked a pebble with my toe, and it bounced off the stone side of the inn with a click. I froze.

"Did you hear something?" Raspy asked.

"It was probably a squirrel. Don't be so paranoid," the man said.

"I have a reason to be paranoid. If this doesn't go through, I'm ruined."

Beep! Timothy turned into the circular drive and beeped his horn. "Chloe! I'm over here!"

The whispers stopped. I heard rustles as the pair moved away. I peeked around the side of the building.

Whoever had been there talking was gone and knew I had been there. I leaned against the building's stone face and closed my eyes for a brief second.

I waved at Timothy and then ran around the building, hoping to catch up with the pair. They were nowhere to be seen. They must have slipped inside one of the inn's many doors. Going into the inn to search for them would be no use. By that time, they would have blended with the other tour bus passengers.

Timothy met me on the other side of the building. "What are you doing? You just took off."

I caught my breath. "I think I just overheard someone scheming on the other side of the building. I ran around to see if I could catch them."

Timothy's brow creased in concern. "What was it about?"

"I don't know." I kicked at the pebbles on the walk. "It sounded suspicious. One of them was threatening the other." I bit my lip. "And I think they may have overheard when you called my name."

Timothy took a step in the direction of the building as if he were trying to decide if he should run after whoever had been there. "You think that's a problem."

"I don't know, but I think it would be better if they didn't know I had been listening to their conversation."

Timothy frowned. "Maybe you shouldn't do this, Chloe. This isn't like the other times you helped Greta. When you did this before, most of the people were Amish, and I knew them. We don't know anything about these tourists."

I stopped kicking pebbles. "I promised the chief."

He stepped into my personal space. "I would never recover if something happened to you."

"Nothing is going to happen." I swallowed hard.

"If it does, it will be my fault for announcing you were there."

"For all they know I just came outside and didn't hear a thing."

Timothy appeared unconvinced. "It will be my fault just like this tragedy at the farm was mine."

I pulled back. "How's that?"

His hair fell into his eyes, and he raked it away with his fingers. "It was my idea to let the tourists taste the fresh milk."

"That doesn't mean the killer wouldn't have tried to hurt both Dudley and Ruby some other way."

"True, but my father wouldn't be a murder suspect either." He clenched his teeth for a brief moment. "*Daed* knows who got him into this situation."

"I've messed this up ten times worse than you have." I went on to tell him about Pearl vanishing from the Dutch Inn.

"Nottingham will find her." Timothy walked over to the truck. "Where to? Home?"

I shook my head. "We have to go back to the farm, so I can get my car."

Timothy nodded. "I wanted to drop in on my parents too and make sure the hazmat suits have left." He paused. "*Mamm* and *Daed* are both taking these accusations hard."

We got in the truck and rode in silence to the farm. I considered mentioning my run in with Curt Fanning to Timothy but decided to wait.

On the Troyer farm, a police cruiser idled in the middle of the driveway.

Timothy parked his pickup in the grass next to my Beetle. "Did Greta say she was coming back here?"

"No, but she doesn't typically tell me what she's up to."

Timothy and I climbed out of the pickup and crossed the yard. Officer Riley lumbered around the side of the barn. He nodded at Timothy and me. He held several plants in his hands. Some were clearly cut from bushes and trees, and others appeared to be pulled from the ground.

The farmhouse was quiet. There was no sign of Timothy's parents, grandfather, or the children. *Were they all barricaded in the house?*

"What are you still doing here, Riley?" Timothy asked.

He placed the plants into the plastic bag. "Doc sent me back to collect some samples."

My forehead creased. "Plant samples? Why?"

Riley hooked a thumb through his belt loop. "You will have to ask the chief about that."

"We will," Timothy said.

Riley tipped his police officer's ball cap and moseyed to his cruiser.

After the cruiser was out of sight, the back door of the Troyer home slammed opened. Thomas shot out the back door. Grandfather Zook followed at a much slower pace. Thomas ran at his brother and catapulted himself in the air. Timothy scooped the boy into his arms and held the child over his head as if he weighed no more than Naomi's favorite doll. Thomas crowed in laughter.

Grandfather Zook grinned. "Thomas has been chomping at the bit to run outside, but Martha wouldn't let him out until that police officer left."

Thomas began to kick his legs, and Timothy set him on the ground. "I need to talk to *Daed.*"

Grandfather Zook nodded. "I thought you might. Your *daed* is in a bad way and may not be up for talking."

"When is he ever up for talking?" Timothy asked.

Grandfather Zook adjusted his stance on his braces. "You know your *daed* is a *gut* Amish man. He is not one to complain or share his troubles."

"This is not just his trouble. It affects the entire family, the entire district."

"*Ya*, I have tried to tell him, but he will not listen to me."

"He's inside," Timothy said it more as statement than a question.

His grandfather nodded.

Timothy headed to the farmhouse, and I followed. The back door opened into a narrow mudroom where the Troyers shed their work boots and mud-speckled coats after working on the farm. Pegs lined both walls with jackets from the smallest Troyer, Naomi, to the biggest, her father. The mudroom opened up into the kitchen, which was the center of Mrs. Troyer's domain.

Even before I stepped inside, I knew she was well on her way into making the evening meal by the enticing smell of onions and lemon in the air. No matter what good or bad befell the family, Mrs. Troyer's cooking was a constant. She found comfort in the kitchen and saw it as her main responsibility as the lady of the house. Many times I wondered if Mrs. Troyer found I was a poor match for Timothy since I didn't know how to cook anything more elaborate than a grilled cheese sandwich and didn't have any interest in learning.

The cabinets were high-polished wood. A pantry hutch stood along one wall laden with home-baked goods and jars of fruits and vegetables, which Mrs. Troyer canned herself in the fall. Mr. Troyer sat in his place at the head of the twelve foot pine wood table. There were chairs on either end of the table, one for Mr. Troyer and one for Grandfather Zook. Everyone else sat on either side of the table on backless benches.

A steaming mug of coffee sat on the tabletop in front of Timothy's father. The austere Amish man stared into the pool of dark liquid.

Mrs. Troyer wiped her hands on an embroidered tea towel. She spoke to Timothy in their language. I shrunk back. Typically the Troyers spoke English in my presence so that I could follow the conversation. The use of Pennsylvania Dutch was intentional. She didn't want me to know what she said.

Timothy frowned and answered her in English. "We've just come from the Dutch Inn. That's where the *Englischers* are staying."

She replied in their language.

"*Mamm*, Chloe is here. Please speak English. It is rude not to."

Mr. Troyer's head snapped up then. In English, he said, "Do not correct your *mamm*. You are the *kind* not she."

A muscle in Timothy's jaw twitched.

I took two steps back into the mudroom. "Maybe I should step outside so that you can talk for a moment."

"No. You have as much a right to be a part of the conversation as anyone." He reached for me and grabbed my hand, folding it into his own. The statement could not be clearer. Timothy and I were a team. "Chloe is trying to help find out who did this. She's riding on the bus the rest of the time it's in Ohio to find out what happened, to clear your name, *Daed*."

Mr. Troyer glowered at our intertwined fingers. "No one asked her to do that."

Mrs. Troyer turned away and busied herself at the stove.

I pulled my hand away from Timothy's.

CHAPTER TWELVE

Timothy pursed his lips as I inched away from him. He knew better than I did that public displays of affection were frowned upon in the Amish world. I wanted the Troyers to accept me just as much as Timothy did, but I wouldn't force them, nor would I offend them in their own home.

Grandfather Zook, who still stood in the doorway to the mudroom, stepped forward and looped his arm through mine. "Come, Chloe, help me check on the cows. They've had a worse day than all of us. Those lab rats stuck them with their prods and needles. They could do with a visit from some friendly faces."

Timothy's eyes softened. Of all the people in his family, he trusted his grandfather's judgment the most. I followed

Grandfather Zook back through the mudroom and out the door. Mabel greeted me with her tongue hanging out of the side of her mouth and her black tail wagging. She sniffed our hands for treats.

I scratched between her ears. "Sorry, girl, I don't have any snacks."

The dog whimpered but quickly recovered from her disappointment as she led the way to dairy barn.

Grandfather Zook didn't seem the least bit bothered by the bite in the air as the sleeves of his dark blue work shirt were rolled up to the elbows.

I folded my arms across my chest in order to conserve as much heat as possible. "Did you see what Officer Riley took from the grounds? They were plants. He said the coroner asked him to collect them. I plan to ask Chief Rose about it. Do you know anything about the plants he chose?"

The old man removed his straw hat. "They were poisonous. Every single plant he cut could kill someone."

A chill rocked through my body. "There are poisonous plants on the farm? Isn't that dangerous for the animals?"

"The plants are from our land. All are from the woods or the garden. They are contained in places the livestock cannot go. Simon is very careful that any dangerous plants are out of the reach of the animals. See that plant there." He used his brace to point to the corner of the garden at a large berry bush with clusters of white flowers blooming on it. "That's an elderberry bush."

"It's poisonous?"

"Parts of it are. The leaves, bark, and roots are all very poisonous. Even the berries themselves can make you ill if you eat them raw. Just because they have that quality does not make the plant all bad. My daughter makes delicious elderberry jam."

"Did Riley take part of that bush?" I asked.

Grandfather propped his brace against the bench. "He did. The poisonous plants my daughter has here in the garden have parts that can be eaten, or they can be used for medicines. We do not go to the *Englicsh* doctor if we suffer from something that we can heal here at home."

I swallowed. I would think about that the next time Mrs. Troyer offered me a piece of an elderberry pie.

Grandfather Zook patted the pocket where he hid his harmonica. "Just like with all Creation, including people, plants have both virtue and depravity within them because this is a fallen earth. There is nothing perfect on this side of heaven."

Thomas threw the tennis ball at us, and I caught it before it walloped Grandfather Zook in the head. Mabel bounded toward us. Thomas raced after the dog. The seven-year-old skidded to a stop.

I handed him back the ball. "Thomas, you need to be careful. You could have hit your grandfather with that."

"*Ya*, I'm sorry *Grossdaddi*. I didn't want to smack you in the head." His eyes were laughing. Of all the Troyer children, Thomas was the most like Grandfather Zook.

The old man grinned. "That comes as a great relief, *Kind*."

The back door to the house opened, and Timothy stepped out. To my surprise he was followed by his father. Mr. Troyer and Timothy strode to us. Neither one looked particularly happy.

I stood, but Grandfather Zook remained in his spot on the bench. Thomas and Mabel took off back toward the tree. I hesitated for a moment.

Timothy and his father walked with purpose to the garden.

"Go to them," Grandfather Zook whispered. "They want to talk to you."

I glanced down at him. "How do you know that?"

"Because I know. When you get to be my age, you will know such things too."

I met Timothy and his father halfway to the garden. "Is everything all right?"

"Timothy tells me you are trying to find the person who hurt those people. Please stop," Mr. Troyer said.

I looked at Timothy. Why had he told his father I was helping Chief Rose with the investigation? I knew that had been a mistake the moment he'd said it in the kitchen.

Timothy's father clenched his fists at his sides. "I won't allow it."

I took two steps backward. "I'm sorry it upsets you, but Chief Rose asked for my assistance." I paused. "And I want to help your family."

Timothy, who stood between us, winced.

Timothy's father closed his eyes for a moment. *Was he preparing to kick me off of the farm, or was he praying?*

"The lady officer is not concerned with your safety. I am." He looked away from me, toward his barn. "I know Timothy cares for you. My son has not had the easiest time because of his own mistakes but also because of my shortcomings as his father."

"*Daed*—" Timothy started to argue.

His father held up a hand to silence him. "He is the happiest when he is with you." He sighed. "It's not your fault you're not Amish."

I suddenly felt lighter. I wanted to wrap my arms around Timothy's father and give him a hug. I stopped myself because I knew it would only embarrass him. Instead I squinted to hold back the tears gathering in my eyes. Those would embarrass him too.

"So I am asking you for my son to stop this foolishness. The *Englisch* police can find whoever did this."

My heart thudded to the bottom of my sneakers because I knew I couldn't walk away from the bus tour. It wasn't just about the Troyers anymore. There was Pearl, who was missing because of me, too. "It is only for a few days. The tour bus leaves for Indiana before dawn on Wednesday morning."

He met my gaze again. "I see I cannot convince you to change your mind. Timothy warned me this would be the case. I can see why my son is so fond of you. The Troyer men are attracted to decisive women. My Martha is a bear when she makes her mind up one way or another. There's no swaying her."

I tried to imagine Timothy's sweet, quiet mother arguing with her husband about anything. The image didn't fit.

Mr. Troyer sighed again. "Please be careful for the sake of my son and for my Rebecca. I know she is very fond of you too."

I couldn't miss the opportunity to mention Becky. "Becky wants to see you."

He clasped his hands in front of himself. "We're hurt. It is a hurt you as an *Englischer* can never understand." He turned and headed back to the farmhouse.

How could he accept me and not his own daughter? Mr. Troyer was right I couldn't understand it. Or could I? I took a couple of steps after him. "I understand betrayal and abandonment."

Mr. Troyer froze.

Quietly, I said, "I know those very well. Becky didn't leave the Amish to hurt you."

"I do not want to talk about Rebecca." His tone was firm.

I swallowed. "You can help me though. Who would want to hurt your farm and your family like this?"

He frowned. "The only person who may be angry with our family is Deacon Sutter, but there are easier ways for him to hurt my family, ones that would not bring so much

disgrace to the district. With the help of the bishop, I believe the deacon has finally accepted us."

Timothy's jaw twitched. He didn't believe that, and neither did I.

"Maybe the person wasn't Amish," I said. "Grandfather
Zook mentioned a commercial farm coming into the area."

Mr. Troyer nodded. "Yes, a commercial farm bought the
old Gundy place, but they have no reason to even notice us."

"I heard someone bought the Gundy place, but I didn't
know they were English," Timothy said. "Is it someone
from town?"

"All I know is his name is Tate," Mr. Troyer said.

Timothy frowned. "I don't know anyone by that name."

Mr. Troyer resumed his course to the house.

I jogged after him. "Do you know the police took poisonous plants from your farm?"

He turned, and his brown eyes bore into me. "Every
farm has poisonous plants. We have to be careful to keep
them away from the cows and other livestock."

Timothy raised his eyebrows in question at me.

"Could you identify them if you needed to?" I asked.

"*Ya.* Any farmer could. We have to know to protect our
animals and families. Why are you asking these questions?"

"I think one of those plants killed those people."

Timothy's father paled. "A plant from my land?"

"Maybe," I admitted.

Mr. Troyer turned and walked to the house without
another word. This time I let him go.

As Timothy and I were about to leave, my cell phone rang. I check the readout and frowned.

"Who is it?" he asked. "Greta?"

"I don't know. I don't recognize the area code." I placed the phone to my ear. "Hello?"

"Where are you?" A sharp male voice asked.

I unlocked the Beetle with my key fob. "Who's this?"

"It's Hudson," he snapped in my ear. "Who do you think it is?"

Timothy watched me closely.

"I'm on my way home," I said.

"Home? Who said you could go home? Dinner is about to begin and the guests are waiting for you."

"Waiting for me?" I squeaked.

"Yes, they are waiting for you to host the dinner conversation."

"Dinner conversation?"

"Part of Blue Suede Tour's full service includes dinner conversation about the sights the group saw that day. Dudley even had a slide show on his laptop for most of the stops. The police took his computer. You will have to make do without it."

I opened my car door and sat with my legs facing out of the car. "Hudson, I'm not giving a talk tonight."

"You have to. It's part of the tour. Have you ever seen these people complain about not getting what they paid for?"

"If it's so important, why don't you do it?"

"I can't do that. I drive the bus," he said. "This is a full service tour. You need to be on the ground to assist the guests with whatever they might need."

I didn't like the sound of that. "What does 'everything they might need' mean?"

I heard him grit his teeth. "If they have an emergency in the middle of the night, you need to be there."

"Hudson, do you think I am spending the night at the Dutch Inn?"

Timothy's scowl deepened.

More teeth grinding. "It's part of your job."

"Hudson, this isn't really my job at all."

"This isn't optional."

"Give them my cell number to call me if there is a problem in the middle of the night."

"That's not good enough," he snapped.

"Then hire someone to do it."

"If you don't do this, I will have no choice but to cancel the tour and take all these people home," he threatened.

Did Hudson know I agreed to be on the tour to protect the Troyers? I bit my lip. "I'll be there in an hour."

"They are ready to eat now."

"If you expect me to spend the night, I need to go home and grab my toothbrush."

He grumbled something I didn't catch.

"Tell them because of what happened this morning, dinner will be less formal."

"Fine, but you had better be here by dessert."

I hung up the cell without saying good-bye.

Timothy stared at me. "What just happened?"

I stared at the phone in my hand. "I'm spending the night at the Dutch Inn."

His eyes widened. "Why?"

I told him what Hudson said about Blue Suede Tours full service.

Timothy put his hand on the roof of my Beetle. "That ogre of a bus driver can't tell you to do it."

I chuckled as I swung my legs into the car.

He shut the door after me and leaned inside through the open window. "What's so funny?"

"I never thought I'd hear you say ogre."

Some of his frustration melted away. "I have seen the *Lord of the Rings* since I left home. Apparently, there is something called the Smurfs that I need to see too."

I smiled. "You do."

His expression grew serious again. "I don't think you should do it."

"I can't give these people an excuse to leave Knox County. The moment they're gone your father becomes the focus again." The image of Officer Riley carrying the plant samples struck me.

Timothy stepped back from the car. "If you are spending the night at the Dutch Inn, so am I."

There was nothing I could say to change his mind.

CHAPTER THIRTEEN

I pulled into the short driveway of the small, mid-twentieth century colonial I shared with Becky. The house sat across the street from Harshberger's campus. A tiny guard house stood in the middle of the road leading onto campus.

This was my third home since I moved to Appleseed Creek eight months ago. If I had it my way, it would be my last. I was tired of moving.

Becky's bicycle lay on its side in the middle of postage stamp yard. I would have to talk to her about that again. Our landlord, a sweet elderly lady who lived a block away, was very particular about how the grass should be treated. She did not approve of Becky's tire tracks back and forth across the lawn. Seeing how she was the most stable land-lord I'd had in Appleseed Creek, I didn't want her to kick Becky and me out over a bicycle.

I moved the bike to the side of the garage as Timothy parked his truck behind my Beetle. He stepped out of the truck while I wondered how I would talk him out of staying at the inn. I opened my mouth.

He shook his head. "I know what you're going to say, but it won't work. If you're staying at the Dutch Inn, then I am too."

"Okay," I said.

He narrowed his eyes. "Okay?"

I nodded. "Okay. You can stay at the inn too."

He stood toe to toe with me and studied my face. "That's quite agreeable of you."

"I'm an agreeable girl."

"Since when?" He chuckled and followed me to the front door.

The front door opened into the living room. Becky, wearing jeans and a Harshberger T-shirt, lay in front of the television on top of her favorite dog pillow, which she still didn't realize was a dog pillow despite "Woof" being stitched on the side of it. At this point, I saw no harm in keeping that knowledge to myself.

As always, Food Network was on the TV. It was the only station Becky watched. I had never met anyone with such a love of cooking programs.

My Siamese cat, Gigabyte, strolled over to me and wove in and around my legs. He meowed at a pitch and decibel level that only a true Siamese could hit.

"Don't let him fool you." Becky glanced over her shoulder. "I just gave him a snack."

I dropped my purse on the couch and picked up the cat. He nuzzled my chin. "Becky, what did I tell you about giving Gig snacks? Remember what the vet said. We have to watch what he eats."

Gig's tummy had begun to hang low with extra weight since we'd moved to Appleseed Creek. As if he understood my words, the feline hissed and fought to escape my arms, and I hadn't even said the "D" word. "Diet." I let him go.

She sat up. "He's hungry. I always gave snacks to the barn cats on the farm and there was never a problem for them."

"There is a big difference between a cat living outside on an Amish farm and a pampered house cat with two attendants waiting on his every need."

Gig arched his back at me. Clearly, he understood everything I said.

"The vet doesn't know what he's talking about." Becky rolled off her dog pillow onto the beige carpet. "I thought you would be home before now. You left Young's a while ago."

"We stopped at the farm to check on the family."

Becky jumped to her feet. "I thought you were going to go there with me."

I had forgotten that I promised to go with Becky to the farm. "I'm sorry, Becky. Timothy took me there to get my car, and now I'm only here to grab an overnight bag."

Becky hopped onto the couch. "A bag for what? Where are you going?"

"I'll be staying at the Dutch Inn for the next few days."

Her brow creased and her expression was so much like Timothy's when he was confused or concerned, it made me smile. "Why?"

"It's where the people from the bus tour are staying. Apparently, bunking with them is part of my job."

"How long will you be gone?"

"Four nights at most, but I hope I won't have to stay there every night. I'm going to have to slip away now and again to check in at the office."

Becky wrapped her arms around her waist. "How was *Daed*?"

I glanced at Timothy. "Why don't I go pack, and the two of you can talk."

I jogged upstairs and threw whatever I could think of into my small suitcase. Jane had said that there was no Wi-Fi in the hotel, but I packed my laptop and iPad anyway. If I needed to, I could make my own hotspot with my smartphone. I threw in an extra pair of socks and rolled my suitcase down the stairs. "I hope I didn't forget anything. I hate packing without a list."

Timothy met me halfway down the stairs and took my suitcase. "You should have told me you were finished. I can carry this for you."

My stomach fluttered. It hadn't even occurred to me to ask for help. Most of my life, I did everything on my own.

Becky sat cross-legged on her dog pillow. "You hate to do anything without a list."

That was true.

Timothy set the suitcase by the couch. "We can stop at my place so I can pack a bag too."

"You're staying at the inn too?" Becky asked.

Timothy nodded.

She pulled her knees up under her chin. "Don't tell *Mamm* and *Daed*. They wouldn't like it if they knew you and Chloe were sleeping in the same place."

Timothy scowled at his younger sister. "They should know us well enough to trust us."

I felt my cheeks turn bright red. *Why did I have to blush so easily?*

"I know that." Becky's cheeks flushed too. "But I just wouldn't tell them; that's all. I learned not telling them things—even when you haven't done anything wrong—is the best way to go."

I picked Gig up, and he climbed onto my shoulder like a parrot on a pirate. "You couldn't have kept your hair a secret forever."

She turned around to face the television. "I know that."

I gave Timothy a half smile. "Go home and grab your stuff. I'll drive myself to the inn. I don't want to be without a car again."

Timothy kissed me on the cheek and left.

I perched on the couch close to Becky's head. "Will you be all right here by yourself for a few days?"

She offered me an easy smile. I was relieved she wasn't upset at my comment about her hair.

Becky sat up. "I'll be fine. Gigabyte and I will watch all the Food Network we want."

I laughed. "You already do." I scooted a little closer to her. "Did you look at those college applications I printed for you?"

Becky frowned. "I will."

Growing up Amish, Becky's formal education stopped at the eighth grade. After weeks of studying, she easily passed the GED. Now, she had to decide where she wanted to do with the rest of her life.

"What's the point of looking at them now? I don't have nearly enough money saved up to go to school."

"You should have a goal," I said, sounding like a mother hen, a quality that I hadn't known I had until I met Becky. Becky turned twenty in January, and I was twenty-four. There was little difference in our ages, but I had twice the life experience, and as an academic I knew how important an education was for Becky's future. "And if you still don't have the money when you are ready, you'll get a loan. I have loans that I'll be paying back until I'm fifty."

"That seems like a strange way to do it."

I wasn't surprised at Becky's hesitation toward a loan. Most Amish were reluctant to be indebted to someone, even to a bank. The Amish lived within their means. "There are many good programs at reasonable costs at the community college level or at state universities. True, you will probably need a loan for these too, but it won't be nearly as much if you went to a school like Harshberger."

She frowned. "Harshberger is the closest."

I laughed. "It is across the street, and I would love it if you could go there. However, it's not realistic."

She picked up the remote and turned off the television. "I don't know if I even want to go to college."

For a moment I reveled in the quiet. I was really tired of hearing about another summer barbeque recipe. "That's your decision, but I think you should do something."

She hopped to her feet in one easy motion. "Not everyone likes school as much as you do, Chloe."

"I know that, but I want you to have every opportunity. You have so much potential..." I stopped myself from going on. I sounded like a graduation card. "What about culinary school?"

She glanced back at the blank TV screen. "Maybe..." She trailed off.

I would take a maybe for now, but our conversation wasn't over. "You're sure you will be okay here by yourself?"

"I'll be fine."

I removed Gig from my shoulder and stood. "Just promise me that you will read the applications?"

"I'll read them if you promise me you'll be careful around those bus people."

I picked up my suitcase. "Done."

CHAPTER FOURTEEN

As I parked my Beetle in the small lot next to the Dutch Inn, my cell phone rang. The readout told me it was Chief Rose.

"Did you find Pearl?" I asked.

"That's why I'm calling," the police chief said in her gruff way. "We tracked her down with her credit card. She checked into a chain hotel in Mount Vernon. Nottingham is over there now talking to her."

My shoulders sagged in relief. "Is she okay?"

"Nottingham said she appeared fine."

"Is she coming back to the Dutch Inn?"

"I haven't heard a verdict about that yet from my officer."

I rolled up my car's windows. "I'm relieved you found her."

"I am too," she said. "I've got to go, Humphrey."

"Wait! I was just at the Troyer farm. Officer Riley was there collecting plant samples."

"I know," she said.

"What were they for?" I asked.

"The crime lab needs to test them." She sounded as if she didn't want to say more.

"You think one of those plants killed Ruby and Dudley."

"That's for Doc to determine." Her voice had an edge to it. "What time are you back on tour duty tomorrow?"

"I'm still on it," I said and explained I was staying at the Dutch Inn.

The chief chortled. "Sounds like you're in over your head, Humphrey."

"Whose fault is that?"

Her laughter rang in my ear long after she hung up.

The only other vehicle in the parking lot was the tour bus. Perhaps no other tourists were staying at the inn. That would mean the two voices I overheard earlier that afternoon had to be from the bus.

I carried my suitcase across the cobblestone walkway leading from the parking lot to the front door of the inn. It was close to seven and my stomach rumbled. I should have eaten something before I left home. Dinner would be long over for the tour guests by now, but I hoped the dining room remained open.

Jane folded a copy of the Amish newspaper, *The Budget*, on the countertop. "I see you're back. Ready to check in?"

Cheetos, who was on the counter, lazily batted at the edge of the newspaper.

"Did Hudson tell you I was coming back?"

"He did. He also told me the tour company would pay for your stay, so you don't have to worry about that."

That came as a relief because I hadn't thought to ask Hudson about who was paying for my room while he had been yelling at me on the phone.

The front door opened, and Timothy entered, carrying a backpack as his only luggage. What a typical guy. Jane's smile widened when he stepped in. "It is *gut* to see you Timothy Troyer. I have heard your business is doing well. You did a *gut* job on the Young's flea market. Everyone in the district is quite pleased it will be open all year round."

"It's nice to see you again too. How are your children?" Timothy said, giving her his thousand watt smile.

"*Gut.* Both teenagers now working here at the inn. What can I help you with?"

He set his backpack on the floor. "I'd like to check in too."

"To stay with Chloe?" She raised her eyebrows at me.

There was that blush again. "No. He needs his own room," I said.

Her hands fluttered to her ledger. "*Ya, ya,* I wasn't thinking anything differently. I do have two vacant rooms." She frowned. "How will you be paying for the room? The tour company said they would only pay for your room, Chloe."

"How much is it a night?" Timothy asked.

"One fifty. It includes meals in the dining room, so it's quite a bargain."

I touched Timothy's arm. "That's too expensive," I said under my breath. "Maybe you should forget this idea. Go home. I'll be fine."

"I'm staying." Timothy's jaw was set.

"I have an idea," Jane said. "I have several odd jobs that need to be done around the inn, from fixing doors to mending furniture. If you do those, I will let you stay here for free."

I opened my mouth to object. Timothy had more contracting work than he knew what to do with. He didn't need to be tied down with a bunch of little jobs at the inn. "He—"

"That sounds fair," Timothy said.

"Excellent." She grinned and turned, removing two keys from the pegboard.

I frowned at Timothy.

He squeezed my hand and whispered as if he could read my mind, "Don't worry. I can do it."

Jane turned back around and handed us both a key. I examined mine. Twenty-eight. "I put you on different floors. Timothy, I put you in room number three. It's one of our best rooms and the closest to the front desk."

Timothy thanked her.

"Is the dining room still open?" I asked.

"It's open until eight. Tonight, the cook made shepherd's pie. We have a set meal for every day. You can see the planned meals for the week on a chalkboard in the dining room. I believe the tour group is still in the dining room."

"Let's drop off our bags and meet in the dining room," Timothy said.

Instead of taking the elevator, I ran up the staircase to the second floor. The hall was quiet and dim as the sun set outside. The buggy-patterned carpet muffled my footsteps.

I peered out the large picture window at the end of the hallway, which overlooked the parking lot, before unlocking my door. Below, I thought I saw movement in the shadow of one of the lilac bushes at the edge of the lot but then nothing. After dinner, I would take a look around the grounds. The sun would be up for at least another hour.

In room number twenty-eight, I dropped my suitcase and purse in the middle of one of the twin beds. As I was on the second floor, I had a balcony instead of a patio at the back of my room. I opened the French doors and scanned the gardens for the shadow. Seeing nothing, I went back into the room and tucked my cell phone and room key into the pockets of my jeans.

Laughter guided me through the lounge to the dining room. Tour guests sat at three of the four large round tables. Hudson sat at the fourth table alone. Half-eaten wedges of Amish pie sat in front of each person.

"Chloe, sit with us," Gertie crowed. She was at a table with Melinda and, by process of elimination, with who I believed to be Duke and Doris, the couple Becky met at Young's. There was one empty seat at their table. I noticed Earl Kepler sat at a table with Fred, Nadine, Bitty, and Charles. They seemed to be having a grand time discussing the state of affairs in Washington. LeeAnne, Raellen, Jimbo, and Bobbi Jo sat at the third table. The three women discussed Amish quilting patterns, and Jimbo looked like he wanted to stick a fork in his eye.

I felt a hand on my back. "You go and sit with them," Timothy said. "I want to talk to Hudson."

I gave him an anxious look.

"There's nothing to be worried about," he said.

I wasn't so sure about that.

Gertie poked Melinda in the side with her index finger. "You move down one. I want to sit next to Chloe. She can tell us all about the Amish."

"I can sit here," I said, pulling out the chair across from Gertie and next to Duke Kite. "Please don't move, Melinda."

"It's fine," Melinda said curtly. She stood and circled to the other side of the table.

Gertie patted Melinda's empty seat. "See, Melinda doesn't mind at all. Sit here next to me."

Embarrassed, I moved to the other side of the table. The vantage point gave me a clear view of Timothy and Hudson. The bus driver didn't seem to be too pleased with the conversation. Occasionally, he grunted at Timothy between bites of Dutch Apple pie.

Ivy came to the table with a glass of water for me. "Would you like dessert too?"

"No thank you. Do you have any shepherd's pie left?"

"We do." She removed her notepad from her apron pocket. "It comes with soup or salad. Which would you like?"

"Just the pie will be fine."

"That will be right out."

I thanked her and sipped my water.

Ivy crossed the room to get Timothy's order.

Gertie wiggled back in forth in her seat. "Who is the hunk?"

I nearly spit out a mouthful of water. Melinda handed me a napkin. I gave her a grateful smile. "The hunk?"

"Why yes. Don't play coy with us. I can see how he looks at you. If a young man watched me like that, I'd never leave his side."

Duke chuckled. "Gertie, I didn't know you were a cougar."

More water threatened to choke me. I set the glass down. I wasn't thirsty anyway.

Doris chuckled as she forked a big piece of apple. "And how did he look at her?"

Gertie's lips curled upwards. "Like she was the last cup-cake on the planet."

Thankfully, I had given up drinking water. Hydration was overrated.

CHAPTER FIFTEEN

Gertie tapped her fork on the side of her dish. "If I were sixty years younger, I'd be giving you a run for your money. How does hunk-o-lovin' feel about older women?"

"I don't know," I squeaked. I couldn't wait to share this conversation with Tanisha. She'd be rolling on the floor by this point. "I'm three years younger than he is."

"His loss," she muttered.

Duke stirred his coffee. "Age is just a number. Right, Gertie?"

Doris cut the remainder of her pie into tiny pieces with her fork and knife. "Gertie, you are a trip."

Melinda looked heavenward.

"I'm sorry this is the first chance I've had to speak to you both," I said to the married couple.

Duke reached across the table and squeezed my fingertips because the table was too large for a proper handshake. "Nothing to apologize for. We really appreciate you jumping in as our tour guide."

Doris forked a bite of pie. "Duke and I have been looking forward to this trip all year long. We were heartbroken when it looked like it would be canceled." She covered her mouth with her hand. "I don't want to sounds callous. We feel terrible about Dudley and Ruby."

Her husband covered her hand with his. "We do."

"I think you met my friend Becky today at Young's Family Restaurant. She was your waitress."

Doris swallowed her pie. "What a stunning girl! I told her that she could be a model. She has the height and body for it."

"She's Timothy's sister."

Everyone at the table looked over at Timothy. "I can see the family resemblance," Doris said. "What a beautiful family."

"Good genes," Gertie said.

Melinda sipped her water. Her pie plate was untouched. "I think I saw him at the farm where we had the accident this morning."

Ivy brought my shepherd's pie to the table. It was a typical Amish-sized serving: extra, extra large. I thanked her and picked up my fork. "He was there. His family owns that farm."

"But he's not Amish."

The steam from the shepherd's pie hit me in the face. "He left the church but is still close with his family."

"Are they allowed to do that? Don't they get shunned? I saw a program on cable television about Amish shunning each other." Gertie pointed her spoon at me. "It's shameful."

I shifted in my seat. "The Amish do shun church members if they leave the church after they have been baptized Amish. At least that's how the Appleseed Creek district operates. Timothy and his sister Becky left the community before either one of them were baptized."

"Still it can't be easy for them to go back. What do they think of you dating their son? You don't look like a runaway Amish." Gertie scrutinized me. "I'd say you are as far from Amish as a girl can get."

"Amish who have left the community don't look any different than any other English—that's what the Amish call non-Amish people—person you might see in town," I said.

"Are you saying you're a runaway Amish?"

I shook my head. "No. I'm from Cleveland."

"Thought so," Gertie said with a victorious nod.

I placed a spoonful of the shepherd's pie in my mouth. It was delicious. It wasn't until I started eating that I realized how hungry I was.

"Do you know where Pearl is?" Gertie asked. "Did the police arrest her? Do they think she's the killer?"

I swallowed. "Pearl is staying at another hotel. It was her choice."

Doris nodded sagely. "It must be difficult for her to be on the tour."

Gertie pointed the business end of her spoon at Doris. "Bah. I bet she's happy to be rid of Ruby. All the two of them ever did was fight."

"They did argue a lot on the bus." Duke added four lumps of sugar to his coffee.

Doris pushed the sugar bowl away. "That's enough for you."

He frowned. "Doris and I sat in the seat right behind the cousins and listened to them squabble all the way across Pennsylvania. I wanted to throw myself off the bus by the time we reached the Ohio border."

"What did they argue about?" I asked.

"Anything and everything. Ruby was the more vocal of the two. She always seemed to have the last word." Duke finger walked toward the sugar bowl.

"Duke, you know what the doctor said about your sweet tooth."

"He's a quack," Duke said as he turned back to me. "Those two made me think about my kids squabbling in the back of my car."

That was interesting. "The bus was half empty, why didn't they sit in separate seats? There was plenty of room."

Duke shook his head. "I don't know."

"Was it mostly minor disagreements?"

Duke nodded. "Maybe Pearl couldn't take Ruby's complaining anymore and snapped."

"Then why would she kill Dudley too?" Melinda asked. "That doesn't make much sense."

Duke shrugged. "To throw the police off the trail. It's what I would do."

"Duke!" Doris yelped. "He's kidding. He's kidding."

Melinda pushed her uneaten pie away from her and folded her hands on the table. "That's a big risk and seems excessive."

"He was joking." Doris swatted her husband with her napkin. "I can't take you anywhere."

Gertie picked up her fork. "Dudley wasn't anything worth writing home about. He wasn't at all enthusiastic about the Amish culture. At times he even sounded like he disliked it. Strange for a man leading tours through Amish Country."

Doris set her water glass on the table. "I agree with Gertie about this. Duke and I spoke about it many times when we were in Lancaster County. Dudley didn't like the Amish. It was clear."

I lost my appetite. "What would he do?"

Gertie sipped her water before answering. "He called everything about the Amish into question."

This was *not* what I wanted to hear.

Melinda clenched her hands together on the table.

When she saw me looking at them, she slid them to her lap.

"Is everything all right, Melinda?" I asked.

Her dark eyes snapped in my direction. "I'm fine. I was just waiting for—"

Gertie interrupted her. "She wants to tuck me into bed so she can have some free time on her own."

"You know that's not true, Gertie." She stirred her ice tea. "But I would like to go for a walk in the gardens before it's too dark."

"Melinda loves plants," Gertie said.

Melinda laughed. "That's a funny statement, Gertie. Almost everyone loves plants."

"Not like you." Gertie scooted back her chair. It barely moved. Melinda stood and pulled Gertie's chair out, helping her to her feet.

My throat was parched from all the talking. I lifted my water glass to my lips.

"It was nice to eat with you, and Chloe," she patted my shoulder with her wrinkled hand. "If you get tired of the hunk-o-lovin' over there, just send him my way. I'll show him a good time."

Again I choked on a mouthful of water. I would have to remember liquids and Gertie did not mix.

"She's a riot," Duke said after Gertie and Melinda left the dining room. The guests at the other tables were beginning to leave too.

I forked a piece of carrot. "Was there anything else in particular you remember from Ruby and Pearl's conversations?"

Duke creased his brow in thought. "No. I can't recall anything. They reminded me a little bit of Laverne and Shirley. They even have the same color of hair."

At my confused look, Duke laughed. "It's an old television sitcom from the 1970s. Way before your time. It was about these two women friends who were funny and bickered."

"Oh," I said.

Duke sighed. "Google it."

Doris laughed. "I think Melinda had the right idea. We should turn in. It's been a trying day."

Duke stood and pulled out his wife's chair. "Don't forget your purse, dear."

She smiled at him as if she were a teenager mooning over a boy she liked. Now, that was a last cupcake look.

I stood too. "Good night."

"Good night, Chloe," they said and shuffled out of the dining room.

Timothy was the only one left in the dining room. I picked up my plate and water and moved to sit across from him. He had finished his dinner. Having been caught up in the conversation with Gertie and the others, I had barely touched mine. Even though it was cold, it was still delicious. "What did Hudson have to say?"

Timothy cut into his slice of pie with his fork. "Not much. That guy grunts a lot."

"I noticed."

"Looks like you had a pretty deep conversation going on at your table."

I told him what I had heard about Ruby and Pearl's relationship. I left out the Laverne and Shirley reference. If I didn't know what it was, I knew Timothy wouldn't.

"Was that all you talked about?"

"No." I smiled slowly. "Gertie said you were a hunk-o-lovin', and she would like to date you."

Timothy choked on his pie. Apparently, Gertie had that effect on people even when she wasn't in the room.

CHAPTER SIXTEEN

I stood. "Come on. I want to have a walk around the grounds before it gets too dark."

Timothy wiped at his mouth with a napkin. "Is this a nice evening stroll or more sleuthing?"

I held out my hand to him. "We will call it a combo."

Timothy and I went out the back door of the inn. The garden was massive. Several of the bus passengers walked through it. LeeAnne and Raellen admired the bluebells, and Charles took photo after photo of the bleeding heart. I couldn't help but wonder how many of those plants were poisonous and which ones could kill a person. I shivered. I didn't see Melinda. Maybe she had changed her mind about touring the garden after she helped Gertie to her room.

"Are you cold?" Timothy asked.

"I'm fine. It's just when we got back to the inn this evening, I thought I saw someone in the garden through the upstairs hall window."

Timothy shrugged. "You might have. What were they doing?"

"That's just it. I don't know. I just caught a glimpse of a figure. I'm half convinced now that I imagined it. Everyone was there when we reached the dining room."

Timothy and I walked around the side of the inn just in time to see Bishop Hooley climb out of a buggy. Deacon Sutter and Ephraim spoke in hushed tones at the hitching post.

Ephraim knew the deacon? Of course, he knew the deacon; everyone in the district did. But how well?

Timothy gave my hand a squeeze and then released it before approaching the two men.

Deacon Sutter tethered the horse to a hitching post. Ephraim hurried away toward the back garden.

"I d-didn't expect to find the two of you here," the bishop said.

"Nor did we expect to see you," I said.

Gravel crushed under the deacon's feet as he joined us.

"Deacon Sutter and I are here to make sure that the p-passengers aren't too upset by today." The bishop paused. "We would have been here sooner, but we had a brief meeting of the district elders to discuss what has happened."

My stomach clenched and I couldn't help but wonder if they discussed the Troyer family at that meeting.

Timothy must have been thinking the same thing because he said, "You must know my father would never have done anything to hurt those people or jeopardize the visit."

The deacon smoothed his black beard. "Perhaps it was simply a case of carelessness. Either way it harms the district."

Timothy balled his fists at his sides. "I can assure you my father had nothing to do with the accident."

"You can assure us of nothing. You are no longer a member of our community. Whatever you have to say is of no consequence to us."

The bishop's eyes darted from Timothy to the deacon and back again. "Deacon Sutter does not mean to offend. At the meeting, we agreed to leave this matter to the police. In this case, the district should not be involved."

The deacon's jaw twitched. He didn't agree.

Had he tampered with the milk to get back at the Troyers? And now, the bishop decided to do nothing?

"C-Chloe, thank you for taking over as the tour guide," the bishop stuttered. "Chief Rose told us that she asked you to do that. We are grateful. It's important that this tour goes well. At least it is important that the rest of the tour goes well." His eyes flicked to the deacon. "However, the elders have decided that having the bus tour here was a mistake. We will not have such an event in the district again."

A faint satisfied smile crossed the deacon's face. Hadn't Grandfather Zook said that morning that the deacon was against the bus tour? Would he go so far as to kill someone to make sure it never happened again?

"I'm happy to help," I said.

The deacon moved a few paces closer to me. "*Ya.* You seem to always want to *help* our community."

Timothy stepped closer to me as if to block the deacon's glare.

"Now, Deacon." Bishop Hooley forced a laugh. "You know Chloe did help us this time."

The deacon scowled but said nothing more.

"Bishop, can I ask you some questions about this morning?" I asked.

He smoothed his beard, and his eyes slid over to the deacon.

"I don't know what the bishop can tell you," Deacon Sutter said. "He was with me the entire time. We know nothing."

"Then maybe you both can answer my questions since you were there this morning."

The deacon shook his head, but the bishop held up a shaky hand. "It is *gut*, Deacon. We can answer her questions."

"We have already spoken to the police. That is enough," the deacon argued.

The bishop frowned. "I will answer her questions."

Before Deacon Sutter could say more, I asked, "Did you speak with Dudley when he arrived with the tour?"

"*Ya.* He was the one I had been in the most contact with to bring Blue Suede Tours to Knox County."

"Did he seem upset or nervous?" I asked.

"*Nee.*" He paused. "He was frustrated that the schedule had to be changed because of the Zugg's sheep getting loose."

I had forgotten that. "How did the sheep get out?"

"There was a hole in the fence. Z-Zugg was lucky only one animal slipped away."

"Did he find it?"

"*Ya.* She hadn't gone very far."

"Did you see anyone near the milk?"

"All the *Englischers* were around the milk," the deacon jumped in. "It would be difficult to see if anyone tampered with it. That's what you are implying, aren't you?"

I nodded.

"It is getting l-late," the bishop said. He looked at me. "Please tell the passengers that we hope that they enjoy the r-remainder of their stay."

The deacon nodded at me. "Be careful as you ride along with the bus tour. We would hate it if anyone else was harmed."

Was that a threat?

After the buggy rocked out onto the street, Timothy said, "I hope you have the deacon on your suspect list."

"You bet I do." I squeezed his hand. "He just jumped up a few notches."

That night in my room at the inn, the events of the day played like a movie reel in my mind. The image that struck me the most was the shock and dismay on Mr. Troyer's proud face right after Ruby and Dudley fell. Coming in a close second was Deacon Sutter's satisfied expression when the bishop said there would be no more Amish bus tours in the district.

CHAPTER SEVENTEEN

I woke up in the middle of the night and wondered where I was, and then I remembered. I hadn't shut my curtains before falling into bed. Moonlight streamed in through the windows in the French doors and shone on my face.

I held a hand over my eyes to block the light. That didn't work. Then, I covered my face with a pillow and felt like I was suffocating. I wriggled out of my cozy cocoon and stumbled to the French doors and opened them. The water of the Kokosing River glimmered like a line of liquid silver under the light of the full moon. A lone doe drank from the water's edge. The sight took my breath away. The crisp spring night air floated into the room. The smell of the lilacs and muddy ground washed over me, bringing me fully awake.

I groaned as I shuffled back to bed. I needed sleep. I had a full afternoon of tour guiding the next day. Thankfully, because tomorrow was Sunday, the tour wouldn't begin until after lunch in case any of the guests wanted to attend local church services.

My cell phone made a binging sound. I grabbed it from the night stand. I had an incoming call through Skype.

On the tiny screen, I saw Tanisha sitting at her desk in her classroom in Milan, Italy. Her long black braids fell over her shoulders and she wore plastic-rimmed glasses "for style" even though her vision was twenty-twenty. I had to admit the purple glasses did look good on her, but then again everything looked good on Tanisha. "Hey, you're up. I didn't really expect you to answer," she said.

I rubbed my eyes.

"Did I wake you?" She sounded worried.

I dropped my hand. "No, can't sleep."

"Turn a light on. I can't see you. You look like the shadow of death."

That was cheerful. I reached across the bed and turned on the lamp at the nightstand. "Better?" I asked.

"Much." Tanisha moved her head back and forth as if trying to find a better angle to see me. "Where are you? That doesn't look like your bedroom."

"I'm staying at the Dutch Inn."

Tanisha sipped espresso from a tiny coffee cup. "Did you go on vacation?"

"Not exactly. I'm still on Appleseed Creek. I guess you would say I'm on an assignment of sorts for Chief Rose."

Tanisha had met the chief when she visited me over Christmas. "Tell me everything." Tee rubbed her hands together. "This will be good."

"Where do I start?" I rubbed my other eye. Maybe I should close the French doors. As much as I loved the lilac scent in the room, I think I was having an allergic reaction to it.

"From the beginning, don't skip anything."

"I was at the Troyer farm…"

She wiggled in her desk chair. "I knew this would have something to do with Timothy." She pretended to fan herself. "Mr. Amish Hotness."

I laughed, thinking of Gertie. "You have some competition."

"You?"

"Oh no, not me, a hundred-year-old woman."

"You'd better start at the beginning. I have ten minutes left in my free period, so hurry up."

After I had told her the story, she said, "Chloe, you are like a magnet for dead people."

That wasn't exactly a title to be proud of. "I just happen to be at the wrong place at the wrong time." I paused. "A lot."

"No kidding." She twirled one of her braids around her index finger. "I wish I could help you. You know I'd be there in a minute if I could."

I smiled, wishing I could give my best friend a hug. "Timothy, your hero, is here."

"That's true. I can count on him to take care of you. Let me tell you I gave him a talking to about how special you were when I was there."

I knocked the heel of my hand on my forehead. "Tee…"

She laughed. "As your best friend, it's my job. It wouldn't have mattered if I had given him the talk or not. He already knew. He's smitten."

"Smitten?"

"It's a vocabulary word this week," she said. "Timothy is staying there too?"

"He's on a different floor," I said dryly.

"That is so sweet. He's your Amish knight in shining armor. I need to find me a Timothy too. Not too many hot former Amish guys running around Milan. I've looked."

"What about Rocco?"

Tanisha had started dating an Italian teacher at the school where she taught English as a second language. She groaned. "Rocco is history. More importantly, how could there possibly be another murder in Appleseed Creek?"

That was an excellent question.

Sunday in Amish Country was a quiet time. According to the itinerary, the travelers could have the morning to sleep in or go to church, so I assumed I was free to go to church myself. Before Timothy and I left, I knocked on Hudson's door. The only answer was snores. I decided waking him up was a very bad idea.

Jane was again at the desk that morning. I wondered if she ever got a break from it. It was the only place I had seen her the entire time we had been at the inn. She chatted with Timothy about the weather.

"Jane," I said. "Can you tell Hudson whenever he emerges from his room that I went to church and will be back by lunchtime?"

She straightened up. "Yes, I'll slip a message under his door. The children and I will be leaving soon for the Sutter farm. That's where the district service will be today."

I thanked her and was about to open the inn's front door to meet Timothy at his truck, when it flew open. A figure stomped into the room and knocked into my shoulder, sending me stumbling to the side. He had his head bent. "Excuse me."

"Mr. Kepler," Jane said. "Are you all right?"

"I'm fine," Earl said without looking up. He went straight for the elevator and jabbed at the button.

Timothy appeared in the doorway. "Chloe, are you ready to go?"

"I--," I stared as the elevator doors closed on Earl's face. He looked like he had been crying. "Yes, I'm ready."

Timothy and I arrived at church early because he was in the choir. Becky was a member too. She'd walked from our house and waited for us on the lawn. I was disappointed to see Hannah Hilty and her two henchwomen, red-cheeked Emily and rail-thin Kim, waiting on the lawn with Becky. Becky didn't appear pleased with the company.

Hannah ignored the girls and only had eyes for Timothy. "Timothy," Hannah crooned. "We were just talking about you."

I bet.

Becky sidled up to my side and rolled her eyes.

"Hi, Hannah," I said.

"Oh, hello, Chloe." She pretended to be surprised to see me with Timothy. "How are you?"

Becky smoothed an imaginary wrinkle in her A-line skirt. "Where's your boyfriend? Shouldn't he be out of school for the summer?"

Hannah's boyfriend played basketball for Kentucky State.

Hannah sighed. "He's back home, but we are no longer together. I don't know what happened. It was going so well."

"He went running for his life," Becky muttered under her breath.

I stepped on her foot.

She suppressed a cry and scooted away from me.

"Maybe it was the long distance," Timothy said.

I inwardly groaned. Timothy's natural concern for others played right into Hannah's clutches.

"I don't know," Hannah said in a pathetic, 'please come rescue me' voice.

Becky opened her mouth as if she was going to offer up another suggestion. I shook my head just once. She closed her mouth and grinned. It must have been a whopper.

Hannah reached out and touched Timothy's arm. He didn't recoil from her touch as I would have liked him to. "He just didn't have substance. He wasn't the right guy for me."

"Chloe, I heard you're the leader of the bus tour that killed those people," Kim, who towered over me, said.

I didn't even bother to ask how Kim knew this. Appleseed Creek was small and everyone knew everything about everyone, English, Amish, Mennonite, it didn't matter. Also, Hannah and her friends took a particular interest in finding out information about me.

"The bus tour didn't kill anyone. But, yes, two people on the tour died under suspicious circumstances."

"It seems like you always find your way into trouble." Hannah blinked innocently at me.

"It happened at our farm," Timothy said with a frown.

"Oh, Timothy." Hannah backpedaled like a champ. "I would never, ever imply your family had anything to do with what happened to those poor people." Hannah glared at her friends. Kim and Emily inched toward the church.

Hannah cleared her throat. "Chloe." She pointed over my shoulder and into the church parking lot. "Someone is waiting for you."

I glanced back and saw Curt in the parking lot leaning against his green truck. He waved at me. My gaze flitted back to Timothy. The skin around his eyes tightened.

Hannah hooked her arm through Timothy's. "Curt loves to talk about you, Chloe. I overheard your name when he spoke to the pastor a little bit ago. It was so darling. Someone has a crush."

"Hannah, that might be the dumbest thing you've ever said," Becky snapped. "Curt knows Chloe and Timothy are together." She leaned closer to Hannah. "And so do you."

For a millisecond, Hannah's right eye narrowed, but then her face cleared. "Becky, you are too cute." She tugged on Timothy's arm. "We'll just be off to choir and let you and your *friend* visit."

CHAPTER EIGHTEEN

I returned Curt's wave, and he walked over to me, carrying a plastic grocery bag in his right hand.

"You're here early," I said.

"I figured you'd be here because Becky had choir."

I noted he didn't say Timothy, but that didn't *mean* anything. "It's nice to see a friendly face after a run in with Hannah."

Curt pulled at the sleeve of his flannel shirt. The plastic bag swung back and forth as he moved. "She's a brat."

I grinned.

Curt shook the bag. "I have something to show you."

"What is it?"

He laughed. "It's a surprise. Follow me." He circled to the back of the building.

I glanced back at the church. Blue sky and cotton clouds outlined its white steeple. Members trickled in for the service. It wouldn't start for another twenty minutes.

"Red, are you coming?"

Behind the church was a small playground for the children. It wasn't much, just a swing set and a slide, but on such a beautiful day, a half dozen girls and boys ran around whooping with joy. Their mothers and fathers stood a few feet away, supervising and hoping the playtime would wear out the children enough they would be quiet in church.

With all the kids and parents, the only open seat was a bench swing suspended from a metal frame. Curt headed straight for it and sat. I perched on the other end of the swing, careful not to get too close. "So what's in the bag?"

He handed it to me. "Open it."

The plastic crinkled as I pulled out a black T-shirt and unfolded it. A silver dove flying out of the cage was on the front. Under the image it said, "Faith Beyond Bars."

"It's pretty. What does it mean?"

Curt licked his lips. "You know I talked to Pastor Chris about making up for my mistakes and doing something good." He pointed at the T-shirt. "That's what I came up with. It's a prison ministry. I read about another on the Internet. Every few weeks, I'll visit the Knox County Jail, and tell the guys my story and how I changed." He spoke quickly as if he were afraid he might not say everything he needed to. "I've been inside the county jail enough times to know what it's like. Maybe if someone came in there and talked to me about my life and what it could be, I would have changed my ways a lot sooner. The pastor and a few volunteers from church will go with me. They can tell the guys all the Bible stuff that I'm just learning."

My mouth fell open. Of all the things Curt could have told me, I never would have guessed this.

"The church is going to help out too by donating a small portion of the mission money. It's a just a hundred dollars, but it will be enough for me to buy snacks for a couple of meetings at the prison. This summer, I'd like to have some type of picnic for a fundraiser. I'm not sure yet." He yanked on his father's dog tags. "Why are you looking at me like that?"

I closed my mouth. "I—I—wow, Curt."

He flipped the dog tags over and over again with his fingers. "Maybe it's a dumb idea."

"No," I yelped. "No, it's not. It's a wonderful idea."

He let out a breath. "You don't think it's stupid."

"Never. I don't know if I could do such a selfless thing."

"You could, Red. You could do anything."

I bit the inside of my cheek.

Curt sat up a little straighter. "Can you help out?"

I shifted my position on the swing to face him dead on. "What do you need me to do?"

His shoulders relaxed. "I thought since you are so good with computers, maybe you could make a website for us. Pastor said that he would share the link through the church's website."

"That's very easy for me to do. I'm happy to help. I can get started after the bus tour leaves. Until they're gone, I'm going to be pretty busy."

"Why?"

"I'm their temporary tour guide and staying with them at the Dutch Inn for the next few days."

"Do you think that's safe? One of them might be a killer."

Even after all this time, it felt strange to have Curt worry about my safety. Our friendship certainly had come a long way.

"Timothy is staying there too."

"Oh, he is." Something flashed in his eyes. "I don't think it's right of Troyer to use you like that."

"Use me?"

"He's making you stay there because he wants you to clear his father's name."

I scooted away from him. "Why do you think that?"

"Hannah said so this morning."

"You spoke to Hannah about me? You said yourself Hannah is a brat. Timothy doesn't want me on the bus. It was Chief Rose's idea."

He balled his hands on the top on his jean-clad thighs. "That's even worse. All she cares about is making an arrest." There was bitterness in his voice.

I refolded the T-shirt. "There's nothing to worry about."

"I worry."

Part of me wanted to ask him why, but a large part was afraid he'd tell me. "Is this what you wanted to meet with me about over coffee?"

"Most of it." He took a breath. "There's something else I need to tell you but not today. I need more time."

I didn't like the sound of that. I started to hand the T-shirt back to him.

He shook his head. "No, you keep it."

"Thank you." I held it on my lap. "I'm proud of you. This is an amazing idea, and I'm so glad you've talked to the pastor about getting the church involved."

He looked down at his white knuckles. "You think I can do it?" he whispered.

I touched his arm. "Of course. You have so much to offer these men and women in trouble."

He reached up and covered my hand with his. I felt his gaze on my face, but I didn't meet his eyes. Delicately as possible, I slid my hand from his grasp and clamped it onto the T-shirt.

A father whistled. "Kids! Play time is over. Head into church."

The children squealed and dashed for one more ride down the slide, one more kick on the swing.

I stood. Curt grabbed my wrist. "Thank you."

I smiled even though I wasn't sure what he thanked me for.

CHAPTER NINETEEN

After church, Becky followed Timothy and me back to his truck. I fell back with Becky, and she grabbed my hand. "Can I go with you?"

I eyed her. "You could read over those applications."

She frowned. "That's not very subtle, Chloe."

I laughed. "I'm just teasing. Of course, you can come with us. You can even ride in the bus today if you like."

"Where's the tour going?" Becky asked.

I removed the agenda from my purse. "It's a short day because almost everything is closed. We're going for a drive through the countryside and then a stop in Utica at an ice cream factory."

"I love that place," Becky said. "Sign me up."

I grinned. "You wouldn't rather stay at home and read those college applications?"

She gave me a look that would put the most sullen English teenager to shame.

I chuckled.

Her face brightened. "Maybe I can help with the tour too. I can tell some great stories about what it's really like to grow up Amish. It will be nice to tell people the truth instead of the stuff they see online or in movies. People either think Amish life is peaceful perfect bliss or a cult."

What Becky said was true. Even I had thought that once about the Amish life before arriving in Knox County. That preconception changed quickly.

Becky placed her hands on her hips. "It's neither. We just choose to live a different way. It's not perfect. It's not wrong."

"This crowd can be tough," I said thinking of grumpy Fred and some of the other men. "They may ask you some tough questions about Amish life. Maybe even be combative."

"I can take it," she said confidently. "I've heard worse waitressing at Young's. Someone asked me if I could read."

I grimaced. "What did you say?"

"I said, 'Yes and your shirt says you're a jerk.' He said, 'no it doesn't.' So I picked up his paper menu wrote 'jerk' across it and slapped it on his chest."

I stopped walking. Parishioners dodged us on their way to the parking lot. "Then what happened?"

"He left, which I didn't mind at all. A guy like that doesn't tip. If they do, they unload the change from their pockets, which is more insulting than not tipping at all. I don't want your lint-covered pennies, buddy."

"What did Ellie say?" I asked. "Did she know?"

"Oh, yeah, she knew," Becky sighed. "Ellie put me in the kitchen for a week after that. She said I couldn't insult the customers no matter what stupid things they say."

"That's probably a good policy." I couldn't help but grin. I wrapped my arm around her thin shoulders. "And I think you're right. You do have a lot to share with the tour group, and it will add to the tour and help their outlook on Amish life."

"Will I get paid for this?"

"Umm, no."

"Oh well, it will still be fun." She snapped her fingers. "I left my music for next Sunday in the choir room. Let me go grab it." She dashed back for the church, yelling over her shoulder. "Don't let Timothy leave without me."

Timothy waited by the truck. The sunlight shone on his head, and I was struck again by how handsome he was, but it wasn't just his looks that drew me to him. There was something more, deeper. I forced myself to stop staring as I grew closer. Mabel hung her fluffy head over the pickup's tailgate. Timothy scratched her between the ears. Timothy's affection for his dog made me love him more, and his tolerance for my temperamental Siamese made him a prince.

"Ready to go?" he asked.

"In a minute. Becky had to run back inside for her choir music. She's coming with us and is going to ride with me on the bus today."

"Good. I'm glad you won't be alone. That's a strange crowd you have on that bus, and I'm not certain they are all trustworthy." He paused. "What do you think Hudson will say about Becky joining you?"

"He might grumble, but I think the group would love to talk to Becky about her experiences."

"Hey, what about me?" Timothy asked.

I cocked my head. "You want to talk in front of the bus?"

He grinned. "Good point. Anyway, since Becky will be on the bus with you, I should start on those odd jobs for the inn." He cleared his throat. "What did Curt want?"

Briefly, I told Timothy about Faith Beyond Bars.

"And he wants you to do what exactly?"

"Just build a website. It's nothing. I can do that in my sleep."

"I don't think that's all he wants," Timothy muttered.

"Timothy Troyer, are you jealous?" I teased, hoping to diffuse the situation.

Heat flashed in his eyes. "Yes."

I swallowed as he stepped toward me. "Timothy, we are in the church parking lot."

A young family walked by on their way to their mini-van. I smiled at them.

He didn't pay any attention to my warning. "Of course, I'm jealous."

"That's silly. You have nothing to worry about."

He kissed my forehead. "Not from you. I know that."

He stepped closer to me. The silver charm necklace of a hammer and computer mouse, which he had given me for Christmas, burned into my clavicle bone.

Becky ran toward us, waving her music in the air. "I got it. I'm ready to go!"

Timothy stepped back, and I remembered how to move air in and out of my lungs.

On the drive back to the Dutch Inn, I was happy Becky sat between us, so that I could recover.

An hour and a half later, Becky and I stood outside of the Dutch Inn, helping the guests onto the bus.

"Charles," Bitty said to her husband over her shoulder. "Did you use your Sensodyne this morning? You know how cold food bothers your teeth, and you have a soft spot for ice cream."

The top of Charles's bald head turned red. "Bitty, please just get on the bus." He clutched his huge camera in his hands.

Becky's forehead wrinkled. "What's Sensodyne?"

"I'll tell you later," I said out of the side of my mouth.

Gertie stopped in front of Becky and jabbed a fist into one hip. The top of her curly head was level with Becky's shoulder. "I hope you have some good Amish stories for us. I don't want just the happy stuff neither. I want the dirt."

Becky scrunched her nose. She certainly had some uncomfortable stories about Amish life she could tell.

Melinda gave us an apologetic smile. "I'm sure Becky has many wonderful stories to share."

"Remember, I want dirt, Kiddo," Gertie crowed over her shoulder. "Melinda, did you remember my fish jerky? It will go real swell with ice cream."

Melinda sighed. "Yes, Gertie, I have it."

When they were on the bus, Becky looked at me. Her eyes were the size of Oreos.

"Don't worry. Gertie is harmless… I think."

"Chloe…"

"Just share what you are comfortable sharing. If you're not sure if you should tell a story, don't tell it. It's better to err on the side of caution than say too much. Whatever you have to say will be more authentic than anything they've heard. You don't have to confess your life story." I hoped Becky understood that last part as code for, "Don't tell them about the buggy accident."

Her worried expression cleared.

"This ice cream better be as good as you say it is," Jimbo said as he struggled up the bus steps.

"It's better," Becky assured him.

My cell rang as I gave LeeAnne a hand up onto the first step. It was Chief Rose. "Becky, can you help these folks onto the bus?"

She took my spot without question.

I moved a few feet away. "Hello?"

"Humphrey, I need you to come down to the station."

"Now?"

"Yes, now, what do you think, I called to schedule an appointment for next week?" The chief sounded more irritated than usual, and that was saying something.

"The tour bus is about to leave. I thought you wanted me on the bus."

While I was on the phone, Becky chatted with the bus guests like they were old friends. It was a rare person who could resist Becky's charms.

"I do, but this is more important at the moment. Pearl's here and wants to talk to you. Only you."

"What about the tour?"

"Drop them off somewhere and come over here." She sounded as if she spoke through gritted teeth.

"It's not that easy. There aren't many places opened on Sunday."

"Think of something and get over here. This is not a multiple choice situation."

All the passengers were on the bus now. Hudson stamped his foot. Becky raised her eyebrows at me, which gave me an idea.

CHAPTER TWENTY

As I drove into town, I felt guilty for sending Becky on the tour alone. She insisted she would be okay, but there could be a killer on that bus.

The police station was one quarter of Appleseed Creek's town hall located on the town square. The town hall and city official offices had a grand entrance facing the square flanked by Georgian pillars. In contrast, the entrance to the police station was a reinforced metal door from the back parking lot. A sign marked the parking space closest to the door with Chief Rose's name. Her white and blue patrol car was in the spot.

I stepped into the police station, which appeared the same as it always did with the no nonsense metal desk, fake plants, and terribly uncomfortable plastic molded chairs. Chief Rose finally admitted to me once she chose those chairs because they were the most uncomfortable she could find. She was thoughtful like that.

As it was Sunday, the chief's receptionist was off. Pearl sat in one of the painful chairs. The police chief sat at her receptionist's desk. She stood. "Thanks for coming."

"You're welcome," I said, caught surprised. The chief typically didn't thank me for following any of her edicts.

Pearl didn't lift her head.

"She's barely holding it together. It's like the loss of her cousin just hit her," the chief whispered.

"How did she get here?" I whispered back. "Did you ask her to come in?"

"I needed her to sign her statement, but I planned to send Riley out to her hotel to collect her signature. She showed up here about an hour ago."

"What did she say?"

"I asked her how she got here, and she told me she took a taxi. After that she said she wanted to talk to you and hasn't spoken a word since."

Still Pearl didn't raise her head.

I crossed the room and pulled one of the empty plastic chairs in front of the older woman. Chief Rose remained on the other side of the room, but she wouldn't miss a thing.

"Pearl, it's Chloe. You wanted to talk to me?"

The older woman stared at her hands gripping the leather strap of her handbag so tightly it left red indentations in her skin.

"Pearl, what did you want to talk to me about?"

Slowly, Pearl lifted her head. "Chloe?" She blinked at me. "I want to go home."

I glanced at Chief Rose. She shook her head.

"I told you we can help you get home. You don't have to stay with the tour."

"I can't leave without Ruby." She fumbled in her purse for a tissue. "She's all the family I have—had—in the world. I need her to be able to go back with me."

Again I looked to the chief for guidance. She mouthed, "Two more days."

"Her body will be released in two days."

She crushed the tissue in her hand. "I can't stay that long. I can't. I'm afraid."

Goosebumps sprang up on my forearms. "Why? Did something happen? Did someone threaten you?"

Her voice dropped to a whisper. "No."

I shifted on the uncomfortable chair. "Then, why do you feel differently than you did yesterday?"

She gave a shuddered breath. "Spending last night in the hotel alone was terrible. I don't know when I've ever been so afraid. I don't travel." Her southern accent became thicker. "I have never been in a hotel like that with no one I know. Every slam of a door, every creak of the floorboards above my head sent me into a panic. I spent the night sitting up in an armchair, reading my Bible and asking the Lord to deliver me."

I reached across the space between us and squeezed her hand. "Pearl, you should have called me. I would have brought you back to the Dutch Inn."

Tears filled her eyes. "To that place where I would be alone to be with people who may have hurt my cousin, my dearest friend?"

"You wouldn't be alone. I am staying there now too."

A tear fell onto the strap of her purse, and she brushed it away. "You are? Why?"

"As the new tour guide, it's part of the job." I offered her a crooked smile. "Starting tonight, I will be leading the dinner conversations."

"I never liked those conversations."

I loved her for saying that.

"I promise no slideshow."

That comment won me the tiniest of smiles.

"So why don't you come back to the Dutch Inn? I can drive you over to your hotel now, and you can pack your things and check out. We'll have you settled in a room at the inn within the hour."

"I would like that," she said.

Chief Rose joined us. "I think this is a wise move, Pearl. Humphrey may be small but she is scrappy."

Umm, thanks?

That got a true smile out of Pearl. "I thought that about Chloe when I met her." She met my eyes. "You set a goal and you reach it. You are like many modern women of this time. In my day, it was different and not as easy. I wish I had been fearless enough to set my own course for my life. Instead, I let others choose it for me."

My brow wrinkled. *Should I ask Pearl what she meant by the comment?*

"Humphrey, I need to speak to you for a moment in the conference room before you leave."

I frowned.

Pearl patted my knee. "Go ahead. I can wait here a few more minutes. I'm in no rush to leave."

I followed the chief into the interrogation room and appreciated it that she referred to it as the "conference" room in front of Pearl.

As I sat at the table, I received a text from Becky. "All good. They're literally eating up the ice cream and my Amish stories. It's a hit. Maybe I should be a travel agent."

I winced at the idea of another career change. When Becky first left the Amish she wanted to be a fine art painter, then an art teacher, then a chef, then a Food Network star, and now a travel agent. It was hard to keep up. I hope she didn't tell her parents any of these ideas before she settled on the final one. It was not the Amish way to be indecisive about one's future, but she was right on target for the average young adult.

Chief Rose got right to the point. "It wasn't just bad milk."

"What do you mean?"

"Those people were poisoned."

My jaw dropped. "With what?"

"Yew."

"Me?" I squeaked.

"Not you, you. Yew. Y-E-W. It's a plant, a bush actually. Grows native in the area and a good portion of the northern half of the country."

The image of Officer Riley sticking those plants into an evidence bag hit me.

The chief opened a manila folder sitting in the middle of the table. She opened it. Inside there was a photo of the spiny pine branch Riley cut from the Troyer's yard. "Yew," she said simply.

"They ate that?"

She nodded. "We found traces of it in the milk cups."

"All the cups?" I yelped.

"No, only three."

"Three. Was someone else supposed to drink it and," I paused, "die."

"That I don't know. Maybe the killer had a backup cup in case."

"How could it be in the milk? Wouldn't it have a taste?"

"Maybe. Doc said the taste would have been a mild, bitter flavor, and the person drinking it might not have noticed."

I examined the photograph. "Would they have choked on the spines?"

She laughed. "Doc believes the poison was extracted by making a tea from the bark or the needles of the plant."

I tapped my nails on the table top. "That takes time and planning."

The chief closed the folder. "It's called premeditated murder. As of this morning, this is officially a homicide investigation."

Relief washed over me. "This means Mr. Troyer is off the hook."

Chief Rose narrowed her purple-lined eyes. "Not so fast."

"Are you kidding me? Why would he make a tea of this?" I pointed at the folder. "And give it to tourists? He would have made it before they arrived. He never met any of those people before they stepped onto his farm. Not to mention, such an act could destroy his family and ruin his business." I took a breath.

She crossed her hands on the tabletop with palms facing down. "I see your point, and no, I don't think he did it. However, until I find the real killer, no suspect is off of my list."

"You said that poison was found in the cups. What about the milk in the tank and the cows. Is that okay? Can he sell it to the milkman?"

"It's not my call."

"The cows have to be milked. What should they do with all that milk? It will go to waste."

Chief Rose frowned. "I don't have the authority to give the Troyers the go-ahead there. The state health inspectors have to do it, especially if the milk is to be sold to consumers."

"When will that be?"

She pulled the folder across the table with her index finger. "I don't know, but in my experience, government agencies are not known for their speed."

"It's the Troyers' livelihood."

"I am well aware of that. I will give the health department a call to encourage them to release the farm from the quarantine, but I have to warn you, they won't pay much attention to a small town cop like me."

That's what I was afraid of.

CHAPTER TWENTY-ONE

I waited in the hotel lobby as Pearl went to her room to pack. A television bolted to the stand in a high corner of the wall blared twenty-four hour news about a civil war on the other side of the world. The newscaster reminded me, Knox County wasn't such a bad place to live.

A teenaged guy with floppy hair and bad skin stood behind the registration desk and winked at me.

I smiled and scooted to the other side of the lobby.

He snapped his gum. "You're with that old lady, aren't you?"

I gave a small nod. I wasn't in the mood to chitchat with the obviously bored teenager.

The teen flicked his hair out of his eyes in a practiced move. "She's really popular."

I crossed the lobby. "What do you mean?"

He clicked his computer mouse on the counter. "Lots of folks have come back here looking for her. There was a cop for one."

Officer Nottingham.

"And then there was this old dude. I thought maybe it was her husband. I called up to her room, but she refused to come down. My girlfriend said she was probably running away from him. That's why the cop was here. Maybe he beat her or something."

"Your girlfriend works here at the hotel?"

He squished up his face. "Naw. But sometimes she hangs with me when it's slow. Don't tell my boss. He wouldn't like it."

"I won't," I promised. *Like I know who your boss is.* "The man who was here, what was his name?"

The teen twisted his mouth as he dug into his memory banks to retrieve the name. "I don't remember. He was old though, and the dude was way mad when the old lady said she wasn't coming. He wanted to know what her room number was, but my girlfriend told me I shouldn't tell him."

"You have a smart girlfriend."

"I know," the teen said in awe. "She's going to college."

"When you say old, how old do you mean?"

He cocked his head. "Older than you, like by a lot."

Great. At twenty-four, I qualified as old.

"Definitely grandpa age. That's why I was surprised the old dude got so mad. I mean, grandpas are supposed to be mellow. At least, my Gramps is. He sleeps most of the day and likes his food straight from the blender."

It had to be one of the men from the bus tour.

"What did he look like?" I asked.

The teen hair fell into his eyes again. "He was a white dude."

That ruled out Duke at least.

"Anything else about his appearance that you can tell me?" I asked.

"He had a wicked mustache."

"Wicked?"

"My girlfriend grew up in Massachusetts, and she says *wicked* all the time. She says it's like *sweet* or *cool* around here."

The older man with the mustache had to be Earl. What was he doing at Pearl's hotel? How did he get there? Did he take a taxi like Pearl had? The hair stood up on the back of my neck. Could Earl be the killer? The image of Earl crying in the elevator sprang to my mind.

"Red, are you giving Cameron a hard time?" a voice asked from behind me.

A chill ran down my spine. Only two people on the planet called me Red. Curt was one, and Brock Buckley was the other.

Cameron cracked his gum more quickly, and his eyes dilated slightly. I didn't know what Brock had done to the poor kid, but Cameron was afraid of him.

I spun around. "What are you doing here?"

Brock was over six feet tall and built like a bulldozer. His bald head gleamed under the lobby's fluorescent lights. He wore the same hotel uniform Cameron had on. His deceptive baby-like face smirked at me. "Aww, Red, I thought you would be friendlier, you being a *Christian* and all. Isn't being nice required for your kind of people?"

I glanced behind me. Cameron was gone.

Brock laughed. "Don't look to that wimp for help. He's in the back room wetting his pants."

I straightened to my full five-four height. "You work here?"

"Surprised someone gave me a job, Red?"

The simple answer was "yes," but I knew better than to say that.

He laughed again and brushed across my body as he slipped behind the registration counter.

I recoiled.

"Checking in?" he asked.

"No. I'm waiting for a friend."

"Ahh." He removed a cigarette from the breast pocket of his shirt and lit up.

"You're not supposed to smoke indoors. State law," I said.

He took a long drag from his cigarette. "Are you going to tattle on me? I know wimpy Cameron knows better than to do that." He clicked on the mouse and smiled at something he saw on the screen. "Your *friend* must be that old lady from the bus tour. Too bad about her sister."

"It was her cousin," I corrected automatically.

He smiled as if he found it quaint I bothered to correct him.

"How's Curt doing?" Brock's lip curled up in distaste.

"He misses you."

Brock laughed. "He should have thought about our friendship before he went Goody Two Shoes on me."

"Maybe if you talk to him…" I couldn't believe what I heard myself say. Why was I encouraging Brock to see Curt? Brock was the last person Curt needed in his life. He was doing so well without Brock. "Curt started a prison ministry."

Brock laughed so hard he gripped the counter for support.

I crossed my arms. "He's turning his life around."

"Curt means nothing to me. Just like you mean nothing to me. I'm working here to save enough money to leave this worthless county. I'm headed to Florida. I always wanted to live on the beach."

I felt bad for the people in Florida.

The grin was back. "I hope you two will be very happy together."

I blinked. "Who?"

"You and Curt."

"What are you talking about?" I asked, but I knew.

A malicious smile spread across his face. "You don't know?" He laughed. "Can't say I'm that surprised. You never were the swiftest on the uptake about these things."

My eyes drifted to the elevator's doors. I hoped Pearl appeared soon, so that we could leave.

He put the cigarette out in Cameron's coffee mug. "Curt's in *love* with you."

I felt like someone had dropped a grand piano on my head. "You don't know what you are talking about."

"Don't I?" He stalked around the counter. "I know Curt the best."

I shook my head. "You don't know him anymore. He's changed."

"And why did he change? Because he really believed in your God? Or because he thought it would bring him closer to you?"

"You're wrong." The back of my leg bumped into a potted plant.

"This could certainly make your little fairy tale with the buggy rider more difficult. What a shame if that was ruined." False compassion laced his words.

"Don't you have to get back to work?"

The bing of the elevator's arrival interrupted us. A minute later, Pearl appeared rolling her suitcase and carrying her Blue Suede Tours roll bag. She hesitated when she saw me standing in the middle of the lobby with Brock.

Brock smiled at her and said as nice as you please, "Good afternoon. Are you ready to check out?"

Pearl gave me a questioning look. "Yes, thank you."

I took the roll bag and suitcase from Pearl's hands and watched as she returned her keycard, and Brock printed her receipt.

All-the-while, my heart thundered in my chest. *Was Brock right? Did Curt have feelings for me? That couldn't be possible. He knew Timothy and I were very much together.* But after my conversation with Curt that morning in the churchyard, I had my own suspicions about Curt's feelings. Maybe he had a small crush, but that didn't mean it was love. It didn't, I told myself.

"Thank you for staying with us," Brock said to Pearl, but he stared directly at me.

CHAPTER TWENTY-TWO

"Who was that nice young man?" Pearl asked as I hurried her out through the hotel's sliding glass doors.

I almost threw up. Brock Buckley was not a nice young man. "Just someone who works at the hotel. Have you eaten today?" I unlocked my car with my fob and popped the hatchback trunk.

Her forehead creased. "No?" she said as if she wasn't sure.

"I bet you haven't. Let me take you to a late lunch. This way if you eat enough and get a to-go bag, you can skip the dinner at the inn tonight and avoid the dinner conversation." I winked at her.

She laughed. "That sounds nice. Not that I think you will host a bad dinner conversation."

"Actually, I haven't even thought about what the topic of today's conversation will be. I'm hoping Becky will come back from Utica with some good ideas." I placed the suitcase and roll bag in the trunk.

"Can you do me one small favor about the lunch?" she asked as she followed me to my Beetle.

I slammed the trunk closed. "Sure, what it is?"

"No, Amish food."

It was my turn to laugh. "I know the perfect place, and it's not far from here."

I took Pearl to a small Italian restaurant in Mount Vernon. The building was a block from the tiny city's main square. The dark interior smelled like garlic. It was the most non-Amish place I could think of.

We stood just inside the door for a moment to allow our eyes to adjust to the dim lighting. A man in a suit jacket showed us to our table. A votive candle sat in the middle of the table under a red glass dome and gave off just enough light so we could see our silverware.

Pearl held her menu close to her face. "This is perfect. It's not like any place we have visited on the tour, and I love Italian food."

I tilted the menu to the candle to see it better. It didn't help that much. I wondered if it would be rude if I asked the waiter for a flashlight. "I'm glad you like it. I've only been here once, but the ravioli I had was excellent. I've been looking forward to coming back."

"Did you come with that handsome beau of yours?"

My cheeks grew hot, and it wasn't from the candle. "Yes."

She set her menu aside. "He seems to be enamored with you."

My eyes finally adjusted to the dark room, and Pearl looked the most alert that I had seen her during the entire trip.

"Are you two going to marry?"

The waiter returned to take our orders and saved me from having to answer that question. Pearl ordered manicotti, and I chose a small, four-inch personal pizza. I wanted to steer the conversation away from Timothy and me and back on Pearl and her cousin Ruby. I also wanted to ask her what Earl was doing at the hotel. "You live in Tupelo? What's it like? I've never been to Mississippi before."

"You should visit it. It's a lovely southern state. I've lived there most of my life, and can't imagine moving. Ohio is lovely too though."

I smiled. "Every state has its own charm."

She sipped her water. "You're right. To be honest, I'm surprised at the difference between Lancaster County and Ohio. I thought it would be much the same, but it's not. The Amish are different here. Maybe not as outgoing, and they dress differently too. The women's prayer caps in Lancaster were almost heart-shaped. Here, they are much simpler."

The waiter placed Pearl's salad in front of her.

After he left, I said, "Don't forget the buggies. Lancaster buggies are gray. Ohio's are black."

"That's right. I never knew there was so much variety among the Amish."

I smiled. "I didn't either before I moved here."

"Have you been to Lancaster?" she asked.

I shook my head. "But Timothy's grandfather is from there, and he talks about it all the time." I sipped my water. "You said Ruby was your only family."

"Yes." She stared down at her plate. "We share a small ranch home in Tupelo. We decided to live together after my husband passed away. The ranch is Ruby's house." Worry creased her forehead. "That will be something else I will have to deal with when I return home. There are so many details. Ruby and I tried to plan ahead for something like this. We aren't young anymore, but there are so many things we didn't do or put off." She sighed. "We thought we had more time, and I always thought I would go first."

"Why?" I asked.

She cut into salad. "Despite her heart trouble, Ruby was the stronger one between us. She had an inner strength that I don't."

"What do you mean?" I asked.

The corners of Pearl's eyes drooped downwards. "This trip, for example. That was so like Ruby. She was decisive and always knew what to do. I don't."

The waiter returned with our food. He set the small mushroom pizza in front of me and despite the huge lunch I'd eaten at the inn, I was suddenly starving. The waiter placed the manicotti in front of Pearl, and she turned a light shade of green. "Enjoy," he said with a nod and walked away.

"Can you say grace, Chloe?" Pearl asked.

"Of course." We bowed our heads, and I said a short prayer.

I picked up one of the tiny pieces of pizza. The hot cheese burned my fingertips, but the taste was heavenly. Pearl poked at her manicotti with her fork, and her salad remained untouched.

"How else was Ruby decisive?"

Pearl placed her fork on the edge of her plate. "She always knew what she wanted. She went to nursing school, graduated at the top of her class, and worked at a local hospital for thirty years. She had a loving husband who would do anything for her."

"No children though."

She touched the fork with the tip of French manicured nail. "Ruby didn't want children. She was a career girl. It's not like today; back in the late fifties and early sixties women chose between a career and children. It was one or the other."

"And her husband?"

"He wanted whatever Ruby wanted. I've never seen a man who adored a woman so much." She lifted her water glass. "Well, until I saw you with your Timothy. That's how Ruby and Merv were." Her voice was distant. "I didn't have the same relationship with my husband. I wasn't a career girl like Ruby, but I lost my chance to have children."

"Your husband didn't want children?" I asked.

She shook her head as if trying to displace a bad memory. "He did, but we were never blessed with a child."

"I'm so sorry."

She twisted her cloth napkin. "It was a long time ago. My husband died five years ago. Ruby's husband died even longer ago. She's been a widow for nearly ten years. She never complained even though I knew she missed Merv desperately." Tears glistened on her face. "After her husband died, she picked up and carried on. Ruby never needed help from anyone. If I had died first, she would have been fine. I'm the one who needs someone to keep me from falling apart."

I set my pizza slice down and was surprised to see the pizza was half gone from the plate. "Ruby would have been devastated."

"Maybe." She dabbed at her eyes with a white napkin. "This is not how she would like it to happen. She protected me. She always made the tough decisions for me when I was unable to do something myself."

What does that mean?

The waiter was back to refill our water glasses. He frowned at Pearl's untouched dishes. "Is something wrong with your meal?"

"Oh no," she said quickly. "I'm not very hungry that's all. Can I get a doggy bag to go?"

The austere waiter picked up her plates. "It would be my pleasure." He cocked an eyebrow at the remainders of my pizza crust. "I see you don't need a to-go box."

I swallowed. "Nope."

The waiter left the table.

"I am feeling a little tired, Chloe. Is it all right if we leave as soon as he returns?"

I swallowed my bite of pizza. "That's fine, Pearl. I do have one more question."

She bopped a wedge of lemon in her water glass with the tip of her spoon. "What is it?"

"Why did Earl try to talk to you at the hotel in Mount Vernon?"

She dropped the spoon, and it bounced off the edge of the table and hit the floor. "I'm so clumsy." She started to bend down to retrieve it.

"It slid under the table. I'll get it." I bent over and slid my head beneath the table. I touched the handle of the spoon with the tip of my finger. If my arm was just a bit longer, I could have reached it. I folded my body in half and snatched the spoon for the tiled floor. In one motion, I slipped out from under the table and hit something soft with my shoulder.

As if in slow motion the Styrofoam box the waiter had been holding flew into the air and landed on a neighboring table with a splat. Tomato sauce and spaghetti went flying. The woman sitting at the table now wore her meal and part of Pearl's. "My blouse! This is dry clean only," the woman cried.

I wanted to die. "I'm so sorry. I didn't mean to do that," I started to babble.

The waiter wiped marinara sauce off of his cheek with a napkin.

"Don't worry, Chloe. I really wasn't that hungry," Pearl said.

I left the restaurant under a cloud of embarrassment and a lighter wallet because I offered to pay for the marinara victim's meal in addition to Pearl's and my bills. I would never be able to show my face in that restaurant again, which was a pity because the pizza was excellent. It wasn't until we reached the Dutch Inn I realized Pearl never answered my question about Earl.

CHAPTER TWENTY-THREE

B ack at the Dutch Inn, Jane and Ivy stood behind the registration desk. Cheetos hung limply in Ivy's thin arms. "Welcome back, Mrs. Kennerwell," Jane said. "We have your room all ready for you." She handed Pearl a key for room seven.

Her eyes flitted around the lobby as if she were searching for someone. "Thank you," she murmured.

"The bus tour is still out," Jane said.

Ephraim appeared and picked up Pearl's luggage. For some reason, I felt like the teenager avoided eye contact with me. *What was his story?* And I still didn't know why he was at the Troyer farm yesterday morning. However, asking him in front his mother, who thought he was at the inn working, was probably a bad idea.

"I can go up with you to your room and help you get settled if you like," I said to Pearl.

"No, Chloe, you have already done too much for me. This nice young man can see me to my room. I would like to rest before the tour returns." She followed Ephraim to the elevator.

"Ivy, can you make Mrs. Kennerwell a cup a tea and take it her room?"

"Oh that would be lovely," Pearl murmured. "You make a nice herbal tea."

The girl nodded and took the cat with her before her mother could protest.

Jane removed her glasses. "It's a beautiful day to stroll in the gardens while you wait for the bus to return."

"I might just do that," I said. "Thank you for allowing Pearl to come back."

"It's no trouble," Jane said. "Timothy has been doing a wonderful job on the chores around here. By the time he checks out, the inn will be in perfect shape. You're very lucky to have him."

"I know," I said.

"It has been nice to have the help. My husband went home to be with the Lord two years ago."

"I'm sorry. What happened?" I asked and immediately regretted my question.

"He was in a tractor accident on his brother's farm." She concentrated on her ledger to regain her composure.

My heart ached for her. "How awful."

She gave me a small smile. "Ephraim does what he can to keep the inn fixed up, but I know he'd much rather be at a social or working at a barn raising than tied down to this inn, and Ivy is in school for one more year."

"Surely, one of your children will want to run the inn someday?"

"I'm not so sure." She closed her ledger. "Chloe, don't let a *gut* man like Timothy slip between your fingers either. Appreciate the time you have with him, no matter how long or how short it may be."

I wandered into the lounge, wondering at Jane's advice. Why would she think Timothy would slip through my fingers? The room was dark except for the picture windows that looked out over Jane's gardens and onto the bending Kokosing River beyond.

A swinging door led into the kitchen. Timothy stood on a stepstool as he tightened the top hinge of a high cabinet door. He glanced over his shoulder and his face lit up.

He finished his task and jumped off of the stool. "How did the meeting go with the chief? You were gone longer than expected. I thought about calling you but didn't want to irritate Greta more than necessary."

"It went okay. Pearl's here now. She just checked back into the inn." Speaking of Pearl reminded me of my encounter with Brock. Brock had lied to upset me. He was a professional liar. The sooner he moved to Florida, the better.

Timothy dropped the screwdriver into the open tool box. "She did? Why?"

I leaned against the island. "She was afraid to be alone."

"I can understand that." He closed the lid to his toolbox.

"The chief told me something else too. Yew poisoned the milk that killed Dudley and Ruby."

He stepped back. "Me? She thinks I poisoned the milk."

"Not you. Yew. Y-E-W."

"What's that?"

"It's a kind of bush. Remember when we saw Riley take those plants from the farm?"

He nodded.

"It was one of those."

"And Greta still thinks my father had something to do with it."

I shook my head. "No, but she won't officially take him off her list."

Timothy pursed his lips.

I tapped my nails on the island's butcher block. "Right. I've been thinking about the new commercial farm that opened on the Gundy place."

"And?" He stepped toward me and covered my tapping hand with his own. Our fingers intertwined.

"Since the tour is gone for the rest of day, I thought I would go over there and check it out," I said.

"I'm coming too." He squeezed my hand and let go. "I only have two things left on Jane's list and can finish those tonight."

"She probably will have more jobs for you then. She told me about her husband. I'm sorry I didn't know."

He kissed the top of my nose. "You have a big heart, Chloe." He grabbed both of my hands. "While I've been working today, I've been thinking about my business."

"Oh?" I said.

His face split into a smile. "I've been thinking about buying a home and place for the workshop."

"I think that's great. I'm so happy the contracting business is going so well, but I never doubted it would. You do wonderful work. All the men who work under you respect you. I hope you find a place that you like."

He laughed. "Chloe, you're not understanding my meaning. I want to find a place *we* like, to buy a place where I can have the business and a home with you."

"Oh. *Oh!*" My pulse quickened. *Was Timothy going to ask me to marry him in the middle of the Dutch Inn's kitchen?* My mouth felt dry.

"I've looked at a few places, and I even—"

"You have?" I squeaked.

"I have a realtor too. He's an English guy Greta recommended. He helped her buy her house a couple of years back."

Chief Rose knew about Timothy looking for a house, and I didn't. I pulled my hands from his grasp. "Why didn't you tell me? I knew you wanted to do this, but I didn't know you already started your search."

Timothy dropped his hands. "I wanted to be sure I had all my money and affairs in order first. I wanted to su—"

"I have money and affairs too. If we get married, I need to contribute." I lifted my chin. "I have a good job. If *we* are buying a home, I want to be a part of the process. I'm not going to freeload."

A muscle twitched under Timothy's right eye. "Being my wife is *not* freeloading."

My breath caught when he said "wife."

The kitchen door swung in, and Ivy entered into the kitchen. She pulled up short when she saw Timothy and me standing toe to toe. Her hand flew to cover her eyes. "I'm so sorry to interrupt."

I inwardly groaned.

Timothy took a step back from me. "Ivy, there's nothing going on in here. You can drop your hands."

"I'm sorry," Ivy mumbled. "I came in here to make another cup of tea for Mrs. Kennerwell. She's feeling poorly." Ivy's maple-colored eyes flitted back and forth between Timothy and me as if she didn't believe Timothy's declaration that nothing had been going on.

"What's wrong with her?" I asked.

"She's sad," the girl replied.

I touched Timothy's arm. "I'll go check on her, and then we can go to the old Gundy place."

He nodded but looked as if he wanted to say something. Ivy's presence stopped him.

I left the kitchen. *Why did I pick a fight with Timothy like that?* I owed Timothy an apology. I had been on my own since I was fourteen. Yes, the Greens took me in after my father left for California, but I made my own decisions, paid my way through college and graduate school, and chose my own career. No one had taken care of me since my mother died. I didn't know how to be taken care of. I didn't want to be taken care of. I wanted to be an equal partner. How did I explain that to Timothy?

He grew up Amish. For him the idea of the woman paying her own way was foreign. *I bet Hannah would be elated if Timothy did this for her.* I smacked myself on the forehead.

I marched through the lounge and paused as I spotted Pearl sitting alone in the garden. A door leading to the garden stood open in the corner of the room.

"Pearl? Are you all right?" I asked.

She turned. Tears streamed from her eyes.

I sat next to her on the garden bench and put my arm around her shoulder.

She wiped at her eyes. "Thank you, Chloe. You are such a dear girl. If I had a daughter, I hope she would be a bit like you."

I dropped my arm. "Pearl, why did Earl visit you at the hotel?"

She shook her head. "I don't know. I really don't know."

A conversation with Earl was long overdue.

Ephraim walked out of the inn and kicked a tuff of grass as he headed in the direction of the river. I chewed on my lip. I didn't want to leave Pearl alone when she was so distraught, but I needed to talk to the elusive teenager.

The door between the garden and lounge opened, and Ivy came out with a cup of tea for Pearl.

She held the cup out to Pearl, but the older woman would not take it. "I think I would rather have my tea in my room."

"I can help you to your room," Ivy said.

"Thank you, Ivy," Pearl murmured.

I helped Pearl to her feet, and Ivy led her back inside the inn. I texted Timothy, "Meet you at the pickup in twenty minutes." I hoped that was enough time to track down Ephraim before going to the old Gundy farm.

There was a garden path between the inn and river. Tiny white pebbles marked the way. Halfway down the path, I found Cheetos rolling on his back under a Bleeding Heart that was three feet tall. As far as good cat lives go, Cheetos had hit the jackpot. The path ended at a spiny hedge. I touched the hedge, and the needles of its sharp points pricked my fingertips but not enough to break the skin.

It was yew. Chief Rose had said it was a common plant in Ohio, so I shouldn't be surprised there was a yew bush in

Jane's garden. I dropped my hand and the branch sprang back and forth. The tour spent Friday night at the Dutch Inn before going to the Troyer farm the next morning. Anyone on the tour would have had access to the plant and plenty of time to brew a pot of yew tea.

The closer I came to the river, the thicker and higher the grass grew, reaching past my ankles. Ephraim sat on an embankment and tossed stones into the water. He turned and frowned when he saw me standing a few yards away.

I touched the tip of a cattail, and it bobbed back and forth. "This is a beautiful spot."

"Do you need something, Miss?" he asked.

"I would like to talk to you," I said.

He scrambled to his feet. "Is something wrong with your stay?"

"No."

He scooped up the small mound of stones from the ground and waited.

"What were you doing at the Troyer farm yesterday?" I asked.

"I wasn't there."

"I saw you, and Grandfather Zook saw you."

He held the stones palm up and clenched his fist around them. One of the stones fell to the ground. "My *mamm* will be upset if she knows I went there. I was supposed to be in the shed mending fishing tackle."

"Why were you there?"

"I thought I could help out. That's all." He tossed the remaining stones into the river. They bounced off a fallen tree before disappearing into the current.

"Help out how?"

He dipped his black felt hat down over his eyes. "Just help out."

"Were you helping Deacon Sutter?"

"What do you mean by that?"

"You were speaking with him last evening."

"When someone comes to the inn, it's my job to greet them. There's nothing more to it than that." He adjusted his hat back on the crown of his head. "And I don't have to answer your questions."

I took a step closer to him. "Are you close to Ruth or Anna?"

His head snapped in my direction. "What are you talking about?"

"You seemed interested in them at the Troyer farm yesterday morning."

He scowled and scooped up more stones. "The Troyers might be fine with you in their business, but I'm not. Leave me alone, *Englischer*." He threw the stone into the middle of the river and stalked away.

There was definitely something the teen wasn't telling me. The question was did it involve the girls or the deacon? I didn't know which possibility was worse.

CHAPTER TWENTY-FOUR

Timothy's truck rocked on the pitted road leading onto the Old Gundy farm. When we had visited the farm last winter, we trudged across a deep field of snow. Now, the spring revealed a road. Timothy gripped the steering wheel, and Mabel whimpered in the tiny backseat of the pickup. "I hope the new owner makes improving this road a top priority."

I braced myself as the truck wobbled through another rut. "It's strange to be back here." The last time Timothy and I were on the Gundy property was to face down a killer.

I touched Timothy's necklace under my shirt. The memories from here weren't all bad. This was where he'd given me the charms.

The stand of three pine trees and the old Gundy weathered barn were gone. The only indication either had ever been there were the patches of hay protecting the newly planted grass. Its absence came as a shock. Despite all the sadness that had surrounded that barn, it had been beautiful in an old and forgotten way.

Beyond the new grass, three large orange barns stood in a straight row. A fourth building was under construction about twenty yards away from the nearest barn. It could have been a house or a commercial office building. With just the framing up it was hard to tell. A luxury trailer, like ones that rock stars travel around in when on tour, sat in front of the construction.

Mabel hung her head over the seat as if she needed a better look.

"This place is open for business," Timothy said.

"Those are the first orange barns I've ever seen. Interesting color choice," I joked, but Timothy wasn't laughing.

Light brown and white spotted Guernsey dairy cows grazed on the pasture.

I pointed at them. "Look at all those cows. There must be eighty of them. They must be the reason the barns are up before the road was mended."

Timothy shifted the truck into park. "Mabel. Stay."

The dog snuggled into the seat, happy to nap in her favorite spot.

As I hopped out of the pickup, the door to the luxury trailer opened. A man about my age stepped out. He wore khaki pants and a white polo shirt with some kind of logo over the breast pocket. I was too far away to decipher what the logo said. His light brown hair was styled in a short fauxhawk, so short that maybe it was unintentional. He wore black plastic-rimmed glasses that settled perfectly on the planes of his angular face. He gave us a friendly wave. As he approached, I saw the symbol on his shirt was a dairy cow inside of a recycle sign. Under the symbol, the letters read, "Tate and Katts' Organic Growers."

The man smiled. "Can I help you with something? If you came to ask for directions, I might not be much help. I'm new here."

"We don't need directions," Timothy said, holding out his hand. "We stopped by to say hello. I'm Timothy Troyer."

The man eagerly shook his hand. "Alex Tate. It's nice to meet you. I've been here a couple of months, but I admit that I have been too busy to go into town much. I'm glad you dropped by. It's important to know your neighbors." He smiled at me in turn. "Welcome to Katts' Buttermilk Farm."

I was about introduce myself when Timothy said, "This is my girlfriend, Chloe Humphrey."

I hid my surprise that Timothy felt the need to introduce me as his girlfriend. True, Alex Tate was attractive in his urban way. I stifled a smile.

Alex shook my hand. "Nice to meet you, Chloe."

As we shook, I noticed a black tattoo on his forearm. It was some type of elaborate cursive lettering, facing inward. Because of the angle of his arm, I couldn't make out what it said.

"Where's Katts?" Timothy asked.

Alex laughed. "In his comfy home in Westerville. I live on the property and handle the day-to-day operations."

"On your own?" Timothy sounded dubious.

"I have a crew of ten men. One of the great things about moving out here, there are a lot of experienced farmhands in Knox County looking for work. I even have a couple of Amish guys on my payroll."

Timothy shoved his hands into the hip pockets of his jeans. "You seem young to be overseeing such a large farm."

"I'm twenty-five." Alex seemed to be unfazed by Timothy's uncharacteristic rudeness. "I have a BA and an MS in agriculture from Ohio State. I've worked on organic farms since I was nineteen. Sure, I'm young, but I work hard and am passionate about what I do."

"So this is a dairy farm?" I asked. "We couldn't help but notice the cows when we drove up."

"Dairy and vegetables to start. I suppose right now, it's just dairy. We haven't planted yet because so much time was put building the barns for the cattle. I'm afraid we won't have any crops. There's a short window of planting time in Ohio."

"You could grow winter wheat," Timothy suggested.

"I thought about that. It would be a good starter cash crop. By this time next year, we'll be fully operational." He snapped his fingers. "Did you say your name was Troyer? Are you related to the Amish family by that name?"

"My parents own that farm."

Alex looked Timothy up and down. "You don't look Amish." He glanced at me. I definitely didn't look Amish.

"I'm not," Timothy said and left it at that.

Alex rocked back on his heels. "I've driven by there a few times. It looks really charming and the cows appeared healthier than I've seen on other Amish farms. Not all Amish give their livestock the respect they deserve."

Timothy bristled. Alex seemed unaware how that comment could be offensive.

"Does your family farm organically?" Alex asked.

"No," Timothy said.

"Organic is the way to go. It's better for the cows, for us, and for the environment." He took a deep breath as if he were about to scale a soapbox.

Timothy crossed his arms.

It was time for me to step in. "You said you've only been here two months?"

Alex patted the side of his fauxhawk—maybe the hairstyle was on purpose after all. "That's right."

Timothy scanned the grounds. "You've accomplished a lot in that time."

"I wanted to move here sooner. We bought the land in January, but I had to wait for the snow to melt to do much of anything. It was a tough winter, you know."

We knew.

Alex surveyed his land with obvious pride. "I have big plans for this place."

"Like what?" Timothy asked.

"I want to build an organic market and maybe a small boutique restaurant."

I gestured at the construction. "Is that building going in now?"

Alex nodded. "Yep."

I smiled. I couldn't help it when I saw Alex's enthusiasm. Timothy was another story. "You're a long way from town," Timothy said. "How will you attract people to come out here to shop and eat?"

"It will be a challenge at first, but I'm up for it. Look at Young's, that big Amish restaurant and flea market, they are even farther from town, and they are doing a booming business. Do you know it?"

"We know it," Timothy said ironically.

"Have you had any contact with any of the Amish or family-owned farms in the county?" I asked.

"Not yet, but I hope to. Right now, I just want to open for business. A lot of the farmers around here, Amish and non-Amish, watch me with some suspicion." His enthusiasm waned. "Is that why you are here to check out the operation?"

My mind scrambled for the best answer.

"Yes," Timothy said.

Alex laughed. "I respect your honesty, Tim. I plan to work with the Amish farmers, not hurt them. Maybe some of my organic farming techniques can benefit them as well. I don't want to impact their business."

Yet another unintentional insult. Alex reminded me of the guys in my computer science program in grad school, crazy smart with a legendary ability to stick their feet in their mouths.

Timothy's jaw twitched. "You are impacting their business now whether you want to be or not."

Alex put his hands up in a mock surrender sign. "Hey, I have no plans to hurt the Amish farmers. That was never my intention when Katts and I bought this land. If an Amish person wanted to open a farm here, he could have. The land lay fallow for seven years. Why didn't they make their move earlier? You can't begrudge me for making use of a forgotten farm."

He had a point. Timothy relaxed his hands.

"So you've never been to the Troyer farm?" I asked.

His brow creased. "I already told you I haven't."

"Do you know a lot about plants?" I asked.

I felt Timothy tense beside me.

Alex cocked his head and his hair didn't move a millimeter. I wondered how much product it took to keep it so perfect. "I studied agriculture," Alex said. "Yes, I know a lot about plants. I deal with plants every day."

"What about wild plants?"

"Some, not as much."

"Do you know what a yew bush is?" Timothy asked.

"Yew? As in Y-E-W?" he asked. "Yes, I know what it is."

"Have you ever used it before?"

The young farmer stepped back. "Of course not, it's poisonous. It can kill a person or an animal."

How well we knew that, I thought.

He waved his hands in front of his face. "Wait, wait, wait. Do you two think I *did* something?"

I put my hand in my jacket pocket and touched my cell phone. "Two people died at the Troyer farm Saturday morning. They drank milk laced with yew tea. Do you know anything about that?"

Alex stumbled. "No. This is the first I've heard of it. I promise you I had nothing, *nothing*, to do with it."

"How can you not know about it? It's the talk around town," I said.

"I heard some of my guys talking about someone dying on one of the neighboring farms, but I ignored it. They like to gossip about what's going in the county. I don't pay much attention to it." He waved his hands in agitation. "If you want me to testify or something, I will. Is there a cop or someone I can talk to about this?"

"There is an Appleseed Creek Chief of Police," I said.

"I'll talk to him then."

"Her." I removed my empty hand from my pocket.

"Okay, her." He wagged his head. "I'll talk to her."

"She'd like that," I said.

He frowned. "This isn't the welcome I expected. I think it's time for you to go." Alex turned and stomped back to his rock star trailer.

"What do you think?" I asked Timothy as we returned to his pickup. "You think he had anything to do with Dudley and Ruby's deaths?"

"No," he said in a disappointed tone.

"Me either." I held my seat belt away from my throat. "What's wrong?"

"He got on my nerves." Timothy started the truck. "He'd better be careful what he says about the Amish around here or he won't last long in Appleseed Creek."

I silently agreed.

CHAPTER TWENTY-FIVE

B ack at the inn, the Blue Suede Tour bus was in its spot in the tiny parking lot. Timothy followed me into the Inn. Becky's laughter floated into the lobby from the lounge. A group of tourists, including Jimbo, much to my surprise,, sat around her as she told a story about going to a one-room schoolhouse.

In one corner, Duke and Earl played a lively game of checkers, and Bitty curled up in one the massive armchairs reading a novel. With her tiny pin curls she resembled a retired fairy cuddled up for a nap. The only people from the tour who were absent were Pearl, no surprise there, and Hudson, no big surprise either. Of the people in the room, Earl caught my interest first. Why had he gone to Pearl's hotel to see her?

Becky waved to me. "Everyone, Chloe's back."

Becky's fan club clapped.

"Hi," I said confused by the welcome.

Becky laughed. "I told them the story about how you rescued me from Curt and Brock the first day you moved to Appleseed Creek."

"Chloe," Raellen said. "You're a real life hero."

"And you solved three murders too," Nadine said. "We're so glad to have you on our tour. Maybe you will be able to figure out what happened to Dudley and poor Ruby."

My skin prickled. Becky shouldn't have told a busload of suspects I solved a murder before. I'd told her not to share everything about her past. Apparently that rule didn't apply to *my* past.

Timothy touched my back. I turned and met his gaze.

There was no point in correcting Becky. She couldn't take her words back, and she had entertained the guests like I'd asked her to. I hoped their amusement didn't come at too high of a price for me.

I laughed. "Those were all very different situations. I'm strictly filling in here to be your tour guide."

Timothy leaned close to my ear. "I'm going to finish up those odd jobs for Jane." He squeezed my fingers. "And we need to talk later about the house issue."

That sounded ominous. I sat on the corner of a plush footstool.

"What did you all do today?" I asked.

The women all began to talk at once, but unsurprisingly, Gertie was the loudest. "That ice cream factory had the ugliest ducks I've seen in all my life."

Nadine nodded. "They were black and white and had these big red bobbles on their beaks and around their eyes. Maybe they need to see a vet."

Becky covered her mouth to unsuccessfully hide a fit of the giggles. I refused to look her way because I knew I would start laughing too.

"They are Muscovy ducks," Jimbo said. "That's what they look like. They are native to Mexico and South America. The ice cream factory just had them for show."

Bobbi Jo added a stitch to her knitting project. "Jimbo is a retired zoology professor. He knows a lot about animals and nature."

I eyed Jimbo with interest. Did that mean he would know what a yew bush was?

Gertie snorted. "Of all the water fowl in the world, they picked those." She leaned closer to me. "I tell you, they were uglier than sin."

"Did you have a nice time otherwise?" I asked.

"The ice cream was good," Gertie said. "But the people there need a bigger vision. I offered them some of my fish jerky to add to their pistachio ice cream. I think it could be a real winner, and they wouldn't take it. I wasn't even asking for a cut of the profits." She poked my leg. "You still haven't tasted my jerky, have you?"

"Umm, no," I said.

"It's up in the room. I'll make sure you get some."

I swallowed. "Thank you."

From across the room, I felt Earl watching me over the chess board. His mustache gave him a villainous air even if it was undeserved.

Duke moved a knight on the chess board in from of Earl's queen. "Checkmate!"

Earl looked back to his game. "Good play, Duke. You're a pro at this."

Duke began resetting the pieces. "My grandson is in chess club. He challenges me quite often and usually beats me. It's nice to win once in a while." He scanned the room. "Who's next?"

Fred stood up from his seat in front of the unlit fireplace. "I might as well play you since there is no cable." He gave me a narrow look as if I was responsible for the lack of ESPN.

Earl stood. "Have my seat." He met my gaze before leaving the room.

Did Earl want me to follow him?

I waited all of thirty seconds before I went after him. I checked the hallway and the lobby. No Earl. Instead I found Jane dusting the fireplace. "Jane, did you see Earl come through here?"

"Mr. Kepler?" She pointed at the door with her feather duster. "He just went out front." Outside, the sun felt warm on my face and held the promise of summer.

Earl stood by the garden of daffodils in between the two sides of the driveway. He had a pipe in his hand and he tamped down a pinch of tobacco into the bowl with his meaty index finger. "I wondered when you would come find me," he said. "I knew you would after this morning."

I stopped in the middle of the driveway a few feet away from him. "I want to talk to you about Pearl. Why did you go to see her at the other hotel?"

He removed a match from the breast pocket of his short sleeve plaid shirt and struck it on the side of the pipe. The flame caught, and he touched it to the tobacco. "So what Becky told us is true. You're some kind of private detective."

Why, Becky? Why?

I forced laugh. "I'm not a private detective."

"But you helped that lady police chief solve crimes in town." He blew a ring of smoke out of his mouth.

Between the mustache and the smoke tricks, I felt like I was talking to a Walrus/Caterpillar combo from *Alice in Wonderland.* I shrugged.

He stared at the daffodils again. "I wanted to make sure she was all right for Ruby's sake. She had been kind to me on this trip, and I wanted to honor her kindness by helping her cousin."

I moved to the other side of the daffodil garden because I didn't think Earl would appreciate what I said next. "So you were crying this morning because of Ruby?"

"Is that so hard to believe? A woman is dead. Shouldn't I feel bad about it? Is it better to be like the others and be more concerned about what restaurant the bus will visit today?"

"Ruby is not the only one who died. What about Dudley?"

He dropped his pipe. Ashes and tobacco littered the driveway. "That is also a shame."

"But you don't feel the loss as deeply?"

He stomped the smoldering tobacco. "How I feel about Ruby and Dudley has nothing to do with you."

What I said next was rooted in a hunch. "What about the argument you had behind the inn yesterday?"

He stooped to pick up the pipe and froze with his back bent.

"I heard you."

He straightened up and glared at me. "Who have you been talking to? Hudson?"

Hudson. So he was the other voice. I should have known.

"So what if I had," I replied. It wasn't exactly a lie.

"He promised me he wouldn't tell."

I remained quiet.

He dumped the remainder of the tobacco from his pipe into the garden. "Hudson had no right to do it." His hands shook. "I wasn't going to do it. I gave Ruby the money, so that I wouldn't do it."

"What money?"

"What do you mean what money?" he gripped his pipe so tightly I thought he might crush it into a pile of splinters. "Isn't that what you're asking about?"

"Right." I nodded. 'The money." My mind raced. I couldn't let Earl know that I didn't know what he meant. If I led him on, maybe I could figure it out. "Why did you give the money to Ruby?"

His grasp loosened on the pipe. "She saw me struggling, she knew I wanted to quit, and she promised to keep it safe from me."

Was he speaking in riddles?

His jaw twitched. "She was kind to me when everyone else ignored me. She didn't judge like the rest of them would have."

Judge what? What was he talking about?

"So you went to the hotel to get the money?"

He nodded. "After she died, I wanted the money back. It was rightfully mine. I hoped she had given the money to Pearl. She either did that or it's with her things the police took."

"Why did Pearl refuse to see you?"

"I don't think she knew anything about the money. Ruby promised me she wouldn't tell anyone. The fewer people knew about my troubles the better. Pearl must have thought I was there for some other reason."

What troubles? How much longer could I keep up this front, pretending that I knew what he was talking about?

Earl took a step back. "You're not a cop. I don't have talk to you." He stomped away and his pipe swung back and forth in his right hand.

I pulled my cell phone out of my pocket and called Chief Rose. I told her about Earl going to the Mount Vernon hotel to retrieve the money he'd given Ruby from Pearl.

"That could fit," the police chief mused.

"Fit? Fit what?" I asked.

"We found a nice wad of cash in Ruby's luggage," the police chief said.

"How much are you talking?"

"Five hundred. But that's not even close to the money I found in Dudley's things."

"How much did he have?"

"Enough for a down payment on an Amish farm and then some."

I closed my eyes for a moment. "Why are you just telling me now? I could have been following this lead since yesterday."

"It was on a need to know basis."

I gritted my teeth.

"Don't growl at me, Humphrey."

"I wasn't growling."

"Sure you weren't." She laughed. "Nottingham and I are on the way with the thumbscrews."

Great.

CHAPTER TWENTY-SIX

The chief's patrol car turned into the Dutch Inn's circular driveway two minutes later. As Officer Nottingham and Chief Rose slammed their car doors, Timothy walked around the side of the building. "What's going on?"

"I just had a conversation with Earl. It didn't go well, so I called the chief."

He frowned. "Why didn't you call me? I'm right here."

Why hadn't I thought to call Timothy? I cleared my throat. "She was already on her way here."

"Humphrey," the chief said. "Where's Earl?"

"Not sure." I folded my arms. "He didn't enjoy our conversation and wandered off."

"Did he leave the property?" Officer Nottingham asked.

I shook my head. "He went around the north side of the building two minutes ago."

The chief straightened her department ball cap on her curls. "Nottingham, find him and bring him out here. Humphrey and I will be at that prissy little table over there."

I turned to see the chief pointing at a white iron table and chairs.

"Right boss," Officer Nottingham said and jogged around the side of the building.

"Come on." The chief waved at me to follow her to the table. She perched on one of the chairs. "These here are more uncomfortable than the chairs in my waiting room."

Timothy folded his tall frame to sit in one of the delicate chairs. "Not quite," he said.

The chief laughed. "Okay, before surfer cop gets back, I have to tell you what's going on. It looks like Dudley was involved in some type of gambling. Perhaps he was even a bookie."

Timothy looked at me. "Do you know what she's talking about?"

The chief sighed as if we'd let her down in some way. "Dudley was more than a tour guide. He took bets on sporting events, mostly NCAA, which is illegal."

"How do you know this?" I asked.

"There's the wad of money, and then there was his computer. He had a website and everything. The bookie business has gone high tech. You should be able to appreciate that, Humphrey. It took us a while to figure out what was going on because Dudley's side business was located in encrypted files on the laptop. Finally, one of the sheriff's geeks cracked it."

"You should have brought it to me. I could have cracked it."

"I thought about it more than one time, believe me, but by that point it was already at the sheriff's office. It makes the sheriff cranky if I ask him for help and then change my mind. Plus, I needed you on the bus."

"You think he was killed because of this?" I took a quick glance at the corner of the stone-face inn Officer Nottingham had disappeared behind. "Do you think Earl was the one that did it?"

"If only it were that easy. If he had been shot or knifed, I would say yes it was a done deal, but he was poisoned. That's not how the average bookie is supposed to go. It's a girly way to die."

Timothy held onto both of his knees. "A girly way to die?"

"Women are far more likely to use poison as a murder weapon than men. It's clean and controlled and appeals to a woman's sense of propriety."

"Okay," I said. "If Dudley was a bookie, what does that have to do with Earl?"

Officer Nottingham and Earl appeared around the corner. Earl dragged his feet on the driveway.

Quickly, I said, "He thinks I heard about the money and betting from Hudson."

"Did you?"

"No." I lowered my voice. "I figured Earl's was one of the voices I heard around the side of the building yesterday. I didn't know it for sure. It was just a hunch. When he mentioned Hudson, I pretended I knew what he was talking about."

"Nice acting work, Humphrey. I'll suggest your name the next time the county puts on a production of *The Sound of Music*. You would make a believable Leisl. Can you sing?"

"No."

"Too bad." She stood. "Mr. Kepler, how nice of you to join us."

He blew his mustache out of his mouth. "Did I have a choice?"

"Not really." She gestured to the empty chair. "Have a seat."

There were only four chairs around the tiny table. Timothy stood. "You can have my spot, Nottingham."

The young officer thanked him. Timothy leaned against an oak tree a few feet away. He wouldn't miss a thing.

Officer Nottingham removed a tiny notebook from the breast pocket off his uniform.

The chief sat back down in her seat. "What can you tell us about Dudley's gambling racket?"

Earl chewed on his mustache. "I don't know what you're talking about."

"Really? Because the five hundred dollars you gave Ruby Masters tells me otherwise. Why'd you give her that money?"

"You have it."

"Yes, I have it. It was with her things."

He removed his pipe from his pocket but didn't light it. "Can I have it back?"

The chief shook her head. "Sorry, no."

"But it's mine." He flipped the pipe over in hand. "I gave it to Ruby for safe keeping, to protect me."

"Protect you. What about Ruby? She's the one who is dead."

He paled. "You don't think I had something to do with that. I didn't. I owed Ruby. I would never want to hurt her. She stopped me from making a mistake."

"What kind of mistake?" I asked.

"I have a gambling problem." He shifted in the hard seat. "I told you I'm a widower. That's not true. The truth is my wife left me after I lost our life savings." He squeezed the pipe in his hand. "Including wasting all the money we had saved for our son's college education on gambling debts. At the time, I was angry, but I don't blame my ex now."

"After that, you got treatment?" I leaned forward.

He shook his head. "Not right away. No. It wasn't for another twenty years. Finally, I built up the courage to do it." He examined his pipe. "By that time, it was too late to save my relationship with my wife or my son."

I thought of my severed relationship with my father. That had been destroyed by my mother's death. We were finally piecing it back together. "It's never too late."

"Are we done? I'm going to miss dinner for this," Earl muttered.

"I'm sure Jane or her daughter will make you up a plate later," I said.

"Unless you're in jail," Officer Nottingham said out of the side of his mouth.

Earl's eyes seemed to roll back into his head for a moment.

Chief Rose grunted. "Okay. So you are addicted to gambling. Sorry to hear that. Where does Dudley come into this story?"

"I'm in recovery, but it's a struggle every day. I joined Gamblers Anonymous. My mentor convinced me this trip to Amish Country would do me good because I wouldn't be tempted to gamble. He was wrong. He didn't know Dudley would be on the bus." His mustache drooped. "The moment I arrived it was as if Dudley knew about my condition. At our first dinner in Lancaster County, Dudley asked me how much I was putting on the College World Series. I broke out into a cold sweat right there. All the next day, he talked about the bets he'd make *if* he were a betting man. By the second night, he told me he could place bets for me and he only needed a couple hundred bucks. He guaranteed he could turn that into five figures or better."

Officer Nottingham twirled his pencil between two fingers. "You placed a bet."

His mustache fluffed out in walrus mode again. "No, but I almost did. The night before we left Lancaster County, I sat on the hotel patio. That's where Ruby found me. She found me at a weak moment, and I ended up telling her my whole story. There was no one else around, and I had to tell someone."

"You gave her the money," Chief Rose said as if she wanted to hurry the story along.

"Yes, but I didn't ask her. She offered. She said, 'Let me take your burden. It's what I do best.' So I gave her the money, and she promised to give it back to me when we arrived back home in Tupelo. That five hundred was all the cash I brought with me on the trip as spending money. I don't trust credit cards." He looked the chief square in the eye. "But I'm telling you I had nothing to do with Ruby's death."

"Dudley's a different story though, isn't he? You haven't shed any tears over his death, have you? Maybe you bumped him off because he was about to drive you back into the gambling abyss, and Ruby was an unfortunate accident."

"No, that's not what happened." He pointed at Timothy. "It was his father who killed them. He's a crazed Amish man."

Timothy balled his fists at his side, but he didn't come any closer.

Earl cowered. He wasn't in any danger from Timothy, but Earl didn't know that.

Officer Nottingham tapped his pencil on the notepad. "Do you have any houseplants, Mr. Kepler?"

"Houseplants?"

"Just answer the question," Chief Rose said.

"I have a spider plant my sister gave me to make my apartment homier, but it died."

Officer Nottingham drew a circle on his notepad. "Do you garden?"

"I just said I live in an apartment. Of course I don't garden. Crazy Yankee cop," he muttered under his breath.

Officer Nottingham simply shook his head at the chief, and she nodded.

"You're free to go to dinner, Mr. Kepler," the chief said.

"That's it?" He looked back and forth between the two officers. "You have nothing else to ask me?"

"If you want to hang out at the station with me, we can talk all day." She slipped her aviator sunglasses out of the breast pocket of her uniform and unfolded the arms.

He bit his mustache. "No—no, that's fine. What about my money?"

"Your money is evidence. When I am able, I will mail it back to you. You won't get it before you leave Ohio though."

He nodded. "Maybe it's for the best. I may have used it wrongly in the end." Slowly he stood, and there was a cracking sound.

I glanced at Officer Nottingham half-expecting to see he'd snapped his pencil in two.

"Are you all right?" Timothy asked. Sympathy replaced anger on his face.

"It's just my bum knee. You will understand when you're older." He limped in the direction of the inn.

I jumped up from my white chair. "Earl, wait! You said before Hudson knew about Dudley's side business."

"I expected he did. He was there many times when Dudley tried to talk me into placing a bet, and he wanted to know everything I knew about it after Dudley died. That's what we argued about behind the inn."

"Did he work with Dudley?" I asked.

"I don't think so, but Dudley must have given him something to keep him quiet. A man like that doesn't do anything for free."

After Earl hobbled halfway to the inn, the chief braced her hands on her knees and stood. "He didn't do it. He wanted the money back, but it was still with Ruby's things. That would have been the motive for her murder. Even though he has a tentative motive for Dudley's offing, he doesn't know a lick about plants." She shook his head. "He's not the guy."

"What about Hudson? He must play a part in this gambling thing," Timothy said.

"Probably," the chief said. "Nottingham and I will talk to him before we go."

"Do you want me there?" I asked.

She shook her head. "No, you still have to work with him on the tour tomorrow. He might think even less of you if you interrogate him tonight."

I bit my lip. I wanted to hear what Hudson had to say and badly, but the chief had a valid point. "I doubt he would dislike me any more than he does already. We aren't exactly best buds."

"All right, you can come." She slipped her sunglasses over her eyes. "But it's hard for me to believe you and Hudson don't get along. I thought you made friends with everyone."

Yeah right. Deacon Sutter and Brock Buckley beg to differ.

CHAPTER TWENTY-SEVEN

Hudson sat alone at a round table in the dining room. The tourists gathered around the three other tables. Becky held court at the center table. This time she told the story of her brother Thomas letting the sheep loose at the schoolhouse's Christmas pageant last year. Earl sat at a table with Jimbo and Bobbi Jo. He had his head down and concentrated on his food.

The room fell silent when Chief Rose and Officer Nottingham followed me into the room.

Officer Nottingham approached the bus driver's table. "Mr. Dugan, we would like to speak with you in the lobby."

Hudson cut into his roast beef. "What about?"

"We would prefer to discuss that in private."

Earl shoved a spoonful of mashed potatoes into his mouth, and a bead of sweat rolled down the side of his face.

Hudson lifted his head from his plate and his eyes trained on Earl. More mashed potatoes went into Earl's mouth. His cheeks were so full, he resembled a chipmunk.

"Fine." Hudson dropped his fork onto the table. It spun across the smooth surface and fell to the floor. He didn't bother to pick it up as he followed the two officers from the room. Before I left, I quietly set the fork on the edge of the table as Ivy cleared away his dishes.

In the lobby, Hudson glared at me from the couch. "What is she doing here?"

Chief Rose stood in front of the river stone fireplace. "Chloe spoke to Earl earlier, so I thought it would be helpful if she sits in while we talk."

"Whatever," the bus driver muttered.

I glanced at the registration desk. Jane wasn't there as she helped Ivy in the kitchen with dinner. However, Cheetos lay across the counter blinking at me.

"What do you know about Dudley's side business?" the chief asked.

"You mean Dudley's gambling?" Hudson said. "If you spoke to Earl, that's what this must be about."

Chief Rose held onto the mantle. "Yes."

"He was a bookie, so what? It didn't make any difference to me. I didn't have anything to do with it."

Officer Nottingham had his notepad out again. "You never reported him?"

"Not my job. I just drive the bus."

"How long had Dudley had this side business?" the chief asked.

Hudson scraped at his front teeth with his pinkie nail. "Just the last year or so. He was tired of being on the road. Can't say I blame him."

"He planned to leave Blue Suede Tours?"

Hudson nodded. "He thought this would be his last tour."

His last tour? It certainly was that.

I spoke for the first time. "When he said this would be his last tour, what did he mean?"

Chief Rose shot me an irritated glance. I'd forgotten I was there strictly as an observer.

"He was going to take his money and run," Hudson said.

"And he didn't plan to share it with you even though you had kept his secret?" I asked.

Hudson was up and off the couch. An inch from my face, he said, "You think I killed Dudley and that old lady?"

I stepped back and ran into Timothy. I hadn't even known he was in the room.

"Because I didn't." He threw up his arms. "If you have to know, Dudley would give me a *tip* every now and again for keeping my mouth shut. Why would I kill my source of easy money?"

Chief Rose dropped her hand to her side. "Because the easy money would dry up if Dudley left the tour bus for good. Maybe you tried to talk him into changing his mind, and he refused."

Hudson grunted. "I would have just shot him. Sure, I wasn't happy that Dudley was leaving because of the money, but I wasn't broken hearted over it either. He wasn't the easiest guy in the world to get along with. I hoped the tour company would put me with some young buck, who I could boss around. I'm the driver. I should be the one in control."

Officer Nottingham scribbled more notes.

"It's good news for you we didn't find Dudley with a bullet hole in his head then," Chief Rose said dryly.

"I guess so," Hudson said. "Was that all, *officer?*" he asked.

"For now," the chief replied.

Hudson stomped up the stairs to the second floor, and Officer Nottingham and Chief Rose left shortly afterward.

I petted Cheetos and felt homesick for Gigabyte. "Another suspect off the list," I said with a frown.

Timothy pulled me into a hug.

I bent my neck back so I could see his face. "What's that for?"

A slow smile crossed his face. "I can't hug you whenever I want?"

"You can."

He looked worried. "Chloe, I know this case is taking all of our time, but I need to tell you—"

"Chloe!" Becky cried as she bounded into the lobby.

Timothy groaned. I patted his chest and pulled away from him

"Chloe, can you give me a lift home? After you and the cops took Hudson away, dinner broke up."

I turned to Timothy.

"You might as well take her. I still haven't finished those odd jobs for Jane yet. I really want to get them done tonight."

"Let me grab my purse," I said.

Ten minutes later, I turned the Beetle onto the state route in front of the inn. "Have you—"

Becky slumped in her seat. "If you ask me one more time about those college applications, I will scream."

"Okay, I promise to drop the college apps, but honestly, I wasn't asking about that."

"Then what?" she asked.

"Do you still want to talk to your parents?"

She covered her face with her elbow. "That's worse."

"You need to talk to them. The silence between you can't go on."

"They didn't even acknowledge me on my birthday," Becky said.

"And you refused to see them on Easter," I reminded her gently. "I'm not saying how they have treated you is right, but you may have to be the person who reaches out. There's no shame in that."

"But I didn't do anything wrong," her voice pitched up an octave in a whine. "All I did was cut my hair. What is the big deal? I already left the community. Why did they freak out so much over the hair?"

"It's the finality of the haircut." I paused at a four-way stop. "You know that."

She folded her arm and stared out the window. "They're the parents. I'm the child. Aren't they supposed to come to me?"

I understood how she felt. For over a decade, I thought the same about my relationship with my father. If he loved me, he would reach out to me. If I mattered to him, he would make an effort. He never did. It wasn't until I saw the coldness of an Amish shunning that I knew the act of isolation hurt the shunner as much as the shunned. "I don't want you to have the same relationship with your parents that I had with my father."

"My situation is different. *Daed* will be angry." Her voice cracked. "*Mamm* will cry."

"Silence is worse," I said, speaking from experience. "Silence and indifference are so much worse."

She dropped her gaze to her hands. "I'm afraid they'll say they don't want to see me anymore. I'm afraid to hear that to my face."

"They won't. Look at how much you've gone through together." I gripped the steering wheel. "If they were going to shun you, they would have last summer when you were in the car accident, but they didn't. When everyone else in the district told them to avoid you, they didn't."

A tear fell on her folded hands. "You're right."

I patted her leg.

She placed her hands on the dashboard and leaned forward. "Can we go now?"

I made a right turn. "Now? What if they're busy?"

"They're not. I lived in that house for nineteen years, and I can tell you exactly what's happening there on a Sunday evening. Dinner is over, and they are all in the living room. *Daed*'s reading to them from *The Budget* or they are playing a game led by *Grossdaddi*." Her voice caught as she remembered what she was missing, what she gave up for her independence.

"Okay, we'll go now." I pulled into a parking lot, so that I could turn around and head to the farm.

She leaned over and hugged my right arm.

I clung to the steering wheel. "Careful. I'm driving."

"Oh, right." She let me go but grinned from ear to ear.

I hoped she'd be able to retain her smile when we reached the farm.

CHAPTER TWENTY-EIGHT

On an Amish farm, the sound of a car engine is unique enough to attract attention right away. Even before the Beetle was all way up the driveway, the front screen door of the Troyers' two story white farmhouse flew open. Thomas and, to my surprise, Ruth hurried down the front steps.

I parked the car. Becky didn't move. I balanced my car keys in my hand. "They are waiting for you."

Becky gave me a wobbly smile. Her smile reminded me so much of the teenager I met on the side of the road eight months ago. There was an anxious resolve in her face. She unbuckled her seatbelt and slid out of the car. When Ruth saw her sister, she burst into tears and ran to Becky. She slammed her thin body into her older sister and wrapped her arms around Becky like rope.

Into Becky's shoulder Ruth cried and mumbled in their language. Becky shushed her and whispered back to her in Pennsylvania Dutch. As she bent forward to comfort her sister, her cut blond hair fell over her face like a silken curtain.

My knuckles ached from holding the steering wheel so tightly. One by one, I pried my fingers free of the molded plastic. However, I didn't leave the car. I didn't want to interrupt the moment between sisters. I lowered my car windows so that I could hear even though I didn't understand the words they said.

Mr. Troyer stood in the doorway of the house. He didn't move. Grandfather Zook appeared and poked his son-in-law in the back. Mr. Troyer shot an annoyed look at his father-in-law but proceeded down the steps onto the yard. Mr. Troyer's glance shifted over to me sitting in the front seat of my car. "Becky," Mr. Troyer said. "Your *mamm* and I want to talk to you. Alone." He went back into the house.

Becky pried herself away from her sister's arms, whispering to Ruth in their language as she freed herself. Ruth let go and scrubbed at her face with the back of her hand. Becky glanced back at me.

I shot her a thumbs up sign, and she went inside the house.

Ruth grabbed her brother's hand and the pair dashed for the cow barn. Thomas waved to me as he went. Ruth did not.

A moment later, the screen door opened again, and Grandfather Zook navigated the three porch steps into the yard. I jumped out of the Beetle and jogged across the grass to lend him my arm.

"*Danki,* Chloe," he said. "Would you like to sit on our bench in the garden?"

I smiled when he called it "our bench." We'd had long talks there many times over the last few months.

When we were settled, I told Grandfather Zook about the poisoned milk.

"I thought it would be something like that. As soon as the officer was here cutting plants I knew it was because of the murder."

"Do you know what a yew bush is?"

"Is that the plant that killed those people?"

I nodded.

"*Ya,* I know what it is. Simon does too. It's part of the job of an Amish farmer to know natural and unnatural dangers on your land that could ruin your crops or harm your livestock. If our cows got a bit of yew, they would become ill. We don't have it near the pasture land, but there are some bushes at the tree line that leads into the woods." He pointed to the tree line several hundred yards ahead. "You see that dark spiny bush there about five feet high? That's yew."

I removed my phone from my jacket pocket. "I had better let Timothy know where we are."

Grandfather Zook watched as my thin fingers flew across the touchscreen. "What are you up to with that?"

"I'm telling Timothy where I am and that I will be late getting back to the inn."

"Why can't you wait to tell him when you see him again?"

I shrugged. "He worries."

A smile spread across the older man's face. "Your little message there won't make him worry any less about you."

Grandfather Zook placed a hand on my arm. "Chloe, did you hear that?"

My head snapped up from my phone. "Hear what?" Then, I did. It was a vehicle approaching, but not from the road. It came from the other side of the barn.

The cows in the pasture mooed and shuffled away from the noise as it drew closer.

"Somebody's coming!" Thomas cried and streaked across the yard.

"Thomas!" I jumped off of the bench and raced after him.

He disappeared around the back of the dairy barn. I came around the corner of the barn and pulled up short. Just a few feet from the seven hundred gallon milk tank, Alex Tate sat absolutely still on a four wheeler. Ruth held a pitchfork just a few inches from his chest.

"Ruth, put the pitchfork down," I said.

"*Nee*. He's the *Englischer* who's trying to ruin our farm." The pitchfork shook in her small hands.

Alex's eyes widened. "No, I'm not. I'm your new neighbor." He licked his lips. "I know I should have stopped over sooner. I've been working so hard on the farm."

Ruth glared at him. "So you can close ours down."

I took the pitchfork from Ruth hands. She didn't fight me. I jabbed it into the ground beside to me. "Alex, what are you doing here?"

Ruth scowled. "You know him?"

"Timothy and I met him earlier today."

"That's right," Alex nodded. "And that meeting convinced me to drop by and say hello. I don't want to close your farm. Really."

"That's not what *Daed* said," Ruth mumbled under her breath.

Grandfather Zook appeared around the side of the barn. "What do we have here?"

I made introductions.

Grandfather Zook squinted. "Ahh, so you are the young *Englischer* running that fancy farm. I heard your barns are orange."

Alex slowly climbed off the four-wheeler all the while keeping an eye on Ruth. "They are."

Grandfather Zook pulled on his beard. "Seems like an odd color choice for a barn."

"Orange is my favorite color, so I thought why not?"

Grandfather Zook cocked his head as if he didn't know what to make out of that answer.

Alex swallowed. "I'm sorry for all the trouble your family has had. Chloe and Timothy told me about it when they stopped by my farm this afternoon. I had nothing to do with what happened to those two people. This is the first time I've been on your land."

"Chloe!" Becky called my name from the other side of the dairy barn.

I left Alex with Grandfather Zook and the children and found Becky standing in the middle yard between the farmhouse and the barn with Naomi and her parents. Becky's cheeks were tear-streaked, but she was smiling.

To my surprise, Alex followed me around the side of the barn. I inwardly groaned as a scowl appeared on Mr. Troyer's face.

"Wait here," I ordered Alex and jogged over to Becky and her parents.

"Chloe," Mr. Troyer said. "Who is that man?"

"It's Alex Tate. He's one of the owners of the commercial farm on the Gundys' old land. Timothy and I met him earlier today."

Mrs. Troyer twisted a tea towel in her hands. "What is he doing here?"

"He said he wanted to introduce himself to you."

Mr. Troyer's frown deepened. "Did you ask him to come here?"

"No," I said quickly. I was going to say more, but then my attention was caught by a blush creeping up Becky's cheeks. I followed her line of sight to Alex, who stared at her just as intently. *Uh-oh.*

I stepped in front of Becky's line of sight, and she blinked as if coming out of a trance. I cleared my throat. "The farm's called Katts' Buttermilk Farm, and Alex says they specialize in organic farming."

"I have heard of them," Mr. Troyer said and strode across the yard. Mrs. Troyer followed him.

Naomi tugged on my jeans. "Chloe, *Mamm* and *Daed* said Becky can visit us again. Isn't that *gut?*"

I smiled at her. "It's very *gut*, Naomi."

She laughed at my use of the Pennsylvania Dutch word and then ran to join the rest of the family talking to Alex. In the meantime, Becky skirted around for a better look at Alex.

"Becky, you just made up with your parents. I don't think mooning over the competition is the best thing to do right now."

She glanced at me. "Mooning? What does that mean?"

"You're gawking at Alex Tate."

She touched her flushed cheek. "I was not."

"I think it's time for us to go."

"We can't go without saying good-bye," she said and headed to the rest of the family standing around Alex Tate.

"I have a herd of ninety Guernsey cows," Alex told Becky's father. "I plan to keep the herd at around that size. We are already producing milk. I also want to plant some crops but don't know if we will be able to do that this planting season. We still have so much of the farm under construction."

Mr. Troyer nodded. "This is my oldest daughter, Rebecca."

Alex stared at Becky in her jeans, pink sweater, and canvas sneakers. "You're not Amish."

Mr. Troyer cleared his throat. "She has chosen another path in life, which as her family, we have accepted."

Becky tore her eyes away from Alex to smile at her father. I prayed Mr. and Mrs. Troyer didn't notice Becky's instant infatuation with the young commercial farmer. Grandfather Zook winked at me. He knew. Becky's grandfather never missed a thing.

"After Chloe and Timothy's visit to my farm earlier today, it reminded me of something. Early Saturday morning, I saw someone headed out this way to your farm. I don't know if that's where they were planning to go."

"What time was this?" I asked.

"Near six in the morning. I didn't think much of because I've noticed Amish folks cut across each other's farms all the time."

I glanced at Grandfather Zook. That was just about the time he heard something in the milk parlor.

"The person you saw was Amish?" I asked.

"I thought so, but I can't be sure. He wore dark cloth-ing, but I wasn't paying that much attention. It was a chilly morning, and I wanted to finish my rounds, so I could go back to my trailer and make breakfast."

"Do you remember anything else?"

He shook his head. "No, I'm sorry." His shoulders drooped.

"That was kind of you to tell us," Becky said.

He straightened up. "Thank you. I'm so sorry about the trouble that you're having. If there is any way I can be of help please let me know. I plan to be a good neighbor to you."

"*Danki*," Mr. Troyer said.

"It's getting late, and I won't keep you. It was nice to meet all of you." His eyes lingered on Becky a little too long.

Thomas jumped up and down. "Can I go for a ride on your four-wheeler?"

Alex glanced at Mr. Troyer who frowned at Thomas's request. "Not today. Maybe another time." He waved good-bye and walked around the side of the barn back to his vehicle. We heard the engine fire up. The Troyer children, including Becky, ran around the side of the barn to watch Alex drive away.

"He seemed nice," Mrs. Troyer said.

"*Ya*, but his business is still a threat to our farm whether or not he intends it to be." Mr. Troyer turned and headed back to the house.

And that's why Becky needs to stay away from Alex Tate.

⊫⊰ ⊱⊨

Naomi, Thomas, and Becky skipped around the barn, hand in hand, and I couldn't help but smile. The children were so happy to have their oldest sister with them again. Ruth wasn't with them though and neither was Grandfather Zook.

Curious, I walked around the barn. Ruth pulled the pitchfork out of the ground.

"Now, *kinner*, you can't go around trying to poke *Englischers* with pitchforks. Most of them don't like it."

Ruth bowed her head. "*Ya, Grossdaddi.*"

Grandfather Zook wiggled his bushy white eyebrows under his straw hat. "I think it's time to go back to the house for a piece of your *mamm*'s strawberry pie."

That got a small smile out of Ruth.

"You coming, Chloe?" Grandfather Zook asked as he hobbled by on his braces.

Ruth looked up at the mention of my name and frowned.

"I'll be there in a moment. I'd like to talk to Ruth."

The older man stroked his beard and glanced back at his granddaughter. "Well, don't be too long. I can't promise there will be any pie left for you if you delay."

"We won't be long," I promised.

Ruth leaned the pitchfork against the side of the barn. "What do you want?"

"Why was Ephraim Shetler behind the barn at six o'clock Saturday morning?" I asked.

Her mouth fell open. "How did you know?"

"Why was he here?"

She folded her arms.

"Is he your boyfriend?" I asked the question, knowing I would receive an angry response in return.

"*Nee.*" Her face turned bright red. "*Nee.* He and Anna are sweethearts."

It was my turn to be surprised at the image of sweet, shy Anna Lambright sneaking around with a boy.

"They are just talking," Ruth said defensively. "They use our farm to do that."

"That puts you in an awkward position."

"She is my *freind*," Ruth said as if that were explanation enough.

"How long has this been going on?"

She chewed on her bottom lip. "A month or so. Ephraim always liked Anna. All the boys do. She's the prettiest girl in our school. It wasn't until Eastertime that Anna told me she was sweet on him. They started courting."

"Isn't Anna a little young to be courted?" I asked.

Ruth narrowed her Troyer-blue eyes. "Anna and I are thirteen. Next year will be our last year of school. We aren't too young to court."

The thought of Ruth leaving school at fourteen made me terribly sad. I knew to stop at an eighth grade education was the Amish way, but the professional student in me couldn't wrap her head around it. School had been my safe place when my family crumbled.

I rested my back against the rough barn siding. "Why do they meet here?"

"They can't meet at the Gundy barn since that *Englischer* tore it down."

The Gundy barn had been Anna and Ruth's special meeting place.

She kicked at the grass. "And anywhere else is too far for Anna to walk without her *daed* noticing she'd gone."

"So Ephraim walks all the way from the Dutch Inn. How far is that?"

"Four miles. He rides his bicycle most of the way."

"Why doesn't she want her father to know about Ephraim?"

"Because of what happened with Katie. Katie always had trouble with sweethearts."

How well I knew. Katie's trouble in the romance department had contributed to her murder last December.

She started back around the barn. "I have to go help *Mamm* in the kitchen."

"I saw Ephraim here Saturday morning when the tourists were here. Grandfather Zook saw him too."

She jabbed her fists into the side of her tiny waist. "He didn't poison those *Englischers* if that's what you are trying to say."

I held up a hand. "I wasn't saying that."

She dropped her hands. "Oh."

"Why was he here, if he and Anna want to keep their courting a secret?"

She started walking again. "I don't know. I just know Anna was happy to see him."

Ruth disappeared around the side of the barn.

I stomped down the tuft of grass she had dug up with her toe. The case of Grandfather Zook's mysterious noise was solved, but a murderer was still on the loose.

CHAPTER TWENTY-NINE

That evening in my room at the inn, my phone beeped at ten thirty. It was a reminder it was seven thirty in California and time to call my father for our weekly talk.

"Hello, Chloe, your father has been waiting for your call," Sabrina, my evil stepmother, answered.

I translated this from Sabrina-speak to mean, "You're wasting my husband's valuable time." I hated it when she answered the phone for my father. I closed my eyes for a moment. "I'm glad to hear it. Can I talk to him?"

She sniffed. "He's finishing up a work email. He will be able to talk to you in a minute."

Ahh, so it wouldn't have mattered if I had called on time. As badly as I wanted to say that to her, I held my tongue. I was rebuilding my relationship with my father and whether I liked it or not—whether Sabrina liked it or not—that included my relationship with my step-mother.

"How are the kids?" I asked.

"They are very well, excelling in school. We just hired a new tutor. The company guarantees if the children complete their program, Brin and Blake will be accepted to the college they choose."

"They're eight and six. How could the company make a promise like that?" As soon as I said it, I wished I could reach into the phone and pull the words back.

Sabrina took a quick intake of breath. "They have very high standards. Higher than anything in Ohio."

I rolled my eyes. It was a good thing Sabrina and I were not in the same room. "I'm glad they're doing so well. How is the house?"

"Thankfully, the remodel of the kitchen is finished. It looks like something right out of *Architectural Digest*. We're moving on to the pool next by having it resurfaced and making it a salt water pool. It will be much easier for the pool boy to take care of."

"Sounds great." I tapped my fingers on the bedspread.

"The next time you visit it will look like a whole new place."

Every time I visited, their house looked like a new place. Despite being a beautiful multi-million dollar home in the San Diego area, my stepmother kept it in a constant state of remodeling. My father could have bought three more homes for as much as he'd put into that house.

"Here's your father," she said.

Finally.

"Hello, Chloe," my father's voice came on the line. "How are you?"

Besides stuck on a bus with geriatric and potentially murderous tourists and arguing with my former Amish boyfriend about a hypothetical house we will maybe own together some day, I'm good.

"Fine," I said.

"And how is work?" he asked.

"Quiet. The semester ended last week. Graduation is over, and most of the students and faculty have gone home for the summer."

"Will you have enough to keep you busy?"

"Plenty."

He cleared his throat. "And Timothy? How is he?"

"Timothy's fine. His contracting business is booming."

"It's good to hear construction is bouncing back after the recession. It's doing quite well out here in California too. You might want to mention that to Timothy. He'd make a much nicer income here than he does in Ohio."

Did my father want Timothy to move to California?

"That's true, but the cost of living is higher out there too, and his entire family is here."

"Yes, well, I would just mention it to him."

Time to change the subject. "Sabrina told me about the new tutoring company for the children. She was very enthused about it."

His breath caught. It wasn't exactly a laugh, but was the closest he'd ever come to one from something I'd said. "You know Sabrina. She's passionate about the children's future."

"She's a good mom," I said, and it was true. Sabrina guarded my half-sister and half-brother like a mother bear.

"That is kind of you to say." He paused. "I know the two of you haven't had the best relationship, but I hope it's improving."

"Little by little," I said.

He laughed a real laugh. "That's the most I can ask for."

We chatted for a few more minutes and then said good-bye. I hung up thinking "little by little" summed up my relationship with my father too.

I plugged my phone back into the charger when it binged, telling me I had an incoming Skype call. I answered it and Tee's tiny face appeared on my screen. "I've been trying to Skype you for the last ten minutes. Why didn't you answer?" she asked.

"Weekly Dad call."

"Oh right. I forgot you do that on Sunday night. So how is dear old dad?"

"Fine." I smiled. Tee still held a grudge against my father for abandoning me after my mother's death.

"And Sabrina the Suburban Witch?" She gave me a wicked grin.

I laughed. "She's fine too. She's turning the pool into a salt water pool."

Tee snorted.

"Why are you calling so late, or is it early? It has to be almost five in the morning there."

"Four forty-five actually. I couldn't sleep and figured you'd still be up."

I sat cross-legged in the middle of the bed. "You'll be tired in the morning."

She waved away my concern. "I'll have a double Italian espresso. It will make you lose the ability to blink."

"Sounds terrific."

"I love the stuff." She leaned in closer to her laptop screen. "What's wrong with you?"

"How can you tell anything is wrong with me over Skype?"

"Because I know you, that's how. Spill. Dad stuff?"

"No."

"Murder stuff?"

"To some extent, but it's mostly Timothy stuff."

She jerked back from her screen. "Don't tell me you and golden boy are fighting."

"We had a disagreement." I went on tell her about our argument about the house Timothy wanted to buy.

"Whoa, whoa, whoa, you'd better hold up there. Why are you talking about a house before you're engaged?"

I came to Timothy's defense. "He's just being practical. It makes sense he would want to talk to me about a house. If we were ever to marry, I'm going to live there too. He's just thinking ahead."

"You make it sound like you're planning a merger. Where's the romance in that?"

She had a point.

"Before there is any more house talk, buggy boy better put a ring on it."

"Okay, Beyonce," I drawled.

"And you had better get used to arguing with Timothy," Tanisha said.

"Get used to it? Why?" I bit my lip.

"Because this won't be the first thing you argue over. It's just the start. What about kids?"

"Kids? Who said anything about kids?"

She shook her finger at me. "It's something that will come up. Don't the Amish have like forty-six children or something? You'd better find out about that too."

"That's a gross exaggeration," I said. "And I'm so not ready for that conversation."

"Get ready because if Timothy is talking house, the next stop is the cradle. And what about schooling for the kids?"

"There's only one school district in Appleseed Creek."

"There are a lot of things you and Timothy need to know about each other before you're off buying houses. You get what I mean."

I did. Loud and clear. "I feel like you have just given me some of your Italian espresso. How will I sleep tonight?"

She leaned into the screen again. "Oh, rats, I upset you. I didn't mean to do that. Chloe, just talk to him. He loves you. Trust in that."

"I know."

She twirled a braid. "All this other stuff will work out."

"I know."

"Can we talk about crazed Amish murderers now?" she asked.

"Yes," I said. "I'm much more comfortable with that topic."

CHAPTER THIRTY

O n Monday, the bus tour's main event was a tour of Holmes County, which had the largest population of Amish in the world. Even with that in mind, I hurried to the college in the early morning to grab a few files from my office and to tell my staff, Clark and Miller, where I would be the next couple of days. As expected, both men seemed unconcerned with my absence.

Our first bus stop in Holmes County was an Anabaptist education center that had a panoramic Amish and Mennonite history. It had been an educational stop for me as well as the tourists because although I had been in entrenched in Amish culture between Becky and Timothy, I knew little about how the religion began.

We were only there for an hour. Hudson was determined to keep on schedule today or even ahead of it. I couldn't help but wonder if he had a reason to want to hurry back to the inn.

"Head 'em up, move 'em out," Hudson cried as the tourists shuffled in a single file line back onto the blue tour bus.

"Does he think he's running a cattle drive because I might take offense to being treated like a cow." Gertie, who stood next to me, stamped her three-prong cane on the ground.

Melinda's cheek twitched as if she physically bit down on her tongue to stop herself from saying something. "I'm sure it's just an expression," Melinda managed to say.

Gertie pointed her cane at Melinda. "You wouldn't feel that way if he had a cattle prod."

Charles clutched his professional-grade camera in his hands. "I don't understand why that man wouldn't let us take photographs of the panorama. What did he think we would do, plaster them on the Internet? What difference would that make?"

Nadine rooted through her purse and came up with a tube of lipstick. "The Amish don't like photographs, dear."

"If that guy was Amish, I'm an ancient Egyptian. He had a cell phone strapped to his belt."

"He said he was Mennonite." Nadine reapplied bright pink lipstick.

"I still think it wouldn't have hurt him if I took one picture," Charles groused.

His wife dropped the lipstick into her straw purse. "You couldn't have taken just one. Photographs are your potato chips, honey."

I glanced at the readout on my cell phone, and worry gripped me. Time was running out. The bus would leave for Indiana on Wednesday morning.

"In a hurry to be somewhere?" Doris asked.

I shook my head. "I'm just checking to see if we are on schedule."

"We are," Duke said. "We aren't a second behind. Hudson runs a tight ship."

"What about Dudley?" I asked. "What was his...umm... ship like?"

Duke stuck out his lower lip while he considered my question. "He seemed like he was in a hurry too. I can't say I got the impression either one of them enjoyed their work. Miss Chloe, you are a breath of fresh air. Thank you for joining us."

Doris smiled at me one more time before her husband helped her onto the bus.

These were my murder suspects. How could I imagine any of these people were devious enough to orchestrate a murder?

Through the bus window, Hudson watched me intently. Then again, they couldn't all be innocent.

The bus tour's next stop was a cheese-making factory, and I'd hoped that I could talk to Hudson while in the factory. It was easier said than done. The pudgy Amish woman named Mercy, who was leading the tour, did not abide by foolishness.

"These are the rules we need go over before the tour begins. There is no talking on the tour unless you would like to ask a question. In that case, raise your hand, and I will call on you." She scowled at Fred and Nadine who whispered to each other about how to text their granddaughter from Nadine's cell phone. "And no photographs or video are allowed during the tour."

"It's just cheese," Charles yelped. "What difference does it make if I take a few photos of cheddar?"

She stared him down like a seasoned schoolmarm. I suspected she might have been in that line of work before the cheese factory. "Please respect our rules."

"Next year, we are going on the vacation of my choice," Charles muttered. "To the Grand Canyon. No one stops you from taking photographs of the Grand Canyon."

Bitty patted her husband's arm. "That sounds nice."

Two by two, we followed Mercy into the work room of the cheese factory. The Amish women wore hairnets over their prayer caps and latex gloves on their hands. It was another example of the Old World meeting the new.

I slid to the back of the pack.

"You use electricity?" Jimbo asked. Accusingly he pointed to the fluorescent lighting overhead and the sockets along the wall.

Mercy pursed her lips. "You didn't raise your hand."

Jimbo shot up his hand but spoke before he was called on. "You use electricity."

"Our bishop allows the use of electricity for our businesses. Not all Amish districts operate this way. It's up to each individual bishop to decide when and how modern conveniences are allowed."

Jimbo chewed on this for a moment.

Mercy scanned the group. "Any other questions?" she asked as if it was a dare.

Everyone shook their heads.

"*Gut.* Let's move on."

The tour ended forty minutes later and spilled out into the cheese shop where the travelers had the opportunity to shop and taste-test the cheeses.

Jimbo's eyes gleamed when Mercy explained about the tasting.

"Please only take one piece of cheese per flavor per person." Mercy looked pointedly at Jimbo.

He placed a hand to his round stomach and narrowed his eyes.

In the shop, the tourists fanned out with their shopping baskets. I hid a smile as Jimbo stuffed three pieces of baby Swiss in his mouth.

Gertie reached into her purse and pulled out a plastic bag of her fish jerky. She held it up to Mercy.

The Amish woman blinked. "What is this?"

"Give it a taste. It will change your life," Gertie insisted.

Mercy wrinkled her nose. "I don't believe I want to give it a taste."

Gertie shook the jerky at her. "You don't know what you're missing, and this will make an excellent cheese flavor."

Mercy placed a hand to her hip. "But what is it?"

"Fish jerky. I made it myself."

Melinda scanned the room as if on the hunt for the closest window to throw herself out of.

Mercy grimaced. "*Danki*, but I would not like to taste it, nor do I believe our customers would want it as a new flavor of cheese."

"Why not?" Gertie asked.

Mercy pushed the loose tie from her prayer cap behind her ear. "It is not an appealing flavor."

Gertie wagged the jerky at her again. "You have chocolate-mint cheese in this store. You don't think that people gag when they choke that down? Jimbo won't even touch it, and I've seen him eat a hamburger after it has fallen on the floor at a highway rest stop."

Like a prairie dog, Jimbo's head popped up from the tasting table at the mention of his name. A piece of provolone hung from his mouth.

Melinda tugged on the sleeve of Gertie's cardigan. "Gertie, why don't we wait outside?"

"Fine," Gertie said. "I'll enjoy my jerky in the sun."

Outside, I found Hudson sitting on a bench overlooking the valley. The cheese shop was perched on the high hill. From that vantage point, I could see for miles. Below an Amish farmer and his team plowed a field.

Hudson crushed his empty can of Diet Coke in his hand and dropped it into his cooler. "Find your murderer yet?"

I ignored his question. "Everyone should be out of the factory in a few minutes." I rested my hip against a log fence.

He smirked. "It must be hard since I came off free and clear to the police. I know you wanted to pin the murders to on me."

I glared at him. "You're not off my list."

He was in front of me in a second and caused me to lean back on the fence. I felt the wooden boards give slightly under my weight. I prayed it held. It was a long way to the bottom of the valley.

"Don't mess with me, little girl," he growled.

The chatter of the approaching tourists interrupted us, and Hudson took two huge steps back. I remembered how to breathe again.

"Chloe," LeeAnne trilled. "Wasn't that tour delightful? I learned so much about cheese."

I willed my pulse to settle. "It was nice."

"Look at the view," Nadine said

Fred shook the fence. "I wouldn't touch that," he said. "It's not stable and could give at any moment. It would be a bad trip for anyone who sat on it."

Nadine smiled proudly at her husband. "Fred used to work in construction. He knows this type of thing."

I smiled at her, but my eyes trailed to Hudson. He grinned at me. Why did I have the feeling he wouldn't feel the least bit of remorse if I had toppled over the edge?

CHAPTER THIRTY-ONE

Our next stop in Holmes County was Berlin, the most 'touristy' of all the towns in the county. Appleseed Creek had a sleepy quality that Berlin lacked. The town buzzed with automobile, horse and buggy, and pedestrian traffic up and down Main Street.

Shops lined either side of the road and sold everything from Amish gifts to New Age crystals. Clearly, the Amish weren't the only ones taking advantage of the tourists. Hudson parked the bus behind a craft mall. The itinerary scheduled two hours in the picturesque town, which would be plenty of time for the travelers to shop and grab a bite for lunch. An Amish man was at the front of the mall selling homemade ice cream and kettle chips.

Gertie was the last passenger off the bus. "Chloe, why don't you walk with Melinda and me through town? I would like the site described by an Amish expert."

"I wouldn't say I'm an expert, but I'm happy to walk with you and tell you what I know. My legs are feeling a little cramped after so many hours on the bus."

Gertie looped her arm through mine. "Come along, Melinda," she said over her shoulder.

I twisted my neck to see Gertie's companion walking a few paces behind. Melinda grimaced but her face cleared when she caught me looking.

"Do you want to stop in any shops?" I asked Gertie. "You might find a nice souvenir to take home."

"Pish, I have no need for any more trinkets in my home to collect dust. I can't live much longer, and then Melinda will have the task of throwing them away."

"Gertie, that's no way to think," I said.

"Ahh, don't think I'm ready to buy the farm, my dear. But don't begrudge me if I look forward to my great reward either."

I could see her point, but at the same time, it made me terribly sad.

Melinda cleared her throat.

Gertie wagged her finger and continued her forward motion. "Melinda doesn't like it when I talk about death. She'd hated to lose her cushy job."

Melinda sighed so deeply that her breath tousled Gertie's pin curls. "I don't feel that way about you, Gertie."

Gertie snorted. "That's what you may say now. Let's not waste any more time running our mouths. Walk with me, dear."

Melinda followed us. I know she was only doing her job, which was to watch over Gertie, but her eyes bore into my back.

"How is Pearl?" Gertie asked.

"She's doing as well as can be expected. I'm glad she's back at the inn. I know it's difficult for her to be around the bus tour, but the thought of her staying in that other hotel all by herself..." I didn't add Brock Buckley was a big part of that. My relationship with Brock and Curt was far too complicated to tell Gertie during a stroll through Berlin.

"She should rejoin the group. She is missing the trip." Gertie touched the colorful silk scarf knotted around her neck. "Seems to be a waste of money to me not to."

I skirted around a woman with a stroller coming the opposite way on the sidewalk. "She's grieving."

"She and Ruby were close for cousins."

"Aren't cousins typically close?" I asked. I didn't know because I didn't have any. Both of my parents had been only children.

"I suppose," she mused. "Have you figured out who the killer is? After Becky told us about your crime solving, I borrowed Melinda's little computer phone and Googled your name. I must say, Chloe Humphrey, I was surprised how many murders were linked to you in the local news."

I swallowed. "Becky spoke out of turn. I'm here as the stand-in tour guide. I was the first person Chief Rose thought of when she was asked about a replacement."

Gertie walked along with her cane. "If she didn't find a replacement, then the tour might have ended. All of the police chief's suspects would have driven away to Indiana or even back to Mississippi."

I gasped.

"I wasn't born yesterday, you know. Oh!" Gertie dropped my arm as we came across an English man operating an Italian sausage cart. She scrounged through her patchwork handbag and came up with a fist of bills. "Melinda, go buy us three Italian sausages with extra peppers."

I stepped to the side of the walk to let a couple pass. "That's so sweet of you to offer to buy lunch, Gertie, but—"

"You're far too skinny. I know the waif look is in right now, but it's not what real men like your Timothy want. They want someone they can hold onto. You don't want him to leave you for a curvier girl now, do you?"

"I guess not," I said. The sausage did smell good. "No peppers or onions on mine though. Melinda, I'll help you carry."

Melinda gave me the tiniest of smiles. While we stood in the line, which was growing longer by the second, Melinda said, "Gertie can be very persuasive, can't she?

"How did you become her companion?" I asked.

She shook her head. "I asked to work for her. I knew she traveled and needed someone to keep her company. I was tired of my old job."

"What did you do before?"

She removed a stack of napkins from the dispenser and came back to our spot in line. "I was a teacher."

"What did you teach?" I asked.

"Middle school." She didn't elaborate.

"That's a tough age."

"It can be, but I loved my students. But after putting thirty years in, I was done and ready to move on to something else. Working for Gertie, despite all her eccentricities, has been a good fit for me." She paused. "It's given me an opportunity to accomplish my goals."

Just as I was about to ask her what those goals were, Charles caught my eye across the street. He photographed a monarch butterfly balancing on a daffodil leaf. *What other photographs had he taken?* Specifically, what photographs did he take Saturday morning at the Troyer farm?

Melinda and I carried our sandwiches back to the Gertie, who somehow found an empty Adirondack chair in front of a florist shop. She perched on the end of it.

"How'd you find an empty chair, Gertie?" I asked.

She tucked her pocketbook beside her. "I told the young man sitting here I was old enough to be his great-great grandmother and would likely die if I didn't have a place to sit. Never underestimate the power of guilt." She pointed a wrinkled finger down the street. "A fresh squeezed lemonade would hit the spot with these sandwiches."

I handed Gertie her sandwich. "I'll get them."

"No, no. I'll do it," Melinda said. "You visit with Gertie."

Before I could protest, she said, "You are doing me a favor by entertaining her."

"Melinda was telling me how she started working for you."

"I met her at our senior citizen center in Tupelo. She was a volunteer there, and I took a shine to her right away. She has a calm and steady presence. It must have been from all those years of teaching eighth graders how to dissect frogs."

"Dissect frogs? She was a science teacher?" I asked.

Gertie nodded.

"You've been to so many places. How did you pick this trip to Amish Country?" I took a bite of my sandwich.

"It was last minute. We didn't even make the final decision until a week before we were set to leave." She threw a slice of pepper on the grass beside her.

"Do you usually travel on the spur of the moment like that?"

"No, but Melinda was so enthusiastic when she heard about the trip, I thought why not?" She tossed another pepper. "She can be a bit of downer, so to see her excited about something made me excited about it too. People shouldn't go through life like it's a chore. It's an adventure and should be treated as such." A third pepper hit the grass. "Plus, I have never been to Amish Country."

"Umm, Gertie, why are you throwing all your peppers on the grass?"

She wrinkled her nose. "I like them for flavoring, but they are too slimy to eat."

I sat next to her. "Does your family ever want to go on these trips with you?"

She took a bite of her sandwich and thought for a minute. "I have one son still living, but he's in a nursing home in Utah. Poor boy, he took after his father as far as health goes, not me. Everyone else has gone home to be with the Lord. I suppose you could say Melinda is the only family I have. I'm her only family too. She never married and doesn't claim any other relatives."

Melinda returned with our lemonade. She handed the first plastic cup to me. "This one is for you, Chloe." She handed the next cup to Gertie. "And here is yours."

"Thank you, Melinda. I was just telling Chloe how we came on this trip."

Melinda's mouth turned down.

Gertie set her lemonade cup on the grass and shoved her half-eaten Italian sausage at me. "I know just the thing that will go with this lemonade."

Uh-huh.

She stuck her hand in her massive patchwork purse and removed a plastic sandwich bag. Inside was a twisted gray strip of what I assumed was fish. It resembled a molted snakeskin.

Gertie pulled the fish strip and held it out to me. "My fish jerky. It's about time you tried it."

Reluctantly, I took it. I could feel both she and Melinda watching me.

"Go on, now," Gertie urged.

I took a tiny bite. It tasted like crunchy salt rock which had been scraped up from the bottom of the Mississippi.

Gertie watched me intently. "Good, ain't it?"

"Mmmmm." I grabbed my lemonade and took a huge gulp.

The centenarian rubbed her hands together. "I knew you would like it."

I willed my gag reflex to remain calm. "Gertie, I think I will save the rest for later."

"If that's what you want to do. You got a strip of large-mouth bass there. It stays fresh a long time." She handed me the sandwich bag. "Catfish is my favorite, but it doesn't keep as well because it's a fatty fish."

I tucked the fish jerky into my purse and chugged more lemonade.

CHAPTER THIRTY-TWO

By the time we reached the Dutch Inn in Appleseed Creek later that afternoon, my stomach was rolling. I was happy everyone was in a light stupor from too much food and too much information, so no one complained when I said I had no more Amish lessons to share until dinner that evening. The sound of light snoring floated from the back of the bus.

All I wanted to do was crawl to my room and lay down on the bed. A pounding headache throbbed behind my forehead. I placed a hand to my temple. It came away damp. That Italian sausage was a very, very bad idea. Or was it the fish jerky? If I made it back to Knox County alive, I promised myself I would never touch either ever again.

I felt the bus shudder to a halt, and heard the sound of tinny voices next to me in the aisle.

Hudson held onto the railing in front of my seat. "All right. Time for you to get out too."

He had to be kidding. Moving seemed impossible.

"Get out, kid. My number one rule is no hurling on the bus."

Slowly, I opened my eyes and his face blurred. With all the energy I could muster, I gathered my bag and struggled to my feet. *Bed. Get in the inn and go to bed.*

"There's some guy out here waiting for you," Hudson said. His voice was distant too.

Timothy. Timothy would take care of me. Thinking of him brought tears to my eyes.

Somehow, I stumbled to the bus door. The steps looked like a mile down. I teetered, and a hand reached for mine and helped me down. I stared at it. It was a man's hand, but it didn't belong to Timothy. In slow motion, I turned my head. Curt. *What was he doing there?* He helped me down to the blacktop. "Red," was all he said.

"Pull her away from the bus," Hudson barked.

I felt Curt lead me to the grass lawn beside the driveway. Hudson cranked over the engine, and the bus pulled out of the driveway. *Where was he going? Should I follow him?* I could no more follow him than I could fly.

"Red?" Curt's voice dipped with concern. "Are you okay?"

I blinked a blurry goatee-covered face. "No."

"I need to talk to you." His tone was urgent, pleading.

"Another time. I can't talk to you right now, Curt."

How did he know I was here? Has he been watching me again? I thought he changed. My thoughts hit me in a muddled string. I needed to lie down now.

"It can't wait. It's already waited long enough." His father's dog tags hung from his neck.

I closed my eyes for a moment. Mistake. It only seemed to make the earth tilt more. "Is it about the prison ministry? I already told you it's a good idea. I haven't had time to work on the website yet."

"It's not about that." He grasped my upper arms. I didn't know if he did that to keep me upright or hold me in place.

"Whatever it is can we do this another time? Please. I'm not feeling well. I think I might be car sick or—"

His grip tightened on my upper arms. "I just need five minutes. Let's go to the garden. I think I need to sit down. There's a bench there."

"Fine." Arguing with him to leave me alone would just prolong my agony. "But please hurry. I don't feel well."

He guided me into the garden. There was a white wrought iron backless bench in the middle of a bed of red tulips. Curt lowered me onto the bench. Sitting was wonderful. I would never discredit the greatness of sitting again. He sat beside me. The bench was so small our legs pressed up against each other. I didn't care. I was way beyond caring about my personal space.

Curt turned my body to face him. "Chloe, look at me."
I blinked.

"I love you, Chloe," he blurted out.

Brock was right? This wasn't happening. This could not be happening. He called me Chloe. He never calls me Chloe.

"No, you don't," I whispered.

He jerked his head back and even through my blurred vision I could see a small piece of the angry Curt I remembered from months ago.

Curt grabbed my elbow. "I know what I just said must be a shock. I was surprised by it myself. My counselor said if I had to tell someone something that was bothering me, I needed to say it. Bottling it up inside leads to anger."

I wished his counselor hadn't done that. More than anything I wished I could lie down on top of the flowers. He took my hand. "Chloe, I love you." He paused. "I've loved you for a while now, longer than I have even known."

The headache intensified. "Curt, you know Timothy and I are dating."

A muscle in his jaw twitched, or at least I thought it did. It was hard to tell as my vision was still unreliable. "I know, but you could date me too. And between the two of us, you could decide who suits you better."

That wasn't going to happen. Ever. I already knew who suited me better. I didn't want to hurt Curt's feelings more, but I had to put a stop to this.

"You're the only girl for me," he whispered and took my face into his hands.

I tried to pull away. "I can't—"

He kissed me. His goatee felt coarse against my skin, and my insides revolted. I jerked my head away from him, bent over, and threw up on the tulips.

CHAPTER THIRTY-THREE

Gentle fingers held my hair back away from my face as I expelled a series of dry heaves into Jane's beautiful garden. As the last heave shook my body, a water bottle was thrust into my hand. "Here, drink this. It will help. You might want to swish it around in your mouth to get the bad taste out. I've seen a lot of foul stuff, Red, but this might be the winner."

Red? The name hit me like a tennis racket to the side of the head. I jerked my head up so quickly it connected with Curt's chin. "Ouch!" we both cried out.

The head knock forced me to look down. Big mistake. Jane's flowers weren't so pretty anymore. Ugh. I had to look away.

I tried to scramble to stand and Curt grabbed me by the waist to steady me.

"What are you doing to her?" Timothy's voice was razor sharp. "Get away from her."

I felt Curt jerk away from me. Still too weak to stand on my own, I began to falter. Timothy caught me as I was halfway to the ground.

"What did you do to her?" His question came out in a snarl and sounded nothing like Timothy.

I shivered. "Timothy, Curt hasn't done anything wrong. I was sick, and he helped me." Nausea washed over me again. "I think I might be sick again." I doubled over. This time it was Timothy who held my hair.

Vaguely, after my last bout of a turned stomach, I felt Timothy pick me up and carry me to his truck. He laid me across the bench seat and placed my head on his lap. At some point, I must have fallen asleep because the next thing I knew I was aware of was an antiseptic smell assaulting my nostrils.

"Morning, Sunshine."

My eyes opened slowly, fighting against the hospital room's glaring fluorescent lighting.

"There you are." Chief Rose's royal blue-lined brown eyes and short poodle curls seemed even more out place under her police department cap than normal. "Have a nice nap?"

"Terrific." My tongue stuck to the roof of my mouth.

A hand offered me a small plastic cup of water. "Here, drink this." It was the exact phrase Curt used in the garden, but it was Timothy who handed me the water this time.

I accepted the cup and took two small sips. It made my stomach clench, but it was enough to satisfy my dry mouth for the time being.

Chief Rose sat on the edge of my bed. "Humphrey, we have to talk about your latest escapade."

"There will be time for that, Greta." Timothy's voice was firm. "The nurse said Chloe needs to rest."

"She looks perfectly fine to me," Chief Rose argued.

Timothy set the water cup on a side table. "What, are you a doctor now?"

"Troyer, don't take your protective attitude out on me."

"You caused this. It was your idea for her to get on the bus with those people," he said.

"I didn't hear her say 'no.'"

"Like you would let her. You just steamrolled her into doing whatever you wanted."

I lifted my hand from my chest. "Hello, I'm right here, and I know I look half-dead, but I am very much alive and can hear you." I blinked in confusion. "How did Chief Rose cause me to be sick? She wasn't the one who gave me that Italian sausage. I have food poisoning."

The chief turned her head toward me. "It wasn't food poisoning."

"What?" My mouth was dry again. I feared it may become a permanent condition. "Can I have a little more water?"

Timothy was at my side in an instant, forcing Chief Rose to step away. He held the paper cup for me while I drank.

When I was done, I waved him away. "What do you mean this wasn't food poisoning?"

The chief and Timothy shared a look.

"What's going on?" I tried to push myself up in the bed but failed miserably.

The room door swung in. "How is our patient feeling? Awake, I see. Chloe, we have to stop meeting like this," the dark-haired doctor said. His hospital ID read, "Dr. Bryant," and I recognized him from my other stays in the hospital since moving to Appleseed Creek.

"Since we hadn't seen you in a few months, we figured that you were staying out of trouble." He held the breast flaps of his lab coat. "But now here you are. You couldn't stand to be away from us too long."

I wanted him to leave. I wanted to hear what Timothy and Chief Rose had to say. "I didn't plan to come back."

"Most don't." He chuckled.

"Timothy, please tell me what you and Chief Rose meant before the doctor arrived," I said.

Timothy pursed his lips as if considering his words. Chief Rose, who was never as subtle, cut to the chase. "Someone tried to poison you."

"Poison me," I murmured.

She nodded.

"The chief's right. You were in bad shape there for a bit," the good doctor added. "We won't know for sure until we get the lab results back, but I think someone fed you narcissus."

"Narcissus," I whispered. "Isn't that a character in Greek mythology that fell in love with his reflection and died?"

Dr. Bryant picked up an iPad from a rolling medical cart in one corner of the room and consulted it. "It's also a flower. More commonly called a daffodil."

"A daffodil," I whispered. Somehow knowing it was my favorite flower that nearly killed me made it worse. My eyes found Timothy's. His expression was apologetic as if he was somehow responsible for this. He knew what my favorite flower was.

"I see a case like this a couple of times every spring. There was a little boy in here last week who ate a whole plant."

I tried to lift my head. The room swerved. That was a mistake. "Was the little boy okay?"

"He was after we pumped his stomach and a two-day hospital stay." He scrolled down his iPad again. "Even though he ate the plant, it was lucky he didn't get any of the bulb. That's where a majority of the alkaloid poison is. Because of the severity of your illness, I suspect you ingested a bit of a narcissus bulb. It's not toxic enough to kill you but will definitely make you wish you were dead."

"Do you think I ate it today? Right before I got sick?" I willed myself not to think about the Italian sausage. If I threw up again, Dr. Bryant would never let me out of the hospital.

"Narcissus doesn't work that fast. You could have been given it any time in the last few days. We would need to know how much you were given and how susceptible you are to know the time of the reaction. I suspect it was in the last thirty-six to forty-eight hours because of your small size. In a large man it would take much longer for a reaction."

Chief Rose rocked back on her heels. "I sent Nottingham over to the Dutch Inn to collect a sample of the lunch you left behind in the garden."

Ugh. Could the floor open up and swallow me now?

"Don't worry. He may look like a kid, but he's an old hand where puke is concerned. Who do you think collects all those drunk Harshberger students on Thursday nights and carts them back to campus?"

Seriously, floor open up already. I am ready to go.

Dr. Bryant closed the cover over his iPad. "You are going to be fine, but I would like to keep you here overnight for observation."

I shook my head. "I don't want to spend the night in the hospital. I feel fine now. A little weak, but that's to be expected after being that sick. I'll feel a little better after I eat." Even the mention of food made my stomach roll. I tried my best not to make a face as I felt like I rode a Tilt-a-whirl on the deck of a sailboat.

He pursed his lips. "You're vitals and coloring are back to normal. You aren't in any danger, so I'll let you go."

"Maybe you should stay to be sure," Timothy said. "One night in the hospital won't be so bad."

"I will be fine."

"Okay, I'll start the paperwork," the good doctor said. "A nurse will be back within the hour with your discharge papers." He pointed the corner of his iPad in my direction. "Don't make me regret my decision, Chloe, and I don't want to see you around here again."

"I don't want to see you either," I said with a smile.

He winked at me and left the room.

"Okay, Humphrey, start at the beginning. I want to know everything you did the last two days, so we can figure out when you might have been fed daffodil and by whom."

I started talking and shared everything I could remember from the last couple of days.

"I need to know what you ate too."

"There was the fish jerky."

Her pen froze in midair. "Say what?"

"Gertie gave me some fish jerky she brought from Mississippi."

The chief touched her pen to the paper. "And you ate it. You do have a death wish."

"Gertie wouldn't have poisoned me," I said. *At least I don't think she would.*

"I'll have to check it out."

"There's a piece in my purse."

Timothy plucked my purse off a chair in the corner of the room and removed the sandwich bag. He gave it to the chief. She held it in front her like she was examining a bug. "You ate that."

"Just a tiny bite to be polite."

"Polite could have gotten you killed." She placed the bag on the corner of the bed. "What else did you eat?"

I pulled the sheet up closer to my chin. "An Italian sausage."

She just shook her head and recorded what I said. A few minutes later, she snapped her notebook closed. "That will do for now. There is someone else here to see you."

"Who?" I heard myself ask even though I knew.

"Curt."

I hated it when I was right.

"He's waiting out in the hall and as much as I try to chase him away, he won't leave until he sees you. He won't take my word that you're all right." Her eyes slid to Timothy, who had been silent throughout the chief's interrogation. "And we both know he won't believe anything Troyer says."

I could use that cup of water again wherever it was. "I'll talk to him."

The chief nodded, and when I thought she was about to leave the room, she hesitated. "I'm glad you are okay, Humphrey. I like having you around."

Were Chief Rose and I friends? I couldn't really see us braiding each other's hair or having sleepovers, but there are other types of friendship among women. A mutual respect.

The door's latch clicked shut after her.

Timothy's blue eyes were wide. There was fear there. Fear over the possibility of losing me. "I can stay with you while you talk to Fanning."

"No," I whispered. If Timothy heard what Curt had to say to me, it would only make the situation worse. Then again, Timothy wasn't a fool, and he may have known about Curt's feelings for me a lot longer than I had. "I'll be fine. Please send him in."

He took my hand and kissed it. "All right." Timothy opened my room door and poked his head out. "You can come in now," he said in a gruff voice.

Timothy stepped to the side as Curt shuffled into the room.

"I'll be just on the other side of the door." Timothy's voice was heavy with a threat.

The latch to the door clicked shut after him.

Curt stood at the foot of the bed and clenched his hands in front of him. "You threw up on my shoe."

"Sorry about that. I'm sorry you had to witness that whole episode. I'm mortified."

"Don't be." He folded his hands in front of himself. "I'm glad I was there for you. I want to always be the one there to help you, Red."

I squinted as if in pain. "Curt—"

"I shouldn't have approached you like that. When you said you didn't feel well, I should have paid attention and helped you to the hospital before I told you how I felt."

"Curt—"

"Pastor Chris said I need to work on thinking before I act. I need to put others before myself. I'm still learning. Slowly. And after the life I led, it's a struggle every day, but I'm getting better at it. Today is not the best example," he pressed on. I suspected he knew exactly what I was going to say.

"Curt—"

"But even if that was the wrong time to say it," he said in rush. "Everything I said was true. I do love you. You are the only woman for me. I know that in my heart."

"Curt—"

He opened his mouth as if he was going to speak again. This time, I was faster. "No, you said your piece. Now, it's my turn. I'm flattered," I said, realizing I was. After all Curt and I had been through, most of which was turbulent at best, it amazed me he could care for me. "But I'm in love with Timothy. Nothing will change that. We're going to get married."

"You are? I don't see a ring." I stared at my left hand.

The fingers of my left hand involuntarily curled inward. "Even without a ring, I know we are."

His face flushed. "How do you know? Have you talked about it?"

"That's none of your business," I said more harshly than I intended.

"If you are not engaged, you are single, which means I still have a chance."

"You don't." I swallowed and felt like I was going in for the kill, but it had to be said. "Even if Timothy and I weren't together, I wouldn't be with you. I don't love you, not like that."

He dropped his head as if a great weight, like a barbell, had been dropped on the base of his neck.

"I," my voice cracked. "I don't want this to have an impact on how far you've come. I do care about you. I'm so proud, and I still think Faith Beyond Bars is a wonderful idea. I'll help you any way I can." I took a breath. "I must tell you a secret."

He looked up, but the anguish I saw there was almost more than I could bear. It was the face of rejection. The same look I saw on Aaron's face when Becky turned him away, the same look I saw in the mirror when my father turned me away.

I took a shuddered breath. "You're brave. You walked away from a life you were used to and started a new one. You've changed, Curt. I see it, Chief Rose sees it, and everyone sees it. That kind of change takes bravery. I don't know if I could have done it. I doubt I could have done it."

"You would have," he whispered.

I shook my head.

"I did it because of you."

I closed my eyes, and the weight of his words settled onto my chest. "Don't say that."

"Why not? It's the truth."

I gripped the edge of my blanket in my hand. "Honesty is good. Do you accept my honesty back?"

"Yes, but I don't have to like it. Would you like some more water?"

I nodded and accepted the cup from his hand.

CHAPTER THIRTY-FOUR

Dizziness swirled in my head as Timothy pushed my wheelchair through the hospital. As he turned the chair around to back out of the hospital sliding glass doors, I was grateful for the chair. Another wave of nausea swept over me. Timothy helped me into his blue Ford pickup truck waiting at the curb.

Mabel whimpered as I settled into the seat and sniffed the back of my head.

I held up my hand so she could smell it. "I'm fine, Mabel. Don't worry."

She whimpered again.

Through the windshield, I watched as Timothy returned the wheelchair. He moved stiffly, and I sensed the stirring of pent up emotion bubbled just below his skin. I bit my lip.

Quickly, I scanned the parking lot for Curt's green truck. It wasn't there. At least one complication was out of the picture.

Timothy climbed into the truck and slammed the door.

Okay, he was upset. Timothy was not the door slamming sort.

"Timothy, I—"

"I almost lost you. Again." His voice was filled with anguish.

"Dr. Bryant said daffodil poisoning isn't fatal."

Timothy slapped the steering wheel so hard it should have split in two. "I don't care what the doctor said."

I shrank back into the passenger side door. I'd never seen Timothy so angry, so angry at me, before. Through the windshield, I saw a hospital worker sitting on a stone bench outside of the hospital doors. He watched us intently as if considering some type of action to save the damsel in distress. *It's not what you think.*

Timothy stared straight ahead. "You can't keep doing this to me. It's going to kill me. I want you to stop."

"I can't." I swallowed. "You need to take me back to the inn."

His neck snapped in my direction.

"Pearl is there by herself. She could be in danger. I need to take care of her."

"We can go collect her and she can stay at your house until she leaves, but you are not staying at the inn. I forbid it." He started the truck and pulled away from the curb. I felt the hospital worker's eyes on my back as the pickup joined the traffic on Coshocton Avenue.

I bristled. Now I was mad. "You *forbid* it."

"And I don't want you around Curt any more either."

I straightened. "Curt had nothing to do with this. He happened to be there when I was sick. He's not responsible for what happened."

"He's responsible for enough. You know that as well as I do."

"He deserves a second chance."

"Not with you he doesn't. Stay away from him."

I sat up straighter in my seat. "Timothy, I'm not an Amish woman nor will I ever be one. You can't order me around. I want a partner, not a boss for a husband. You'd better figure that out now, or this relationship is going nowhere."

He clenched the steering wheel. The muscles on his arms tightened. The side of his jaw clenched and un-clenched. Just as quickly as the anger overcame him, it was gone. His shoulders sagged and the veins on his fore-arms deflated like the air out of a tire. "I don't want to be your boss, and I love you because you're strong, brilliant, and independent. I don't want to change you or make you to be any other way than what you are. But I do want to protect you, and I'm failing at that. I'm never there when you need me." The smallest of tears gathered in the corner of his eye and slid to his cheekbone.

I reached over and wiped the tear from his cheek. The tear hung from my finger until it fell to the upholstery-covered seat. "I love you for wanting to be the one to protect me, but you can't be there every second. I'll admit I seem to find more trouble than most girlfriends—"

The corner of his mouth tilted up in a wry smile. "You can say that again."

"But you will have to trust me to take care of myself. You know I will come to you when I need help, don't you?"

"I do. The problem is you don't always recognize that you do until it is too late."

We drove in silence the rest of the way to the inn. Timothy thought Pearl would be willing to leave the inn, but I wasn't so sure. Pearl was afraid and for good reason. If she felt she was safest in her own room in the Dutch Inn, there was no way we would be able to convince her to go anywhere else.

The pickup rolled into the circular drive of the Dutch Inn. Timothy parked in the empty spot by my Beetle. Ephraim stood in the middle of Jane's garden, hosing down the flowers. Gross.

Timothy unbuckled my seatbelt and pulled me toward him as if I were a small child. He murmured into my hair, "I'm sorry. I want to kiss you, but I'm afraid you are too sick for it."

I chuckled into his chest. "You can kiss me if you would like. I brushed my teeth at the hospital."

He barked a laugh and then kissed me.

As he kissed me, I couldn't help but be reminded of that last kiss I had received from Curt and wondered how I would tell Timothy about it without upsetting him again. I placed a hand to his smooth cheek and decided that was a conversation for another day.

An hour later, Timothy continued to try to convince Pearl to leave the inn. Pearl wasn't going anywhere. Timothy and I sat with her at a tiny table in one corner of the lounge. Duke and Jimbo played a game of chess on the other side of the room, and in the middle of the room, Bitty, Bobbi Jo, and Raellen compared quilting kits they purchased at a quilt shop in Charm.

Pearl wrung her hands. "I can't leave here. The room Jane gave me is very nice. It's only for two more nights. My cousin's body will be released Wednesday. I've made arrangements to fly home with it." She choked on her words.

I reached across the tiny round table and squeezed her hand. "Then I will stay here too."

Pearl smiled. "Thank you, Chloe. You've been too kind to me, and it's so nice of you to offer your home to me. I'll be much more comfortable here at the inn."

"I think this is a bad idea, but I'll stay too if this is what you want to do," Timothy said. After my "you're not the boss of me" speech, he treaded lightly.

Pearl beamed at him. "Thank you. You two are the perfect couple."

She wouldn't think that if she had been in Timothy's pickup an hour ago.

Pearl struggled to her feet. "I think I will go to bed."

Timothy jumped up to help her.

My cell phone on the table read eight ten in the evening. Outside the light was dimming over the garden with the setting sun.

"Did you eat anything?" Timothy asked Pearl. "I'm sure there's something in the kitchen we could find for you to have."

"I have some crackers in my room," Pearl said. "Those will be fine. I haven't felt much like eating lately."

That I could understand. Food. Ugh. I wondered if I would ever be able to think about food again without wanting to toss my cookies.

"Thank you again," she said and shuffled from the lounge.

Timothy sat back down. "I think you should go to bed now too. It's been a long day, and you're still not feeling well."

I opened my mouth to protest.

"Don't deny it. You're as green as a frog."

I'm sure that looks very holiday festive with my red hair.

I picked my phone up from the table. "Okay, but I'm going to bed because I want to, not because you told me to."

He smiled. "I'm okay with that."

In my room, I'd just changed into my pajamas when the room door burst open, and I literally fell off the bed. "Surprise!" Becky bounced into the room and leaned over me. "Chloe, are you okay?"

"I'll be fine after I shove my heart back behind my sternum."

She tucked her blonde hair behind her ear. "Maybe I should have knocked?"

"That would have been nice," I muttered.

She helped me off of the floor. "You aren't hurt, are you?"

I rubbed my elbow. "Not really."

"Good." She dropped her extra-large overnight bag on the floor.

"What are you doing here?" I sat crossed legged on the bed and set my iPad to the side. "And how did you get inside my room?"

"Jane gave me an extra key for the room." She dangled the key in the air. "And Timothy called me. You don't think he'd let you sleep alone when you had been poisoned. You need to tell me all about that, by the way. I want all the details."

"Trust me, you don't. Most of them are beyond disgusting."

She hopped onto the other twin bed. "Hmmm, never mind. Maybe I don't want to know."

I moved my iPad to the nightstand. "Timothy really didn't have to call you. I'm fine, and he's sleeping on the first floor in this inn too."

"You know my brother. He's protective."

Like a mama tiger.

It was dark outside. "How did you get over here so late?"

"Danny gave me a lift." She beamed. "We'll have a sleepover."

I laughed. "Becky, we live in the same house. I'm not sure that qualifies us as sleepover material."

She hopped off the bed. "I'm putting on my PJs. I just bought some new ones at the Polaris mall last week. They are pink silk with tiny little pies and cookies on them. They're so cute."

I bit my lip to stop myself from telling her she should be saving her money for school—whatever school that might be—not spending it on silk pajamas with baked goods printed them on them. She needed to make her own decisions and choose her own path. Becky didn't like me telling her what to do, as much as I didn't like Timothy telling me what to do. I tried to remember that. She left the Amish so that she could make her own decisions. I had to let her do that.

Becky scooped up her bag and went into the bathroom. "And maybe you can tell me more about the Alex Tate guy."

Oh boy.

"I don't know much about him," I admitted when Becky came out of the bathroom.

She bounced onto her bed. "You don't think he has anything to do with those people who died, do you?"

I shook my head.

"Then who do you think did?"

I leaned back against the headboard. "I don't know."

"What about the deacon?"

"He does have a motive. He doesn't want more bus tours in the district, and the bishop said there wouldn't be any more after what happened. If that was the end the deacon was trying to achieve, he got it."

"Who else?"

"There's the bus driver, Hudson."

Becky wrinkled her nose.

I laughed. "He's not the nicest guy, but Dudley was giving him money to keep quiet about Dudley's gambling business. He won't get that money anymore now that Dudley is dead. And dislikable as he is, I don't see any reason for him to want to hurt Ruby. Along with the gambling, Earl Kepler is a suspect. He's a recovering gambling addict. Dudley may have pushed him too far to try to get him to relapse."

She hugged a pillow to her chest. "So you think Dudley was the intended victim? Not Ruby?"

"I think that's much more likely, but I can't be certain, at least not yet." I placed a hand to my forehead. The headache I had in the hospital returned with a vengeance.

"Chloe, are you okay?"

"I'm fine. I think I just need some rest."

"Of course, you do," Becky said, jumping off of the bed to turn out the overhead light. "Good night."

I heard her even breathing in a matter of seconds. I stared at the ceiling. How I envied her ability to fall asleep so easily.

I woke up in the middle of the night with a start. *What time was it? Where was I?* I hadn't pulled the curtain closed over the French door leading to the balcony, and moonlight filled the small room and slashed across my pillow. Maybe that's what had woken me up. Moonlight hit Becky directly in the face too, but she didn't stir. I climbed out of the bed, and the pine wood floor felt like an iced over pond under my bare feet. I closed the curtain just enough so that the moonlight would not disturb Becky.

I grimaced as my gut churned. I wondered if a cup of tea would help. It would require a walk to the kitchen on the first floor. The Dutch Inn wasn't a coffeemaker/tea bags in the room kind of place. Jane said guests were welcome to the kitchen. I didn't think there would be any Amish cooks in there at this hour. I picked up my phone from nightstand. Two in the morning. I tucked it into the front pouch pocket of my hooded sweatshirt along with the room key.

Quietly as possible I put on a pair of socks and my tennis shoes. I didn't want to walk around the inn in my bare feet. As I straightened, another wave of dizziness overcame me.

Should I wake Becky? In the moonlight, her white-blonde hair fanned out on the pillow like an iridescent halo, making her even more beautiful. Aaron would faint dead away had he seen her like that. My heart ached for Timothy's best friend. He was a kind and cheerful—well, cheerful until Becky told him she didn't love him—man, and deserved happiness. I closed my eyes and whispered a prayer for both of them.

Glancing at Becky one last time, I slipped out the door and tripped over a body.

CHAPTER THIRTY-FIVE

S trong arms caught me before I hit the hall floor. "Chloe, are you okay?" Timothy's hissed whisper was on the edge of frantic.

I lay on top of him and rolled off. "What are you doing here?"

Timothy was fully dressed and lying prostrate across the threshold to my room. He sat up. "I couldn't sleep," he said defensively.

"You were guarding my door?" I asked.

Even in the dimmed light from the wall sconces, I could see Timothy's neck and cheeks turn red. "So what if I was."

"I thought you sent Becky to watch over me."

He snorted. "She's doing a great job since you're out here, and she's in there sound asleep. I'm glad I decided to stay here tonight."

"You were going to sleep on the floor all night."

"I wasn't sleeping," he muttered.

I tried to stifle a smile, but I couldn't. How could I resist the idea of my Mennonite prince standing guard over me while I slept? I took his hand and coaxed him to his feet. When he was standing, I intertwined my fingers with his. "Come on before we wake everyone up." I passed the elevator. "Let's take the stairs. I'm still feeling a little dizzy," I admitted.

His hold tightened on my hand. "I knew you should have stayed at the hospital."

"Were you planning to sleep across my threshold there too?"

"Probably," he admitted.

A grin crossed my face. Timothy caught my expression and relaxed. "You're not mad?"

"No." I kissed him on the cheek when we reached the first landing. "In fact, I think it might be the most adorable thing I've ever seen." I kissed him on the lips.

"Women are so confusing," he murmured against my lips.

"So I hear." I led him down to the first floor.

"What are you doing up anyway?" he asked.

"My stomach is still a little sore. I thought a cup of tea would help."

The grand staircase ended in the lobby. Except for the moonlight coming from the windows and the occasional wall sconce, the first floor was dark. The registration desk was quiet. We crossed in front of the desk into the hallway that led to the first floor guest rooms and the lounge. Of the rooms, the lounge was the best lit because it had floor to ceiling windows which allowed the moonlight to pour in.

A person lay on the floor in front of the sofa. "Oh no," I gasped. I dropped Timothy's hand and fell to my knees next to the person.

Suddenly, the room was awash with glaring yellow light as Timothy hit the light switch.

"Pearl? Pearl?" She was on her side. I placed my head next to her mouth to listen for a breath. I heard it, but it was faint.

Her head lolled to the side. Blood coated my fingers as I pulled my hand away from her shoulder.

A bookend the shape of a horse's head sat on the buggy patterned carpet beside her. One corner of it was caked with blood and a strand of Pearl's crayon red hair.

"Timothy, call 911."

He was already on the phone with the dispatcher. "Yes, we are at the Dutch Inn in Appleseed Creek."

Cheetos was on the chess table and puffed up to twice his normal size. He was a fur pumpkin and hissed repeatedly.

Jimbo's large frame filled the entryway to the lounge. "What's all the racket out here? Don't you know people are trying to sleep? It's two thirty in the morning." He spotted me kneeling next to Pearl. "What did you do to her?"

"Nothing," I snapped.

Timothy stuck his phone back into the hip pocket of his jeans. "The ambulance is on its way."

Jimbo shook a finger at Timothy. "You did this to her."

More sleepy faces appeared behind Jimbo's in the doorway. Raellen had her hair up in curlers with a flowered bedcap covering it.

I didn't move from my spot next to Pearl, and I didn't try to move her. Timothy was on the phone again. "Are you calling Chief Rose?" I asked.

He nodded.

Jane had a robe tightly wrapped around her waist, and she pushed through the crowd of tourist gathered in the lounge doorway. Ivy followed after her, but there was no sign of Ephraim. The girl gasped when she saw the body, but then her eyes landed on Cheetos. She ran to the cat and scooped him up in a cloud of orange fur.

Her mother said something to the girl. Squeezing her eyes closed, she fled the room with her cat under her arm.

"Chloe, what happened?" Jane asked in English. A hand flew to Jane's face, when she saw the bookend. "Oh no, do you think she tripped and hit her head on the bookend. I knew I should have gotten rid of those. Any time a child stays at the inn, I'm certain he will drop it onto his foot."

"Jane, she did not trip and hit her head on the bookend. Her wound is on the back of her head."

"Oh. *Oh!*" She said as she realized what I meant. She half turned and looked at the Blue Suede Tour group and paled. "What can I do?"

"Clear the guests out of the way, so that the police and EMTs can get through," Timothy said.

Jane nodded with a determined look and spun around. "Everyone, please go back to your rooms. The emergency crew will need space to work."

"We aren't going anywhere. Pearl was a member of our group, we have a right to find out what happened to her," Gertie said. Despite the late hour, she was wide awake.

A siren wailed. A second later, the musical doorbell sounded, followed by a Bam, bam, bam, on the door itself.

"Move!" Timothy cried.

To my relief, the crowd backed off and made way for the EMTs. "Please move aside, miss," an EMT said.

I scrambled to my feet.

"Don't touch the bookend," one EMT told the other. "Chief Rose will want to see that."

As if saying her name beckoned her, the petite Appleseed Creek chief of police strode into the room. Officer Nottingham, who looked like he just rode in on a big wave, was a few paces behind her. The chief's purple-lined eyes took in everything in the room. I marveled that she had time to apply eyeliner at this hour and arrive at the scene so quickly. *Did she sleep in it?*

Her eyes stopped at me and then fell to Pearl. A muscle twitched in her cheek. "Nottingham, start taking pictures of the weapon but don't move it."

The surfer turned small town officer jumped into action with his SLR camera.

I felt Timothy's hand on my waist, guiding me out of the way.

"Is she alive?" Chief Rose asked the closest EMT.

He gave her a curt nod in return. "Yes, but the sooner we transport her to the hospital, the better the chance she'll stay that way."

A third EMT ran into the lounge with an orange flat board. Another braced her neck with a foam collar, being very careful of her head wound. Then three men oh-so-carefully rolled Pearl from her side onto her back on the board.

Why had I convinced her to stay in the Dutch Inn? She would have been safer at the motel in Mount Vernon even with Brock Buckley sulking around the halls. I started to shiver. My toes curled in fighting the cold. "This does prove something," I whispered as the EMTs carted Pearl away.

Timothy wrapped an arm around my shoulders. Even his comforting touch did not calm my shivering. "What?"

"The murderer is someone here in the inn."

The sirens started up again as the ambulance left the inn's grounds. Jane reentered the lounge. Now, she wore her apron over her robe.

When the sound of the sirens faded, Chief Rose said, "I want all the guests in the dining room, so that Officer

Nottingham and I can question them. Hopefully, someone heard or noticed something that can give us a clue to
who did this. This inn isn't that large. It's difficult for me
to imagine no one saw or heard anything."

"Humphrey." Chief Rose stood from her squat position. "Tell me what happened."

"I woke up still feeling a little queasy and thought a
cup of tea would make me feel a little better. I headed to
the kitchen to make one. I was shocked when I saw Pearl
on the floor."

"Did you hear any unusual noises during the night?"

I shook my head.

"Timothy, your room is on this floor. Did you hear anything unusual?"

"I was on the second floor all night."

She cocked an eyebrow. "Really?"

His jaw twitched. "I was in the hallway."

A slow smile crossed her face. "Guarding Humphrey's
room, I take it." She looked at the blood soaked into the
buggy-patterned carpet. "Chivalrous and apparently necessary. That could have been Humphrey with a dent in the
back of her skull."

I felt Timothy's entire body quake.

Click, click, click went Officer Nottingham's camera
shutter.

"I think that should be enough, Nottingham." The
chief stood.

He nodded and removed an evidence bag from his kit. With gloved hands he picked up the bookend and gently placed it inside of the plastic bag. He then removed tweezers from his kit and began to collect hair and minuscule pieces of lint from the carpet.

"This is my fault." Tears threatened to fall from my eyes, but I willed them back. "I shouldn't have told Pearl to come here."

"I'm to blame for this too, Humphrey. I wanted her back at the Dutch Inn where you could keep an eye on her." The chief's eyes were sunken in. "This case has been a screw up from the start. I've been too concerned with the tight timeframe of the bus leaving the state to think of the safety of all those involved. I will station Nottingham at the inn for the rest of the night," Chief Rose said.

"They leave Wednesday—I guess that's tomorrow now—and we're no closer to knowing who killed Dudley or Ruby or poisoned me or hit Pearl," I said.

"I am well aware of that." A muscle in her jaw flexed. "What's on the agenda for the bus tour today?"

"To tour the Amish farms in the district, which were missed on Saturday."

"Good. I'm glad you'll be in town. That will make it easier."

"You want the tour to continue?" I asked.

"Yes. It'll keep all the suspects occupied and out of trouble."

"Chloe shouldn't be doing this anymore. It's too dangerous," Timothy said. "Two people have been killed, a third savagely attacked. She was poisoned. It's gone too far."

"That's really up to Humphrey, isn't it?" She turned to me. "What do you say? Are you in?"

Behind me, Timothy's body tensed. I knew the answer he wanted me to say, but the image of Pearl bleeding on the buggy carpet was more powerful. "I'm in."

Timothy made a tiny squeaking sound that only I could hear, but he didn't argue.

The chief nodded. "That's my girl."

I glared at her condescending tone. "Don't make me regret it already."

The chief laughed. "I like your attitude, Humphrey. The truth is you and I aren't all that different."

No, we weren't.

"Now, you might want to go wash that blood off of your hands."

I looked down at my bloody hands, and I felt like I had been poisoned again.

CHAPTER THIRTY-SIX

Becky flew down the inn's staircase in her new silk pajamas and bare feet. "Chloe, what's going on? Why didn't you wake me up? I woke up and found you gone from the room. I thought something happened!" She threw her arms around me.

I hugged her. "Something did happen. Didn't you hear the sirens?" I asked.

She jerked back. "Sirens? What sirens?"

I shook my head. Becky could sleep through anything.

We stood in the tiny lobby, and the Blue Suede Tour guests gathered around us in their pajamas and bathrobes. They were all talking a mile a minute. Jane had no success in convincing them to move to the dining room.

Timothy put two fingers in his mouth and released a piercing whistle.

The room fell silent.

"I didn't know you could do that," I whispered.

He winked at me. "I have all kinds of tricks you don't know about."

Jane, red-faced, cleared her throat. "Thank you, Timothy. Everyone, please move to the dining room." She pointed to the right. "Go this way through the kitchen. The police need to question all of us."

The room erupted into complaints and protests again. Chief Rose poked her head out of the lounge. "Move it, people, or I load you into the bus and take you to the police station for questioning. You will not be happy there. I've been told my chairs are particularly uncomfortable."

That got them shuffling toward the back entrance to the kitchen. Becky and Timothy followed at the rear of the group to make sure no one wandered back to his or her room.

Across the lobby, Ivy, holding Cheetos against her chest, and Ephraim watched the English tourists. Tears rolled down Ivy's face and into her cat's ruff. Even in the commotion, I heard the cat's motorboat purr. Ephraim placed a hand on his sister's shoulder.

Melinda placed a hand on my arm. "Don't blame yourself over this."

I hadn't known she was there and jumped slightly at her touch. "Thank you, Melinda." "Gertie is somewhere in that group, I better find her before she starts a mutiny."

I nodded.

Becky and I dragged ourselves to our room at five. That's when the chief and Officer Nottingham had finished conducting their interviews. I had asked the chief if she had learned anything particularly helpful, but she simply shook her head no.

Timothy followed us to our room. When I opened the door, Becky bounced onto her bed and under the covers in one motion. She was asleep before her head hit the pillow. I wished sleep came that easily to me. As tired as I was, I would be tossing and turning until it was time to get up for the day. There were too many thoughts about the investigations and concerns about Pearl flying through my head to truly rest. Chief Rose had called the hospital before she left, so she could give me an update. Pearl was still alive but unconscious and in intensive care. The doctors worried about permanent brain damage because of her advanced age.

I closed the door behind me in the hallway so I could talk to Timothy without waking Becky. Although I didn't think a foghorn would wake her at that point.

Timothy sat on the carpet.

"Timothy, you're exhausted. You're not spending the rest of the night sitting outside of my door." I gave him my hand and pulled him to standing. His blue eyes were bloodshot, dark circles gathered under his pale lower lashes. I wished I could wipe the dark circles away.

His mouth quirked up in the corners. "Is that a direct order?"

My heart melted. "Yes."

"Hmm... So you can tell me what to do, but I can't tell you what to do. Is that how it works?"

I wrapped my arms around his waist. "That's exactly how it works."

"And what if I don't agree to this arrangement?"

"You don't have any choice."

I watched him until he disappeared down the staircase.

Becky snored softly as I stepped into the room. I climbed into the bed and lay my head on the pillow, but just as I knew I would be, I was wide awake for the rest of the night.

When I stepped out of my room a few hours later, Timothy was back at his post.

Because of the late night, I pushed the bus departing time back to noon. For once, no one protested. As consolation, Jane and Ivy had made a lovely brunch for everyone in the dining room.

After my narcissus cocktail, the thought of food made me want to bolt for the closest bathroom. I pulled my Beetle keys out of my jacket pocket as Becky came down the main stairs with her overnight bag.

"I can take Becky home," Timothy said.

I shook my head. "No. I don't mind. I have to get away from the smell of that food."

He smiled. "I can come with you."

"No. You spent the entire night sleeping on the floor in front of my door. The least you deserve is a decent meal. Stay and eat. You can keep Officer Nottingham company. I think he's starting to buckle under the relentless questions from the tourists."

"They are persistent," Timothy said.

Becky dropped her bag at my feet and yawned. "I don't think I have been this tired since I lived at home and had to get up at four every day to help *Mamm* in the kitchen." She stretched. "I'm happy to be working the lunch and dinner shifts tonight."

I picked up her bag and nearly toppled over from the unexpected weight. "Becky, what do you have in here? Bricks?"

She thought for a moment. "Six pairs of shoes and four outfits, plus makeup and hair products. The basics."

"You created a monster," Timothy said with a smile.

"Don't blame me for this." I handed Becky her bag. "I should be back in half an hour."

Timothy frowned.

"I promise. I'm just going to drop her off, feed Gig, and come straight back."

"Okay." He hit a button on his watch. "I'm timing you."

Becky dozed in the front seat as I drove the few short miles to our rented house. I poked her in the arm. "Wake up, sleepyhead."

She muttered about five more minutes. She sounded like me. I was the one who hated mornings. Finally, I coaxed her out of the car.

A bouquet of red tulips sat on the cement step in front of our door. I froze.

"Oh look, flowers!" Becky dropped her bag in the middle of the yard, ran, and knelt next to the bouquet. "I love tulips. You love them too."

I made a face.

"Oh, right." She covered her mouth. "You got sick in the tulips yesterday." She plucked a florist's card from bouquet. "They're from Curt," Becky said. "Do you want me to read the note to you?"

"N—"

"Red, I'm sorry about yesterday. What I told you was the truth. Curt." She held the card between her thumb and index finger. "What does that mean? What did he tell you?"

"It's not important." I gave her a hand up.

"Is that weird he chose the flowers you got sick on? Someone needs to tell Curt that's poor etiquette."

I laughed, trying to cover my dismay over the flowers. "What do you know about etiquette?"

"They had a special about it on television a couple of months ago. I know what a fish fork is now. Do you?"

"Nope."

"Didn't think so."

Becky placed the flowers in the kitchen window while I fed Gigabyte and listened to his grievances about being abandoned for a night. As I left, the cat followed me all the way to the front door meowing and snarling. It was going to take more than a can of tuna to make up for this, and he wanted me to know it.

The bus wasn't leaving the inn for another two hours, and I told Timothy I'd drop off Becky and return to the inn, but what about Pearl?

I sent him a text before I headed to the county hospital.

CHAPTER THIRTY-SEVEN

Inside the hospital, I stepped up to the receptionist. "I'm here to see Pearl Kennerwell."

She clicked on her keyboard. "She's in room two eleven."

I thanked her and headed for the elevator. As soon as I exited the elevator, I saw Officer Riley standing outside of a room to the right. He folded his arms when he saw me coming. "The chief's in there."

"Can I go in?" I asked.

He looped his thumbs through his duty belt. "Nope."

"Come on, Riley, maybe I can help. Pearl's my friend. I helped Chief Rose talk to her before."

He grunted and opened the door just a crack. Through the narrow opening, I spotted the police chief sitting below an IV drip. The tubing from the drip stopped at the top of Pearl's thin frail hand. Pearl's pink nail polish was chipped. It was all I could see of her.

"What is it, Riley?" the chief asked.

"Humphrey is here, boss," her officer replied.

A sideways smile spread across the chief's face. "Send her in."

Officer Riley pushed the door in for me. After I cleared the threshold, he closed the door again. I pulled a second chair up close to the bed. Pearl's eyes were closed, her cheeks sunken in. Her complexion was the color of a cinderblock.

"Don't worry, Humphrey, she's still with us," the chief whispered.

I blinked at her.

"You looked like you were about to pass out." She eyed me. "You didn't stop for an Italian sausage on the way here, did you?"

I paled.

Chief Rose touched Pearl's arm. "Mrs. Kennerwell, Chloe is here to see you."

Her eyelids fluttered. "Chloe, it was so nice of you to come. You're such a dear, sweet girl. I hope my daughter is just like you."

"Daughter?" Chief Rose barked. "I thought you didn't have any children."

Pearl squeezed her eyes shut. A tear leaked out from her right eye. "I did once."

"Did she die?" The chief asked.

I elbowed the police chief in the side.

"Ouch!" She rubbed the spot on her ribcage.

"Let's talk about the more recent past. What happened last night? What were you doing in the lounge with the bookend?" Chief Rose asked.

The police chief didn't seem to realize she sounded like she was making accusation in the board game Clue. I scanned the tiny hospital room for Colonel Mustard.

"I've had trouble sleeping, and I got up to close the curtains. The moonlight was so bright." She smiled at me. "When I did, I saw your note slipped under the door."

My pulse quickened. "Note? What note?"

Her mouth drooped. "There was a note from you saying you couldn't sleep, and if I woke up, I should join you in the lounge for a cup of tea. It sounded like the perfect alternative to tossing and turning in bed all night. I went to the lounge but was surprised it was dark. Your note implied you'd already be there, but I thought maybe you ran up to your room for something. That's the last thing I remember thinking."

I bent closer to the bed. "Pearl, I promise you I didn't leave you a note."

A tear rolled down her cheek. "Someone tricked me."

"Do you still have the note?" the chief asked.

"I took it with me to the lounge because the handwriting was so nice. I wanted to compliment Chloe on it."

"That proves it wasn't Chloe. She has terrible handwriting. She's from the keyboarding generation," the police chief said.

"Oh, that's a shame. It was very pretty." Pearl moved her hand and flinched as the IV pulled at her skin.

The radio at the police chief's waist crackled.

Chief Rose stood. "We didn't see any evidence of a note near where you fell. I suspect whoever attacked you took it with him or her, but I will have my officers search the inn's lounge again to be certain. I've got a callout, so I have to go." She sidestepped my chair to the door.

Pearl's eyes slid closed again.

Chief Rose opened the door. "You coming, Humphrey?"

I folded my hand on my lap. "I'll stay here a little while longer and visit with Pearl."

She nodded. "Remember what to do if you learn anything significant."

"I do."

She left the room.

"Pearl?" I touched her thumb. "You said before that you and Ruby were alone, that neither of you had children, but now, you mention a daughter. Can you tell me about your daughter?"

Her eyes slowly opened. "Remember when I told you Ruby made all the hard decisions for me. That was the hardest of all."

"What do you mean?"

"It was the nineteen fifties, and I was nineteen and pregnant." She looked out the window, which faced a brick wall. "I wasn't married. In my time, having a child out of wedlock could ruin a girl. My boyfriend didn't want anything to do with me or the child. He told me to get rid of the baby." She shuddered. "Ruby was the only other person I told. We were always close, more like sisters than cousins. She took charge over the situation just like I knew she would. Somehow she convinced both sets of our parents we were accepted to a ladies refinement school in Texas. Our parents gave us money to go because they thought we would return to Mississippi fine, cultured ladies and be able to snatch up rich husbands.

"Instead of going to the school, we went to a little town outside of Austin. Ruby found a job as a waitress, and I stayed in the tiny apartment we rented until the baby was born. It was the worst time in my life. Ruby delivered the baby, a girl. We agreed before the child was born I would give her up for adoption. Ruby found an orphanage in Austin that would take her." She cleared her throat.

"When it came time to sign the release papers to give the baby up, I couldn't do it. I was too weak, but Ruby knew it was the right thing to do. I had to do it if I ever wanted the chance of finding a good husband. It was the right thing to do for the baby too. What kind of life would I give her on my own? Because I couldn't do it, Ruby signed her name on the papers and claimed the baby was hers to give up."

My fingers curled around her thumb. "No wonder you were so close to her."

She turned her face back to me. "She was so strong. She should be the one still here. I don't deserve to be. I'm the weak one."

The door opened and Dr. Bryant strolled inside. "Chloe," he said with surprise. "I thought I told you I didn't want to see you around here anymore."

"I'm not a patient. Just visiting a friend."

He chuckled. "I suppose that makes it all right. How are you feeling, Mrs. Kennerwell?"

"Poorly," she said.

He nodded as his finger zoomed around his iPad's screen. "You had a nasty bump on your head, but I'm happy to tell you there is no sign of concussion. That's a miracle considering your age and the heft of the blunt object. You should be released later today."

"Will I be able to fly home tomorrow?" she asked.

"Certainly," he said.

"Thank you, Doctor." She closed her eyes.

He smiled and pointed his iPad at me. "Remember, Chloe, I don't want to have you as a patient again."

"I remember."

He left the room.

"Pearl, I'm going to have to leave for the inn. It's that last day of the tour here in Ohio."

"I understand," she murmured with her eyes closed.

I released her hand. "Thank you for telling me about Ruby and your daughter."

Her eyes fluttered opened. "You're the first person I've told that story to in a very long time. I hope my daughter is like you."

Pearl's words brought tears to my eyes. For too many years, I was the daughter my father did not want. That was changing, but rejection does not heal overnight. To hear Pearl say she wished her daughter was like *me* meant more to me than she would ever know. "What was her name?"

"I never picked one. I couldn't bear to." She closed eyes.

I kissed her on the top of her head, careful to avoid the bandage, and left the hospital.

CHAPTER THIRTY-EIGHT

I n front of the Dutch Inn, Timothy helped the passengers onto the bus. When the last person climbed on, he said, "I think we should have a new rule."

I folded the day's itinerary and stuck it into the back pocket of my jeans. "What's that?"

"When there is a crazed killer on the loose, text messages are not sufficient means of communication." He gave me a pointed look.

"I'm sorry, but the idea to visit Pearl didn't strike me until after I dropped Becky off. If I drove all the way back here first, there wouldn't have been time to see her before the bus left."

He folded his arms. "You could have called."

"You would have argued against my idea," I said.

"I'm going with you today. You didn't think I would let you go with this group again without me, did you?"

"Nope," I said. I was glad for the company.

"Where are we going first?" Timothy asked.

"It's the Sutter farm." I made a face.

"The deacon won't say anything to you in front the tourists," Timothy said.

I gave him an Are-You-Kidding-Me look. The deacon had never been shy about sharing his opinion about the Troyers or me before, so how would a group from Mississippi stop him?

"Stop standing around talking, and get on the bus," Hudson bellowed.

I gripped the railing and pulled myself up the first large step. "Timothy's coming too." Hudson rubbed his bald head. "You need more muscle?"

Officer Nottingham was already aboard under Chief Rose's orders.

"Yep," I replied.

"Whatever," Hudson said. "Just get on the bus. The sooner this day is over the better."

I couldn't agree more.

On the drive to the Sutters, we passed the Troyer farm. A white van from the State Department of Health idled in the Troyer's driveway. Timothy and I leaned close to the window for a better look. It was yet another time I wished the Troyers had a phone in their farmhouse so that we could call them and ask what was going on. That answer would have to wait until the tour ended for the day.

The Sutter farm was three miles down the road past the Lambright farm where Ruth's closest friend Anna lived. The Sutters ran a small vegetable farm. Most of the deacon's income came from the storefronts he rented to Amish businesses in town.

The deacon, Aaron, and a half dozen other Amish men, including Bishop Hooley, waited for the bus as it rolled up the Sutters' long driveway. Aaron, the men, and the bishop waved. The deacon did not.

"What a beautiful farm," Bitty said.

Charles snapped photographs.

Bitty poked her husband in the ribs. "Charles, put the camera away. You don't want to offend our hosts, do you?"

Charles replaced his camera in its case with an all-suffering sigh.

I needed to see those pictures.

Outside the bus, the guests milled around the bus, and Deacon Sutter flashed a phony smile at the group. If he was surprised to see Officer Nottingham and Timothy with us, he did not show it. "*Wilkim.* We're so happy you are here with us today. We will begin with a short demonstration on thrashing wheat."

"Oh, I always wondered how flour is made," Bobbi Jo said. "Won't this be exciting, Jimbo?"

The large elderly man narrowed his eyes. "Will there be free samples of Amish bread too?"

The deacon held his gaze. "*Nee*. After what happened a few days ago, the district decided that we would not be able to give you any food from any of our farms. It is for your own safety."

Jimbo's mouth fell open. "So we're going to starve?"

"Jimbo," I interrupted. "There will be plenty to eat back at the inn."

He grunted.

Finally, the deacon led the group to the barn. I fell to the back of the pack with Bitty and Charles. "Charles, can I see your camera?" I asked.

He gripped his camera bag tightly in his hand and stopped walking. "Why? I'm not taking any photographs. I can't leave it on the bus where it could walk off. It's an expensive piece of equipment."

"I know that," I said quickly. "I would like to look at the photographs you've taken, especially those from Saturday morning."

Bitty placed her hand over her heart. "Do you think Charles may have taken a picture of whoever hurt Ruby and Dudley?"

I shrugged. "It's worth a look."

Charles's jowls shook. "You can take a peek, but Chief Rose already looked through my pictures and made copies of every photo I took on Saturday. She didn't seem to think they were of much help."

Here I was thinking I was a detecting genius and the police chief was two steps ahead of me. "Can I still have a look? Maybe I will pick up on something she didn't."

He nodded. "All right." He handed me the camera bag. "Do you know how to use it?"

"I do."

"Because if you break it, you buy it. Come on, Bitty, I don't want to miss the wheat."

They continued on their way to the barn. I searched the farm for a shady spot where I could view the photographs on the camera's screen without glare. A toolshed with a small porch in front was a few yards from the barn. I perched on the cement step and opened the camera case.

I whistled. It was the first time I had been able to see Charles' camera up close. It was a Nikon with three interchangeable lenses, easily worth two grand. Carefully, I removed the camera from the case because I knew Charles would hold me to "you break it, you buy it."

I switched it on and changed the setting to view pictures. I groaned. There were over four thousand photos stored on the camera. *This is going to take forever.*

I scrolled back to the beginning of Saturday. It started with images of the group climbing on the bus at the Dutch Inn. It was a shocking to see Dudley and Ruby among those pictured. Ruby smiled brightly at the camera as she stood next to Pearl. Dudley was in the background of a second photograph, making notes on a clipboard. I wondered if those notes were about the tour or about his side gambling business. The camera captured Earl in the same picture. In the image he anxiously watched Dudley. I knew now he was trying to deal with his gambling addiction, but I wondered what Chief Rose thought when she saw the image the first time.

The next fifty frames were shots of the countryside from the bus. I paid closer attention when I recognized the Troyers' farm. Five shots of Naomi and Thomas playing with Mabel. Because of the angle, I could tell Charles was above the children when he took these. He must have still been on the bus. More pictures of buggies, cows, the tourists exploring the farm. There were some Amish in the shots, but mostly in the background. It appeared Charles at least tried to be respectful of the culture's aversion to cameras.

Surprisingly, there were only three interior shots of the Troyer dairy barn. The third shot showed a scowling Mr. Troyer. I was sure he told Charles to put his camera away. I concentrated on the two other pictures. The first was of Mr. Troyer milking the cow. Several of the tourists were in the picture, including Bobbi Jo, Jimbo, Fred, and Nadine. The second shot was of the snack table. Clearly when he took the picture it was before anything happened. The muffins sat in the baskets, and the small plastic cups of milk waited in straight, symmetrical lines. Seeing those milk cups, I couldn't help but wonder if Ruby and Dudley had been poisoned by chance. There was nothing to indicate that one cup was different from the next.

I sighed. If Chief Rose didn't find anything of interest, why did I think I would?

I turned off the camera and repacked it. *Why did I feel like I was back to square one?*

Charles waited for me outside of the barn. I handed over his camera. "You were careful with it, weren't you? You didn't drop it?"

"I was careful," I reassured him. "You have some great pictures there, Charles. You have a great eye."

His jowls wiggled. "Oh, well, I dabble is all." He smiled.

Bitty poked her head out of the barn. "Charles, you're missing the wheat smacking."

Wheat smacking?

Charles and I stepped into the dim barn with the rest of the bus passengers.

Aaron's brother-in-law Amos stood in the middle of the room, holding shafts of wheat bound together by twine. A white sheet lay on the barn's dirt floor. "We do almost all of our threshing with a steam-powered thresher out in the field, but for this demonstration, we'll show you how it is done by hand." Amos hit the wheat over and over again onto the sheet, and the wheat fell away from the shaft.

Across the barn, I studied Aaron's face as he watched his brother-in-law. His lips compressed into a thin line. How much did he wish he was the one giving the demonstration? How much did he wish he wasn't confined to his wheelchair and could do the heavy labor expected of an Amish man?

Aaron caught me staring. His jaw twitched, and he turned away.

Amos collected the wheat from the ground and passed around a handful of the freshly threshed wheat. "At this point," Amos said, "We take it to the local mill to be ground into flour, but we have a small hand crank mill to show you as well." He walked over to a table with the small metal mill clamped to it. A cylinder comprised the third of the mill. He dropped the grain into the cylinder and began to crank. A light tan-colored flour fell into a waiting bowl on the table. The tourists asked dozens of questions. The stop at the Sutter farm went better than I ever suspected it would. I felt myself relax against the barn's door frame.

I let my guard down a moment too soon. A shadow passed over my shoulder, blocking the light from the doorway. I turned and found myself face to face with the deacon. I took a big step back into the barn.

"Deacon." I nodded. The bishop stood a few paces behind the deacon. "Bishop Hooley," I added.

The bishop gave me a half smile. "T-thank you again for what you have done to keep the tour going."

I smiled. "You're welcome." I glanced at the deacon. "Do you still plan to cancel any other tours coming into the district?"

He nodded. "I have realized my error in bringing tourists into our community."

With the deacon's help, I thought.

"I c-can't say that I will be sorry to see them go." The bishop thanked me again and joined the English tourists in the barn.

The deacon did not join him. Instead Deacon Sutter took a step closer to me. "Whatever the bishop may say, you are still unwelcome in our district."

I stared him in the eye. "Duly noted."

"*Daed*, don't you want to show the guests the drying barn next?" Aaron asked from behind me inside the barn.

"*Ya*," the deacon said but didn't take his eyes off of me.

"You had better tell them as soon as Amos is finished or they might wander off."

The deacon nodded and pushed his way into the barn.

"Thanks," I said to Aaron.

"Don't mention it." He rolled down the slight ramp onto the lawn. "I saw you give one of the *Englischers* his camera back. I hope you weren't taking photographs of our farm. That's not the way to get on my *daed*'s good side."

"I wasn't taking photographs. I was looking at photographs Charles took on Saturday to see if he caught something with his camera, which may hint to what happened to those people."

Over the Southern-twanged chatter of the travelers, the deacon said, "We will go to the drying barn next. That's where we hang our fruits and vegetables to be dried for the winter. Please follow Amos out the back door."

Aaron rolled backwards onto the ramp. "His can't be the only camera on the trip. Maybe someone else snapped an incriminating picture."

True. But hadn't Chief Rose told Officer Riley to check all the tourists' cameras for clues? It was worth a shot. I was running out of ideas.

"Aaron, you are a genius." I leaned over and hugged him.

He grinned, and I saw some of the old Aaron sparkle back. Just as quickly, his face grew somber again. "I wish Becky thought that too."

Timothy appeared in the barn door. "Hey, Aaron."

They did a complicated guy handshake.

I arched an eyebrow. "Is a fist pump part of the Amish repertoire?"

Aaron laughed. "Danny taught it to us."

"I'm glad to see you out here with Chloe, buddy." He met my eyes. "You've been gone for a while. I was starting to worry."

Aaron sat straighter in his chair. "Nothing to worry about. I've been keeping an eye on her, but Timothy, I have to tell you, she is a handful."

"Don't I know it," Timothy mumbled.

"Funny," I muttered. "I'm relieved the stop here has gone so well. I've been dreading this one the most. No offense, Aaron."

He smiled. "Where are you off to next?"

"The Zuggs' sheep farm and then a fruit farm," I said.

Timothy gave a sigh of relief. "Two more stops, and then the tour is over."

Timothy was right. The next morning, the group would move on to Indiana where they would meet their new permanent tour guide. Their troubles in Ohio would be forgotten, and someone would get away with murder.

CHAPTER THIRTY-NINE

In the middle of the Zuggs' sheep barn, big and tough Jimbo patted the head on the newborn lamb in his lap. "He's so soft."

"Jimbo, who knew you were such a softy?" Fred said.

The lamb nestled closer to Jimbo's round tummy.

"We have two more baby lambs. Would anyone like to hold them?" Abby Zugg, a seventeen-year-old Amish girl, asked.

Two thirds of the group raised their hands. The Zugg Sheep Farm was an official hit. After watching Abby's mother card and spin wool, which she let the tourists try as well, Abby brought out more lambs for the tourists to pet.

The Mississippians cooed over the baby lambs like they were newborn infants.

All-the-while, I thought about who, other than Charles, had brought a camera on the trip. My eyes felt on Raellen and LeeAnne who patted yearlings' heads through the feed opening in their pen. The yearlings baaed. "Aren't they sweet?" LeeAnne asked in her soft Southern drawl.

I stared. I had heard her ask that question before about Naomi and Thomas because she wanted to take a picture of them in the Troyer barn.

Earl sat in a wooden folding chair next to Jimbo, and Abby settled the lamb with a bottle on Jimbo's lap. "You can feed her if you like."

He smiled as the lamb ate hungrily from the bottle.

I crossed the barn to the yearling pen and LeeAnne and Raellen. "LeeAnne, do you have your camera with you?"

She blinked. "My camera?"

"You had a digital camera with you on Saturday."

Her dark cheeks deepened just a shade. "I did, but I haven't carried it since that older Amish man told me not to take pictures. I'm respectful of the Amish."

"'Course you are, LeeAnne," Raellen said soothingly.

"You took photographs on Saturday though," I said.

"Yes." She frowned. "Do you want me to delete them?"

"No," I said too quickly. "No. I need to see those pictures. You may have captured what happened to Ruby and Dudley."

She straightened. "You think so?"

Raellen grabbed her friend's arm with her bejeweled hand. "LeeAnne, that would make you a hero."

A lamb bumped his head into the back of my knee. "What did the police say about them?"

She licked her lips. "The police?"

"Didn't the officer ask to see your camera on Saturday?"

LeeAnne's upper lip began to sweat. "He did."

My brow furrowed. "So what did he say?"

"Nothing. I may have fibbed and said I didn't have a camera." Her cheeks darkened.

"LeeAnne, how could you?" Raellen yelped.

"I couldn't give it to him, Raellen. My husband once gave the police his video camera after recording a traffic accident in Las Vegas. The police said they would give it back, but we never saw it again."

"The police didn't keep Charles' camera," I said.

"I know, but by that time, I realized that it was too late. I didn't want to look bad by admitting to the police that I lied." She twirled her wedding band around her finger.

So these were pictures even Chief Rose hadn't seen. *Don't get ahead of yourself, Chloe. This could lead to another dead end.* My excitement grew. "Where's your camera?"

She thought a moment. "Well, it's tucked away in my roll bag on the bus."

"Can I go look for it?"

"I suppose," LeeAnne said.

"We can go with you," Raellen said.

I shook my head. "No, no, don't trouble yourself. I can be there and back in two seconds. You enjoy petting the sheep."

"If you're sure…" Raellen trailed off.

"Absolutely," I said, giving her a bright smile.

"Okay. My bags are under the seat in front of me. Do you remember where we sat?"

"Yep," I said over my shoulder because I was already halfway out of the barn. Outside of the sheep barn, I fast-walked through the crowd and then broke into a run toward the bus. To my relief, Hudson wasn't hanging around the bus. I raced up the bus's steps. In the middle of the blue aisle I paused and visualized where LeeAnne and Raellen sat. The left side near the back. LeeAnne sat by the window.

I hurried down the aisle, sliding into the seat and tugging the roll bag out of its spot in one motion. I pulled out three cardigans, slippers, a knitting magazine, socks, granola bar, and a bottle of water. *These bags can hold a lot. Was the camera really in there?* I stuck my hand in again and hit a plastic rounded corner. My fingers curled around the camera, and I pulled it out.

With my heart thumping in my chest, I turned it on and scrolled back to Saturday. There were only ten pictures from that morning, and true to her word, those were the last photographs LeeAnne took on the trip. Two were of her and Raellen on the bus, three were of the scenery of the Troyer farm, but the rest were the inside of the Troyer barn during the milking presentation. I scrolled through the five pictures in disappointment. I didn't see anything right away that gave me a clue. Determined, I went through them again, slowly and deliberately. Mr. Troyer milking the cow. Jimbo and Bobbi Jo behind Mr. Troyer milking the cow. Fred and Nadine standing poised for a picture in front of the milk table. Then, I saw it in the background. Melinda handing Ruby a cup of milk.

Thoughts flashed through my head. Melinda was a science teacher, Melinda asking Gertie to go on this tour, and Gertie mentioning Melinda's love of plants. *But why?*

I heard a release of air, the sound the bus doors made when they closed, followed by a decisive click. My head snapped up.

Melinda stood in the middle of the aisle with a syringe in her hand. "Found what you were looking for, Chloe?"

I pushed all of LeeAnne's roll bag contents off of me and onto the floor and started clamoring to get out of the seat, but I was too slow. Melinda and her syringe were already at my seat.

She twirled the syringe in her hand. "What I have here is extract from Canadian yew. It's much more potent than what I gave Ruby and Dudley and will work more quickly."

Someone shook the bus's door and banged on it. Melinda was unconcerned and slid the needle back and forth along the bare underside of her arm.

My back was up against the metal siding of the bus's interior. There was nowhere to go. *Was the Blue Suede Tour Bus to be my blue coffin? This is so not my first choice.*

"Melinda, everyone can see what is going on. If you hurt me, you will never get away with it."

"This isn't for you. I'm done hurting others." She tipped the syringe point in the crook of her arm.

"No!" I cried. "Don't do it."

She hesitated.

I licked my lips. "Why did you kill them? You had no reason to—"

She glared and me. "No reason? Is that what you think? I had more reason than anyone needs. That woman destroyed me."

I blinked. "How?"

"She was my mother, and she abandoned me to an orphanage as a baby. When the orphanage closed, I moved from one family to the next. No one ever wanted to keep me. I'm a problem no one wanted. I will spare your delicate ears the horrors I faced in those homes, but if you imagine the worst then double it. Finally, I ran away when I was thirteen and made my own life. I *never* forgot what she did to me.

"When I put myself through college and became a teacher, I poured all my free time into research about who my birth mother was and where she was from. The orphanage kept poor records, and the ones that weren't destroyed were scattered." She rolled the needle in her fingers and the tip spun on the top of her skin. "Finally, I found her name. Ruby Carne later to be married and become Ruby Masters. I moved to Tupelo and watched and waited for my opportunity."

In my peripheral vision, I could see people moving around the bus. Someone shouted for Hudson. I thought it might be Timothy.

"When I discovered Ruby and her cousin signed up for this tour, I knew this was my chance. I was already Gertie's traveling companion. It was easy to convince her to join me on a quiet little trip to Amish Country."

She doesn't know Pearl is her mother. I swallowed. "And Dudley? What about him?"

"He was just an aside. I was there, although they didn't know it, when Earl confessed his gambling problem and the pressure Dudley put on him to gamble again to Ruby. Dudley's death would distract the police, or so I thought. It wasn't nearly distracting enough."

Outside I could hear Officer Nottingham and Timothy yelling at Hudson to unlock the bus.

"Why did you hit Pearl on the head then?"

She started to shake. "I wrote her that note pretending to be you because I wanted to talk her about my mother. I wanted to know more about her, but when Pearl came in the room, I realized what a stupid idea that was and that it would give me as the killer. I panicked and hit her with the bookend. I didn't plan it!"

She didn't plan it like she'd planned Ruby's death, I thought.

"Melinda, Ruby wasn't your mother," I said quietly.

Confusion and rage twisted her features. "What? What would you know about it?"

"Pearl told me the story just this morning. *She* was the one who had the baby. She couldn't bring herself to sign the release papers to give you up so Ruby did it for her. She claimed to be your birth mother and signed the papers."

"I don't believe you. I saw the document."

"All you have is a signature on a document. I heard it from Pearl herself who lived it."

Melinda clenched her jaw. "I can't even have the revenge that I earned?"

"You think you earned Ruby's death?" I whispered.

"Yes," she screeched. "Because I died a thousand times as a child."

I inched away from the wall. "Melinda, put the needle away. Maybe you and Pearl can salvage this somehow."

"After I murdered her cousin?" She began to shake. "No. I have to end this." Her tears fell freely. She tipped the needle straight down.

I froze.

The bus door opened and the sound of the agitated tourists and Amish outside filled the bus. At the bus steps, an argument broke out.

"I'm going in," Timothy said. "Chloe's in there!"

"Stay back, Troyer," Officer Nottingham snapped.

"Move! Let me through. I will talk to Melinda." Gertie ordered and she climbed onto the bus. "Stay back!" she shouted at whoever was behind her also trying to climb on. She stamped her cane in the aisle like a lion trainer keeping the wild beasts at bay. Then, the tiny centurion focused all of her attention of Melinda. "Melinda, what are you doing?" She set her cane in the first row of seats.

Melinda shook her head back and forth like a defiant child. The syringe made an indent crease on the inside of Melinda's elbow. She pressed down. "There is no reason to be here. I have no one. No family. No one has ever loved me." A bead of blood appeared where the needle broke her skin.

I was afraid to jump up and grab the syringe from her, afraid I would push the needle in deeper.

"I have no family." Tears coursed down Melinda's face.

Gertie stood in the middle of the aisle with her arms outstretched to Melinda. "What am I, Melinda? What am I?"

Melinda lifted her head.

Gertie held her arms aloft. "My child."

Melinda's body quaked. I forgot how to breathe. The syringe clattered to the aisle floor and skittered beneath a seat behind me as Melinda crumpled to the ground. Blood trickled down her arm, onto her wrist, and onto the blue aisle floor.

Gertie stepped forward and placed her hand on the crown of Melinda's head like a pastor blessing a child.

Officer Nottingham and Timothy bound onto the bus. "Chloe, are you okay?" Timothy cried.

I met his clear blue eyes that were so afraid. I nodded because speech was impossible.

EPILOGUE

Three weeks later, Timothy held my hand as we walked around an old abandoned farm. Paint peeled from the siding of the house and boards covered the windows where glass had once been. The lawn and grounds weren't much better. The grass came midway up my calf and groundhogs had made the landscape into a landmine just asking for a broken ankle.

Mabel barked as she ran around the lawn and stuck her nose in the groundhog holes, searching for the chubby rodents.

"What do you think of this farm?" Timothy watched me expectantly.

"It's lonely," I said.

He laughed. "Come on. Let me show you the house."

We picked our way through the groundhog burrows to the house. The front porch had seen better days. The floorboards were weather-warped, and one of the pillars hung loosely from its pilings. Its disrepair reminded me of the first home I'd lived in in Appleseed Creek. The porch had been even worse off than this. It was also where I'd met Timothy. Becky had called her brother over to fix our broken front door.

So much had changed since that day, I reminded myself as I thought of the events of the last month. The Blue Suede Tour bus was back in Tupelo by now, and for most of the travelers being on a tour bus with a killer would be a good story to entertain the grandchildren with. Over time, the event would move from frightening, to amusing, to a tall tale the grandchildren would doubt. At least that's what it would become for most of the tourists from Mississippi, not all. It was certainly not that for Pearl, who grieved for her cousin and wondered what to do with her new found daughter, nor would it be for Melinda, who was in the Knox County jail awaiting trial. Pearl went back to Mississippi because she could not contend with who Melinda was, but Melinda wasn't alone. Gertie remained in Appleseed Creek and had taken up long-term residence at the Dutch Inn. She taught Jane and Ivy how to make her famous fish jerky. Cheetos was a fan.

I chuckled.

Timothy smiled. "What is it?"

"I was just thinking about Gertie and her fish jerky." My face fell. "I hope they will all be all right."

"Me too," he said and punched a combination on an electronic padlock. The door swung in.

The outside of the barn was bad, but it had not prepared me for the inside. The wallpaper was torn, holes large enough for Mabel to jump through were in the walls, and there was the distinct odor of a cat who may have mistaken what must be the living room for a litter box. "What happened to this place?"

"It's been empty for nearly ten years. The owner died and had no children or family to leave it to. No one seemed interested in buying it. It's been looted a few times. The upstairs is worse. All the copper piping was ripped out. Even the toilet is gone."

I peered up the stairs. They didn't look like they would hold Gigabyte let alone a person. "Who did it?"

"Thugs who were trying to make a profit." His jaw twitched. "I wouldn't be surprised if Curt and Brock weren't some of the guys who did it."

I picked at the edge of a peeling piece of wallpaper. "I don't want to talk about Curt right now."

"You're right. That's not why we are here." He smiled. "Let's go back outside. It doesn't smell that great in here."

I laughed. "I wasn't going to say anything."

Timothy led me through the large kitchen—no surprise, all the appliances and cabinets were ripped out—and out a back door.

Outside, I gasped. The Kokosing River was a basketball court length away from us. In front of the river was a small orchard of apple trees, their white blossoms on full display.

Mabel barked and galloped to the back of the house.

"What a beautiful view," I murmured.

"I hoped you would like it."

"It's great, but why did you bring me here? I thought we were on the way to your parents'."

He grinned. "We are, but I wanted to surprise you with this first. You know I have been looking for a place to buy, and I think this is it. Look at all this space. It's perfect for everything we need."

We.

To our right, a shed the size of a double garage stood. Timothy led me close to the garage. "These I'll turn into my workshop. Eventually, I'll build another garage for our cars, but of course the condition of the house is the first priority. Not only does the place need to be gutted, but this was an Amish farm. Everything has to be wired."

Mabel barked and raced after a groundhog she'd finally tricked out of its hole.

I opened my mouth, but Timothy kept going, "It's not too far from town. I clocked it. It's only two miles from Harshberger. That's not the commute you have now, but it's much closer than when you and Becky lived at the Quills' place."

I watched the groundhog dive into another hole. Mabel tripped over herself trying to catch it. "I don't know what to say."

He paled. "You were upset when I brought up buying a house without your input. I understand that now. I may have been even more upset than you were because I knew I'd made a mistake by not consulting you first." He swallowed. "When we argued that day in the Dutch Inn's kitchen, I had already purchased this property as a surprise. You weren't supposed to see it like this. I wanted to fix it up for you, so the first time you saw it it was move-in ready."

I released his hands and stepped. "Why didn't you talk to me about it *before* you purchased the land?"

"I know I should have. I'm sorry."

I turned away from him. It wasn't until this moment that truly realized that Timothy and I were from two different worlds. How would we ever meet in the middle when we thought so differently from each other? Could I contend with his Amish way of thinking for the rest of my life?

"I understand why you are upset, and we can look for another place. This property is still great for my workshop. I can keep my business here. We don't have to live here. We can find another place that we both like. We don't have to make any decisions right now."

"That sounds expensive," I said with my back still toward him.

"It is," he admitted. "But I just want to make you happy."

I turned around to face him. "You do." I gave him a half smile. "But we are going to have to talk about our communication issues."

He smiled. "Deal."

"And even if you are just using this property for business, you will need my help."

His smile widened. "I will?"

"Sure. It isn't wired yet, so I can pick where the outlets and network drops go. You need Wi-Fi, I mean, that's a given."

He laughed and the worry lines on his face smoothed. "I'll leave all that to you then, and the fact you want to do it makes me love you more."

"I'm glad that's settled." I shook my finger at him. "But you'd better talk to me next time before you make another big purchase, mister."

Timothy's face softened. "I guess this means I have another confession to make."

I blinked. "What?"

"I made another big purchase without consulting with you." He dropped to one knee.

Timothy took my hand. "Chloe Humphrey." He reached into his jacket pocket with his free hand. "I love you. I want to argue with you until we're both old and gray."

"You want to argue the rest of your life?" I heard myself ask. My voice sounded so far away.

He laughed. "If it is with you, yes, that's exactly what I want." He kissed my hand, and then opened the box. A modest white gold diamond ring with a twist in the band on either side of the pearl-cut stone nestled in the velvet. "Will you marry me?"

Breathe. Breathe.

"Yes." I finally managed.

He slipped the ring on my finger, jumped to his feet, and kissed me. "Can you stay out of trouble for a little while now?"

I admired my ring over his shoulder. It was blurry through my tears. "I'll do my best."

He wrapped his arms more tightly around me and laughed. "Why don't I believe you?"

ABOUT THE AUTHOR

Amanda Flower, an Agatha Award-nominated mystery author, started her writing career in elementary school when she read a story she wrote to her sixth grade class and had the class in stitches with her description of being stuck on the top of a Ferris wheel. She knew at that moment she'd found her calling of making people laugh with her words. Her debut mystery, *Maid of Murder*, was an Agatha Award Nominee for Best First Novel, and her children's mystery, *Andi Unexpected*, was an Agatha Award Nominee for Best Children's/YA Novel. She writes the Andi Boggs Series for children, the Appleseed Creek Mystery Series, the Living History Mystery Series, and the India Hayes Mystery Series. She also writes the national bestselling Amish Quilt Shop

Mystery Series as Isabella Alan for Penguin Random House. In addition to being an author, Amanda is an academic librarian for a small college near Cleveland. Visit her online at www.amandaflower.com and www.isabellaalan.com.

Connect with Amanda Online
Facebook: http://www.facebook.com/
authoramandaflower
Twitter: http://twitter.com/aflowerwriter
Blog: http://amandaflower.wordpress.com/

11-16

CPSIA information can be obtained at www.ICGtesting.com
Printed in the USA
LVOW08s1424071016

507221LV00001B/39/P

9 781502 9605